WHISPERS IN THE

PINES

Mark D. Trollinger

Published by Myths and Malts Productions Chandler, AZ

The book is a work of fiction. The author drew the characters, incidents, and dialogue from his imagination and did not construe them as real. Some events from the original cryptid sightings have been retold, modernized, and at times, fictionalized.

This book includes the use of trademarks for realism. Product names, logos, brands, and other trademarks featured or referred to within this manuscript are the property of their respective trademark holders.

These trademark holders are not affiliated with the author or any of the author's representatives. They do not sponsor or endorse the contents, materials, or processes discussed within this book.

Drink responsibly and do not drink and drive

If you or a loved one need help with an alcohol problem, please reach out to SAMHSA's National Helpline: 1-800-662-HELP (4357).

The author will donate 15% of the sales from this book to The Barefoot Trail Foundation in Flagstaff, AZ. I will make donations quarterly. See the Field Notes section at the back of the book for more details.

Myths and Malts Productions LLC

Cover by Nyssa Iñiguez

Library of Congress Control Number: 2025922650

First Edition, first printing

Printed in the United States of America

ISBN: 9781968796907

also by Mark Trollinger

Texans Investigating Mysterious Entities Series:

The Chupacabra and the Bat Rastard

Champ and a Bit of Sunshine

The Red Ghost and a Chocolate Bunny

The Loveland Frog and the Narrow Path

Tegan Stone and the Gibson County Beast

The Ringdocus and a Guy on a Buffalo

Into the Dark with the Maryland Goatman

Kareem Ortiz and the Menehune of Kaua`i

The Jersey Devil and the Silky Intergalactic Pajamas

The Lizard Man of Lee County and the Sope Creek Cryptidweizen

Whispers in the Pines

For Susana, Karmina, Jorge,

Lydia, Enid, and Linda

Legacy endures

OUR STORY SO FAR ...

Carson Quinn was drifting after losing his job as a science teacher. Running into his old friend Tyson Carr pulled him back on course. With Ty, Kareem Ortiz, and Tegan Stone, he found friendship, craft beer, and a new drive to chase the mysteries his grandfather once whispered about. Together they built the T.I.M.E. Agency. Texans Investigating Mysterious Entities.

What started as curiosity and road trips soon opened a hidden world. The Chupacabra. Champ in the lake. Witches. Visitors from the stars. They learned the government had known about such things since the days of the Founding Fathers.

Now, with StarShield closing in and the past refusing to stay buried, the T.I.M.E. team continues its search for answers across America and into the unknown. The hunt is no longer just about cryptids. It is about survival.

This book takes us to Iceland in the winter of 1602. It is a separate thread from Carson and his friends. This is not about the modern team's direct ancestors. But one figure, her ancestor, Ölrún, will rise from this time. That is where her part in the story begins.

TABLE OF CONTENTS

CHAPTER 1

THE DROWNED AND THE DAMNED

Þórsmörk, Iceland – Winter, 1602

Wind tore through the valley like a wolf.

It howled between the mountains and shook the turf halls of the farmsteads. Snow blew in thick sheets. Ice sealed the ground.

No grain came from the fields.

The Danish king had closed the trade. His ships alone brought goods, and his price was too high.

Hunger followed.

The people of Þórsmörk were cold, hungry, and weak in the dark winter.

Inside the turf halls, firelight burned low. Flames spat against the cold air. Smoke clung to the rafters. The smell of charred wood mixed with wet hides.

Men and women moved slow. Their faces were red from frost. They kept their mouths shut. Words cost too much breath.

The men went to the river. They cast their nets, but pulled them back empty. Their eyes were hollow. They dragged their boots through the snow. The earth was frozen. The cattle stood thin. Their breath white in the air. The sheep lay gaunt. Their ribs showed through hide and hair. The land gave nothing. The people took what little they found. It was not enough.

Children sat close to the hearth. They did not cry. They whispered about the sea. How it swallowed men. How it sent worse things back.

The elders gave no answer. They sat in silence.

A raven called from the ridge. The cry was sharp. Harsh. None answered. None cared.

An old woman prayed. Her voice cracked in the smoke. She called on Odin. On Freyja. On the powers that had guarded their kin in ages past. She asked for bread and mercy. Only the wind replied. The others watched her in silence. Once they had called on the gods of the hills and sea. Now the priests spoke of Christ. The old ways lay buried, and the people feared to dig them up.

The people grew desperate. Days without food left them dull. The hunt brought nothing. One morning, the net came back heavy. Cod thrashed in the mesh. Enough to feed them all. But black shapes lay among them. Fins bent the wrong way. Heads hung as if the sea still pulled them back.

At first, the people cheered. Then the sound died.

Jónas, the old fisherman, stared. His face went white. He remembered the tales. Men had pulled such fish before. They came home hollow-eyed. They spoke of the öfuguggi. The backward fish. Feeders on the drowned. Flesh too red. Flesh that killed.

But hunger is cruel.

The people crowded close. They reached for the meat. Jónas gave a warning. No one listened. The black fish went to the fire with the cod. Pots boiled. The smell filled the hall.

They ate.

By nightfall, the first man fell. He spat black fluid. His chest burned. His limbs turned stiff. His eyes rolled white. One man died before dawn. By morning, half the village lay still.

The elders gathered in the hall. Their faces were hard with cold and loss. Jónas stood with them. His voice shook. He spoke of backward fins. Of red flesh. Of warnings cast aside. But the dead lay cold. The living sat in fear. But there was no time to mourn.

The farmsteads had to act quickly to hold back the poison. The elders gave strict orders. No one was to touch the bodies without the rites. Those who showed sickness were driven from their homes, isolated on the edges of the village to prevent further contamination. They were cut off from kin. Fear spread from door to door. They did not know if the curse passed by hand or by air. Fear gripped the village and did not let go.

The dead were carried out. They were laid in the snow beyond the halls. Their limbs were twisted. Their faces stiff. Flesh split in the frost. Decay filled the air. A fog rose from the ground. It spread low. It carried the taste of the grave.

The people grew certain the drowned had not gone in peace. Some whispered that the öfuguggi had struck deeper than flesh. They said the drowned were bound to the land. Their souls did not leave.

Again, the elders gathered in the hall. Smoke hung above them. Their breath showed white in the dark. Jónas spoke of the black fish. Of the curse that followed. The priests told them to bow to Christ and wait. Their words were thin.

The survivors believed they were marked and cursed to live under the shadow of the öfuguggi's evil. The farmsteads, once full of life, now stood hollow and still. The dark presence clung to the mountains and to their halls. The elders whispered in the hall, fearful of what waited to come. The village had been left in despair.

The elders and the people huddled in the cold. They were worn and afraid. The curse from the öfuguggi seemed impossible to fight. The spirits of the dead had not rested. The poison still lingered. It infected their minds as much as their bodies. The elders whispered in the hall, fearful of what waited to come. The villagers were convinced the end was near.

The people looked to one another. No one spoke. None dared call on the old gods. At last Eiríkur rose. His back was bent, his beard white, yet his voice carried. Once he had been a goði. Before the crown and the Christ stripped the name. The people feared the old ways, but they still listened when he spoke.

He leaned on his staff. "There is one who can stand against this curse," he said. "One who has faced the dark before. Ölrún Karlsson. The Valkyrie. Send a rider. She will come."

Murmurs quieted in the hall. The fire spat in the smoke. The people shifted on their benches. Some crossed themselves. A woman gave a low cry. One priest spoke sharply. He called the name a sin. Blasphemy. But no one answered him.

The elders sat in dread. They feared the old ways. They feared the name. Yet no other road lay open. Hunger had broken their bodies. The sickness had filled their halls. The priests gave no hope.

Eiríkur's gaze did not move. "You asked for counsel," he said. "This is the counsel. Call her. Or lie down with the dead."

The elders bowed their heads. One by one, they gave their answer without words.

"Send a rider."

A man rose at once. His breath broke in the cold air. His eyes were wild, but his voice was firm.

"I will ride," he said. "I will find her."

The elders gave him their blessing. A small band went with him. They set out at dawn. Snow lay deep on the paths. The horses strained with each step. Ice cracked under their hooves. The mountains stood black against the pale sky. The men did not speak. Their faces were hard as stone.

Days passed. Wind tore at their cloaks. Frost clung to their beards. Hunger gnawed at their bellies. One by one, the band fell back, too weak to go on. At last, the rider pressed forward alone.

He came to the high valleys where no farmstead stood. Only rock, ice, and shadow. The people said she dwelled there. The Valkyrie. The woman born under a dark sky. The one who smelled of petrichor and pine. Like a storm that drifted through the trees. Her name was carried in whispers. Half in awe. Half in fear. She had fought the dark things of old and left them broken. Her deeds had become legend.

The rider turned his horse toward a narrow pass. The wind cut his face. Snow drove against him. The land itself seemed to bar his way. Yet he pressed on.

At last, he saw her.

Ölrún Karlsson came down from the heights. She stood tall with broad shoulders. Her steps were sure on the ice. Her black eyes did not turn aside. The storm pulled at her cloak of raven feathers. It rose about her like wings. A sword hung at her side. It was bright even in the dim light. Its steel scarred by many battles.

The wind shifted. Rain had darkened the soil below. The smell of pine rose with the damp earth. She carried it with her, as if the storm itself walked at her side.

But it was her hair that struck him first. Red as fire. It lay loose across her back and burned against the pale snow. A flame that would not die.

The rider bowed his head. He did not speak. He dared not.

Ölrún stood before him in silence. Fierce as the winter. Still as stone.

The rider drew his horse to a halt. He dismounted in the snow. His knees sank deep. His head bent low.

"Lady," he said. "Our halls are dying. The curse eats us. Come."

Ölrún's gaze did not waver. Her cloak rose in the wind. Her hand rested on the hilt of her sword.

"You have called," she said. "I have heard."

She turned and walked down the pass. The rider followed. He was too afraid to speak again.

The rider was gone for many nights. The people waited. Each dawn brought more bodies to the snow. The fog spread wider. The halls grew still. Some said the man had perished in the heights. Some said the Valkyrie had slain him.

Then, on the seventh night, hooves struck the frozen ground. The rider came down from the pass. His horse stumbled under him. Foam frothed at its mouth. The man's face was hollow. His eyes were wild.

Beside him walked a tall woman. She did not lean. She did not falter. She set her foot on the ice as if it were bare earth.

The people gathered outside the turf halls. Their faces were grey with hunger. Their breath hung in the air. They had heard the raven's cry. Now they saw the storm she carried with her.

Ölrún stood tall. Her step was sure. Her black eyes cut through the crowd. The wind seized her cloak of raven feathers. It rose about her like wings. At her side hung the blade. The edge caught the moon. Cold light ran along the iron.

The smell of pine drifted with her. The ground lay wet from the thaw. The earth gave off a scent as sharp as the forest after the rain. She carried it with her, as if storm and soil clung to her.

But it was her hair that struck them first. Red as the fire of Hel itself. Wild and untamed, it cascaded down her back. The strands glowed like embers that would not die. Its brightness was a stark contrast against the bleak, frozen landscape.

The people of Þórsmörk stared. Some crossed themselves. Some shrank back. A woman covered her eyes. Others held their tongues. Their hands clenched at their sides.

Ölrún gave no word. She did not bow. She did not bend. She was winter given form.

She walked between the turf halls. Her reputation preceded her. The people drew back. None blocked her path.

Whispers followed her footsteps.

"That is her."

"The red-haired one."

"She fought the dark in the north."

"She is curse and shield alike."

Mothers pulled children close. Old men bowed their heads. Some made the sign of the cross, yet their eyes never left her.

They whispered her name under their breath. None dared speak it loudly. To see her in the heart of their wasted land brought a hope they had not felt in many weeks.

CHAPTER 2

THE PYRES OF KROSSÁ

The elders of the scattered farms came out to meet Ölrún. They gave her respect. They told of the öfuguggi, the fish with fins turned backward, taken from the Krossá when the river ran high with meltwater. Men ate of it and fell to sickness. Fever walked from farm to farm. The dead were laid in the hard earth, yet the earth would not hold them. Pyres were lit, yet the bodies did not catch. The drowned did not rest. A bitter poison clung to the people.

Ölrún listened in silence. Her face did not change. Her shoulders were broad. Her hair was red as fire. The scar at her jaw caught the torchlight. Her eyes were black and without mercy. When they finished, she stood. The task was hers now.

"I will end this," she said. Her voice was iron. "But first I must see where it began."

She walked among the farmsteads like a shadow. Her steps struck hard on the frozen ground as she passed. Her eyes searched and measured. She passed the sick in their doorways. Children whimpered in their mothers' arms. She saw the hunger on the people's faces. She knew the curse was more than the öfuguggi.

The elders told her what they had seen. A net dragged from the Krossá, heavy with a strange fish. Fins turned the wrong way. The folk ate of it and grew weak. Fever came.

Ölrún listened. Her face was stern. She heard the whispers of the drowned in the wind. The farms lay in shadow.

She went to the bank of the Krossá, where the first backward-finned fish had been taken. Her boots ground against the frozen stones as she passed the sick and the dying. The air turned her stomach. Not only death, but something twisted. There was something else. An unnatural presence. Her chest grew tight. Something moved under the dark water.

She crouched. Her eyes cut through the water. The cold bit at her skin. It did not move her. She felt the ground under her boots. It throbbed. The earth was disturbed.

She knelt at the edge of the Krossá. Ice cracked under her boots. The water was black with winter flow. It carried the taint of the drowned. The curse rose from their graves. The öfuguggi was not just a fish. It was a keeper of the dead. A vessel of dark power. The curse had taken not only the bodies. It had crept onto the riverbanks. Into the soil of the fields. Into the timbers of the homes. The whole valley bore its mark.

She stood. The wind pulled at her cloak and hair. Snow shifted on the stones around her feet.

Cold moved through her chest. She saw the truth of it. If she did not act, the curse would spread from farm to farm. The soil would fail. Cattle would starve. Children would cough and weaken. The folk would never be at peace, not in this life nor in death.

Her hand closed on the knife at her belt. Her shoulders tensed as battle-fire stirred within her. She had fought men and beasts. This was not only the dead. It was an old darkness. Older than the names of these valleys. She knew what must be done. She would not turn aside.

Ölrún turned back to the farm folk. They had followed her to the riverbank. They stood in a knot, their faces hollow with hunger and pale with fear. Their breath smoked in the frost. Some clutched staffs. Some clutched children. None spoke. Her voice carried over the wind, steady and hard.

"The curse is not only in your blood," she said. "It is in the soil. The drowned lie near, and they will not go. Their hunger grows. You must burn the bodies. Fire alone will send them on."

She faced them in the frost. The farmers shifted and muttered. A woman cried out. She clutched her shawl as if it were a child. "My son lies in the earth," she said. "You would set him to flame? Fire is for the outcast." Murmurs ran through the gathered crowd. Some made the sign of the cross. Some stared at the earth. Some wept.

Eiríkur came to the front. His cloak was thick with frost. He lifted one hand for silence. "In the old days," he said, "we gave the dead to the fire. Then the souls walked free. The earth holds them now. It is wrong. She speaks true. The ground will not hold them. Only fire will."

Ölrún spoke to them. Her voice carried over the wind. "The dead are not at rest. You weep for them, yet they remain. They are trapped. They are angry."

The elders stood firm. Their faces remained grim. Their breath clouded in the cold air.

"You must return to the old ways," she said. Her eyes were dark and stern. "If you keep them in the ground, the curse will not break. This is no common fever. It is a binding. The drowned cling to the earth. The öfuguggi was sent to guard them."

Silence fell. The birches rattled in the wind. In the sound, the folk thought they heard the dead.

The bodies lay in cloth at the river's edge. The ground was frozen too hard for spades. No grave could be cut. The dead lay above the soil, heavy and still.

Jón spoke. He was a man of the new faith. A wooden cross hung from his hand. "The dead must lie in the earth," he said. "So the priests have taught us. Fire is for the outlaw. Fire is shame. You would have us dishonor our own blood."

The folk crowded close. They muttered to one another. Some made the sign of the cross. Some turned away from the sight. Some stared at the frozen bodies, unable to look away. Hunger had taken their strength. Fear bound them more tightly than frost.

Ölrún was silent. The wind scoured the valley. Rafters groaned. The moon showed thin above the peaks.

She stepped forward. The wind pulled at her hair. "I have walked the fields of war," she said. Her tone was firm. "I saw men torn open and left for crows. I heard their souls cry for release."

Jón did not look away. "The soul is God's," he said. "The earth must keep it. To burn the dead is to shame them. I will not see it done."

Ölrún drew a breath. "Where is your God now?" she said. She pointed to the wrapped bodies by the river. "Did He come to carry them? Or do you still hear them in the wind?"

The villagers shuddered. Some turned their heads, as if trying to shut out the sound. The old woman in the front swallowed hard. Her son lay among the dead. Her hands clutched the edge of his burial cloth as if she could still hold him here.

"They are not at rest," Ölrún said, softer now. "The öfuguggi's curse is not just death. It is torment. They will wander. They will hunger. They will never leave this place unless we set them free."

Jón opened his mouth to answer. His hand lifted the cross as if to strike the air. "The priests…" he began.

Ölrún cut him off. Her eyes fixed on him. "Choose," she said, her voice sharp. She turned to the others. "Hold to the new ways, and the curse will remain. Return to the old, and your dead will go free."

The folk shivered. The old woman looked at the shroud of her son. Her hands pressed to the cloth. She let it fall. Her voice was low. "Do it."

The murmur broke. One after another, the folk bowed their heads. Even Jón dropped his eyes.

Ölrún spoke again. "Build the pyres. Bring them here." The farmers bent to the work. They dragged the dead from the frozen ground. They carried them to the wood. They stacked the bodies with their own hands. The elders stood close by and did not speak.

The men swung axes at the birches until the trunks cracked and fell. They split the timber with dull iron. Women brought brushwood. Children fetched armfuls of twigs. They built the pyres high, though their hands shook from hunger and cold. Each body was laid upon the wood. No priest gave blessing. No earth was turned. The new ways were put aside. The old ways stood again.

Ölrún stepped to the woodpile. She pulled a torch from the fire. The resin had already flared. She lifted it so all could see. Her staff stood upright in the frozen ground. The runes on the shaft shone red in the glow. She spoke to the dead. Her voice was plain, hard. "Go now. The path is open. Walk it. Leave this place."

She thrust the torch into the brushwood. Flame caught. Smoke rolled over the river. Flesh split. Bone broke. Faces turned in the smoke. Mouths opened in silence. Hands rose, then vanished into the dark. The night turned red.

She stood before the rising fire. Heat struck her face. Sparks flew past her eyes. She did not move. She held the staff in both hands. She struck it against the stones. The sound carried over the valley.

"Spirits of the drowned," she said. Her voice was steady. She struck the staff against the frozen ground. "Go now. You have lingered too long. You do not belong in this world. The path is open. Walk it. Leave this place. Be at rest."

WHISPERS IN THE PINES

The fire roared. Timber split. Ash lifted. The smoke bent and curled. Faces showed within it. Still mouths opened. Arms reached for the sky. The folk cried out and fell back. The air was thick.

Ölrún watched the spirits writhe. She had seen worse on fields of war. The sight did not move her.

One by one, the shapes broke apart. They thinned in the smoke. The wind howled. It carried their last cries into the night.

And then, at last, the silence came.

The people stared at the fire. Some clutched their cloaks. Some wept softly. The smell of ash and burnt cloth lay heavy over the ridge. No one moved to speak.

The old woman had fallen to her knees near the pyre. Her hands were raw from clutching the burial cloth. Her son's name slipped once from her lips, a sound barely more than breath. She bowed her head but did not look away from the flames.

Jón kept his gaze on the ground. His hand still gripped the wooden cross, but he did not lift his eyes to meet hers.

Ölrún lowered her staff. She let out a long breath and faced them.

“It is done.”

The curse was lifted. Yet in the high mountains, beyond the reach of firelight, something old and dark still stirred.

CHAPTER 3

THE SHADOW ON THE RIDGE

The mead hall burned hot. Firelight jumped on the walls. Smoke climbed into the rafters. They wanted drink. They wanted comfort.

Laughter broke in bursts. Cups knocked together. There was little food, but the feast had to happen. It was not for plenty. It was for victory.

They boiled the last winter roots. A ram, too weak to last, was slaughtered. Its bones gave marrow to the stew. Dried fish and black bread lay on rough boards. Mead was watered down, stretched to last. No one complained.

Ölrún sat at the high table. Fire lit her hair. It blazed like Hel's own. She drank deep. Her eyes gave nothing.

The elders spoke first. They told of her triumph. She had lifted the curse. The dead now burned. Their restless souls were freed.

"She is Odin's own," one man said and raised his cup.

"A Valkyrie," another said. "Favored above all."

The warriors called for stories. They spoke of her past. The battles that made her name.

"She crushed the Danes when they came for our shores."

"She hunted the draugar in the winter lands."

"She has seen beyond Midgard itself," one elder said. His voice dropped. "She has walked where men cannot go."

Ölrún listened. The tales grew taller, yet none were false. She had done these things. She had shed blood for gods and kin.

Yet she felt no pride. The hall's warmth did not touch her. Something tugged at her mind. A shadow in the snow.

The doors burst wide.

A gust howled through. Flames shook and cast wild shapes on the walls.

A man staggered in. His face was raw with cold. His lips were cracked and blue as he fought for words.

"Something watches from the ridge."

Silence fell. The warmth thinned.

Ölrún set down her cup and rose from her seat. The wooden bench scraped against the floor. Her boots thudded as she crossed the hall. The fire cast her shadow long behind her. The man shivered where he stood. His breath came in ragged gasps.

She took his arm to steady him. "What did you see?"

His eyes darted to the door. He swallowed hard. "A shape," he rasped. "Tall. Wrong. It did not move like a man."

Murmurs spread. Some gripped weapons. Others whispered prayers.

Ölrún's grip tightened. "Speak plainly."

The man licked his lips. "It stood on the ridge, where the trees thin. Blacker than night. Arms too long. Head twisted, as if listening." His voice fell. "It had no eyes. Yet it watched me."

A hush fell. The fire cracked. Wind clawed at the walls.

Ölrún let him go. She turned to the warriors. "I will go."

The words settled like iron.

A young man rose. Thick with muscle. "I ride with you."

A grizzled berserker stood. "And I."

A third warrior, a woman with a scar down her cheek, shoved back her cup. "You will not go alone."

A fourth nodded.

Ölrún's lips curled in approval. "Arm yourselves."

They moved at once. The hall stirred. Axes and spears were taken up. Furs thrown over shoulders.

Outside, the night waited. The wind bit. Snow crunched under boots as they strode to the stables. The horses stamped. Uneasy. They sensed what lay beyond the trees.

Ölrún swung onto her mount. The others followed.

She looked once toward the ridge. The darkness there was thick. Unnatural.

Then she spurred her horse forward. The hunt had begun.

Ölrún rode at the front. Her horse's breath came in thick clouds as steam rolled from its nostrils. The others kept close. The village gates groaned as they swung open. The wood was stiff with ice. The wind cut like knives. Snow drove into their faces. Sharp as glass.

The young man was Hróald. His blond hair stuck to his brow, slick with frost. He gripped his spear tightly. His family had been among those who ate the cursed fish, yet he did not waver.

The berserker was Stigandi. Broad as an ox, wrapped in furs. His beard hung heavy with ice. An axe lay across his back. Its blade notched from years of battle. He rode like a man with nothing left to fear.

The scarred woman was Ylva. Her cloak snapped in the wind. A sword strapped across her chest. Her wolfskin hood threw her face in shadow. She had seen many winters. She did not flinch.

The last was Bjorn, silent and grim. His eyes stared ahead and scanned the dark. He carried a bow with raven-fletched arrows.

They rode into the storm. The village shrank behind them.

Hróald lifted his spear. "If it shows itself, I will strike first."

Stigandi laughed, a rough sound in the gale. "If it bleeds, I will drink of it."

Ylva turned her scarred face toward him. "Save your strength. The thing will not fall to boasting."

Bjorn kept his eyes on the ridge. "Something waits for us."

Ölrún felt it as they passed the last post. The air shifted. The wind bore more than snow. It carried whispers.

Something unseen watched from the dark.

She did not look back. To do so was doubt.

The ridge lay two days ahead. The path was not kind. The first night, the cold burrowed into their bones. Frost crept into their beards and hair. The fire barely held against the wind. They ate little.

By morning, the snow deepened. Horses sank at each step. Their muscles burned from the fight to push forward.

On the second night, the howling came. Low at first. Faint. Then closer.

Not wolves.

Ölrún did not sleep. Nor did the others.

By dawn, the ridge loomed ahead. A black scar against the white. Something waited for them there.

She felt it.

It had waited all along.

A figure stood on the ridge. A shadow against the storm. It did not move. The wind howled, yet snow did not touch it.

Ölrún's breath curled in the cold. Her horse shifted.

The thing on the ridge was neither man nor beast. It was older.

Then it moved.

A slow turn of its head. A glint beneath the hood. Eyes like embers burning in the cold.

The others tensed. Stigandi gripped his axe. Ylva reached for her sword.

The wind carried a sound down the mountain. A voice.

Not words. Something deeper. A whisper that crawled under the skin and clawed at the mind.

Ölrún knew.

A vættr. A spirit of the land, twisted by hunger, famine, and the unburied dead. The curse was not broken. It had taken a new form.

And it was waiting for her.

CHAPTER 4

ONLY FIRE

The vættr stood on the ridge, wrapped in tattered furs. The hides shifted and lifted as if moved by breath, though the wind held still. Its frame was shaped like a man yet twisted. In one place it stretched too thin. In another it swelled thick with shadow. Snow clung to it. Ice hung from its edges. The cold did not touch its flesh. Beneath the hood, a face wavered, half lost in shadow.

Its skin was the color of frostbite. Black and blue. Split with deep red cracks. The mouth stretched too wide. The corners torn by years of screams. Teeth jutted from the dark. Some long and sharp. Some rotten, snapped to stumps. The eyes burned red, like embers sunk deep in their sockets. They shifted like coals stirred in a dying fire.

This was no common spirit. It was born of hunger and grief. A thing that should have stayed buried under ice but clawed its way free. A draugr-kin. A landvættir twisted by famine and cursed deaths of those who ate the öfuguggi. It was bound to this mountain, yet it was awake now because of the blood and fire that had defied it.

Ölrún felt its eyes. It waited for her.

She slid off her horse. The others held back. She raised her hand.

"Stay."

The wind howled through the valley. Snow cut their faces. Ylva's hand tightened on her sword, but she stayed in the saddle. Stigandi muttered the old words of the berserkers, hardening his soul. The young scout shook but did not fall back. Bjorn, the silent one, studied the shadow with sharp eyes.

Ölrún stepped forward. The vættr stood still.

She had seen its kind before. Some were protectors, spirits of the land that kept balance between the living and the dead. But this one had changed. It had been twisted by the famine, by the blood spilled in hunger and fear. The dead who had eaten the cursed fish had fed it.

She pulled off a glove and set her hand to the snow. The cold bit deep. She did not flinch. Her breath slowed. Her body stilled.

She listened.

The mountain whispered.

The land still ached from the deaths. The spirits were not at peace. Fire had burned the bodies, but their souls had not been guided home. The dead wandered, caught between realms. And this vættr, this thing of old magic and restless hunger, had risen in their place.

Ölrún rose. She reached for the seiðr, the old magic that ran in her blood. The runes at her belt thrummed with power. She reached down and took one rune in her hand. A palm-sized antler fragment cut from a tine. Its surface was smooth from centuries of handling. Her fingers brushed against the Algiz deeply carved into its surface. The lines darkened with ash and blood from her early battles. When she closed her fist around it, the rune pulsed with her energy, amplifying her protective aura. She closed her eyes and exhaled.

The dead must be set to rest. The curse must be broken at its source.

She opened her eyes. The fire of the vættr met her own.

"I will not leave until you stand down," she said. Her voice did not waver. "Or until I tear you from this mountain."

The vættr grinned. Its mouth stretched too wide.

The storm thickened.

And then the vættr lunged.

It moved like a shadow that broke free from the earth.

Faster than any man.

Faster than the wind. The furs that clung to its body whipped back to reveal limbs twisted by something older than time.

Its fingers stretched too long.

Its nails were curved and blackened.

Like the claws of something that had dug its way from a grave.

Ölrún did not flinch.

She had fought worse.

She stepped back and drew her seax in one hand. She raised the other.

The runes on her belt burned against her skin.

The power of the seiðr rose within her.

The moment the vættr came close, she struck.

The blade cut its arm.

Black blood burst across the snow.

Steam hissed where it struck the ice.

The vættr shrieked.

A sound that did not belong in this world.

It stumbled, then came on again.

Claws stretched for her throat.

Ylva roared from the saddle. She drove her horse forward with her axe held high.

Ölrún barked.

"Stay back."

Ylva hauled the reins and held.

Ölrún snarled. "Stay back!"

Ylva pulled the horse to a stop, panting hard.

The vættr turned toward the sound. Its ember eyes squinted.

It had been human once, but that was long ago.

 It did not think as men did.

It did not fight as men did.

Ölrún rolled her shoulders. She could not kill it with steel alone.

She spat into the snow. "I know what you are."

The vættr circled her. Its movements were jerky.

Unnatural.

It grinned again.

Black spit dripped from its mouth.

"Then you know you cannot send me back."

Ölrún smirked. "I have sent worse things crawling to Hel."

The vættr lunged again. This time, she did not cut.

She raised her arm and caught its strike.

She twisted as it slammed into her.

Its strength was monstrous.

She let it push her back and used its own force against it. With a sharp exhale, she braced and rammed her knee into its ribs.

It slid across the ice.

The vættr howled. The sound made the horses rear.

Bjorn drew his bow.

"We end it now!"

"No," Ölrún snapped. "Steel and arrows will not stop it."

The vættr laughed.

Ölrún knew what had to be done. The dead clung to the thing. They would not rest until the land was whole.

The curse must be broken at its root.

The fire must finish what it began.

She sheathed her blade and stepped toward the vættr.

Seiðr rose in her chest like a second heartbeat.

The fight was not over.

It had only just begun.

The vættr lunged.

Ölrún braced. It was too fast.

Before she could twist away, claws raked across her side.

Pain tore through her ribs.

Hot and sharp.

Blood darkened the fabric beneath her furs.

She gritted her teeth and staggered back but held her feet.

The vættr smelled the blood.

Its blackened lips split in a grin.

She let out breath through the pain.

Pain was nothing. Pain meant life.

The vættr circled low.

Limbs twitched.

Eyes measured her.

It was not witless.

That made it worse.

Ylva shouted from behind, gripping her axe. "Ölrún…"

"Stay back!" Ölrún snapped. Her eyes never left the creature.

Ölrún pressed her wound.

The gashes ran deep, but not mortally.

The vættr lunged again.

This time, she was ready.

She dropped low and rolled beneath its swinging claws. Her hand shot out and grabbed a handful of the furs draped over its frame.

With a sharp twist, she yanked.

The vættr stumbled.

She drove her seax into its thigh.

It screamed. The sound was raw. Something scraped from the depths of the earth.

It struck her aside.

She fell hard into the snow.

Her breath burst out.

The vættr loomed.

It grinned. It dripped black blood, yet it did not fall.

Ölrún spat blood into the snow.

The others stirred. Hooves shifted. Hands gripped wood and steel. But they could not aid her. Not yet.

The vættr lunged, hands reaching for her throat.

She rolled aside at the last moment and twisted up to her feet.

The wound at her side throbbed, but she ignored it.

She was faster now.

She slashed at its arm. Her blade cut deep.

The vættr shrieked.

It swung again. She bent low.

A claw grazed her cheek. Warm blood slid down her jaw.

It rushed her again. A blur of claw and shadow.

She kicked snow to blind it. Her blade drove into its ribs.

The vættr staggered.

Ölrún fell back. Her chest heaving.

The wind howled thick with ice.

The vættr hissed.

Black blood spilled on the snow. Its eyes burned.

"You fight well, Valkyrie," it rasped.

Ölrún wiped the blood from her mouth.

"And you die poorly."

The vættr grinned. "I do not die."

Ölrún flexed her fingers.

The seiðr beat in her veins. Then she knew.

Steel would not end it.

Fire must. She had to burn it.

She took a slow step back. "Bjorn," she called. "The torches."

The archer reached for the pack at his saddle.

The vættr saw.

It bared its teeth.

Then it charged.

Ölrún readied herself.

The fight was not over.

The vættr lunged again.

Ölrún raised her blade, but the creature was faster.

Its claws slashed across her chest, tearing through blood-soaked fur.

The fabric shredded and exposed raw skin beneath.

Pain seared through her ribs.

She gasped and stumbled back. The wind stole her breath. Snow stuck to the wound as blood spread and mixed with the blood that spilled onto the ice.

The vættr did not stop.

It slammed into her, knocking her off her feet.

She struck the ground. Snow burst high.

Clawed fingers locked around her throat and drove her into the ice.

She fought for breath.

The vættr bent low. Its eyes burned with hunger.

Its grip closed like iron.

Ölrún's vision blurred.

Her vision dimmed at the edges.

She clawed at its wrists but could not break them.

Her chest heaved. Cold gnawed at her skin.

Blood filled her mouth.

Her lungs burned. The cold bit at her exposed skin.

She tried to summon seiðr, but her mind reeled.

Dizzy and dark.

From behind came a cry.

"Ölrún!" Ylva's voice cut through the storm.

Bjorn stepped from the shadows.

His bow bent.

The arrow struck deep in the creature's shoulder.

Black blood spilled on the snow.

Steam rose where it fell.

The vættr shrieked and threw Ölrún aside.

She drew in air, sharp and ragged.

The spirit turned on Bjorn.

Its ember eyes burned with rage.

He stood firm.

His bow was drawn. The raven-fletched shaft dripped with black blood.

"Come, beast. You bleed as any man."

The vættr lashed out.

Claws ripped his chest.

The blow hurled him down.

He struck the ground, blood spreading fast.

His limbs bent wrong. His breath rattled in his throat.

Ölrún's heart pounded.

She saw his fingers twitch. He was still alive, but barely.

Rage burned away the pain in her body.

She would not see him lost.

The vættr faced her again. Its grin split wide with jagged teeth.

"One by one, Valkyrie."

Her hand closed on her sword.

The seiðr beat in her veins.

The wind screamed.

She charged.

Ölrún's feet pounded against the ice-crusted snow.

The creature rushed to meet her. Its claws held high.

She drove low.

Steel cut ribs.

Black blood spilled, smoking in the snow.

An unpleasant smell filled the storm.

Something rotten.

The wind howled. Snow whipped around them in a blinding storm.

The creature staggered but did not fall.

It lashed out again.

She slashed again.

Chest. Arm. Neck.

Each wound closed.

The spirit moved fast. Its claws tore her shoulder.

Warm blood ran down her face.

A burst of pain shot through her.

She gritted her teeth and pressed forward.

The vættr lunged again.

Ölrún did not yield. She stepped in close.

The claws raked her arm, but she struck deep.

Her sword drove into its belly.

Black blood poured out, searing the snow.

The vættr shrieked.

It gripped her arms. Claws pierced flesh.

It lifted her from the ground.

Then it hurled her down.

Ice cracked beneath her.

Her body shuddered.

Ölrún struggled, kicking hard. The vættr slammed her down.

Ice cracked beneath her. The impact rattled her bones.

Her breath left her in a harsh gasp.

The vættr leaned over her.

"You are not invincible," it hissed. "The cold will claim you. The mountain will keep you."

Shadows swam in her sight.

Her breath came harsh and thin.

Blood ran hot across the snow. She tasted iron. She spat red.

It soaked into the snow beneath her.

Another cry cut through the storm.

Ylva charged. A spear in both hands.

She drove the point into the creature's back.

The vættr screamed.

It tore free and staggered away from her.

Ylva and the others attacked.

Arrows whistled through the air.

Spears jabbed into its torso.

The creature barely flinched.

It was beyond death.

Ölrún's mind raced. The stories spoke of such creatures. Spirits that refused to return to the earth.

Weapons could not end them.

Only fire.

A gust of wind nearly knocked her back.

The snow swirled. It was thick and blinding.

The vættr moved through the storm and struck hard.

Ylva cried out as claws tore through her side.

The berserker swung his axe, but the vættr caught it in its taloned grip and hurled him aside like a ragdoll.

Ölrún wiped blood from her face.

Her breath was ragged.

They could not keep fighting like this.

Fire.

She glanced toward the supplies strapped to her horse.

There, bundles of oil-soaked rags and a small flask of mead.

Enough.

She turned and sprinted toward the horse.

The vættr saw her flee and gave chase.

It moved with horrifying speed.

She barely reached the saddlebag in time.

Her hands closed around the flask.

She popped the cork with her teeth.

She doused her sword in the mead.

Then grabbed a torch.

Flint struck against steel.

A spark.

Then flame.

The torch blazed to life just as the vættr reached her.

She turned and thrust the brand into its chest.

The creature screamed.

The sound was like breaking ice.

Like bones snapping in the cold.

The fire spread across its body and ignited the oil-soaked rags from the arrows still embedded in its flesh.

It staggered back. It flailed.

Its form burning like dry wood.

Ölrún wasted no time.

She raised her sword, now slick with mead and fire at the tip.

She drove it through the creature's throat.

Flames erupted from the wound.

The vættr convulsed.

Its body cracked and split as fire consumed it from the inside.

It reached for her one last time.

Then it collapsed.

Its charred remains crumbled into the snow.

The storm began to ease.

The wind died. The shadows receded.

Ölrún stood over the smoldering corpse.

She was bloodied and breathless.

It was over.

CHAPTER 5

THE ROAD OF THE FALLEN

The ride back was silent. The storm had broken, but the air still cut their skin. Ölrún rode at the front. Her horse's hooves struck the frozen crust. Blood marked her fur and her armor. Her face showed exhaustion, yet her eyes carried relief. The vættr lay dead. The threat was ended.

Ylva rode close. Her hand pressed to her side where the claws had cut. She did not slow. Stigandi kept to his saddle. His arm was bound in a rough sling. He gave no word of pain. Hróald and Bjorn rode grim and still. Their weapons carried the dark blood of the spirit.

They crested the hill. The village lay below. Smoke from the pyres thinned. The dark clouds broke and drifted. The grip on Ölrún's chest eased.

At the gates, Ölrún looked back. Bjorn rode behind her. He had fought with fierce strength. Now he sagged in the saddle. His face was pale. Blood darkened his chest.

"Bjorn!"

Ölrún drove her horse to him.

Bjorn gave no answer. His body swayed loose in the saddle. The claws of the vættr had ripped him deep. His life ran out into the snow.

"Bjorn!" she called again. Dread filled her chest.

Bjorn raised his head. His voice broke in the wind.

"It is my time."

He let go of the reins. He fell from the horse. His body struck the snow.

Ölrún spurred her horse and leapt down. She knelt at his side. Cold air cut her skin. Worse was the fading beat under her palm. His chest rose shallow, but each breath was a struggle.

"Stay with me, Bjorn," she said. Her voice shook. Her hand was held against his chest. The faint beat weakened.

His hand slipped from hers. His breath rasped thin in the frost. He looked at her once more.

"You were right," he said. His voice barely rose above the wind. "I fought to the end. You said I would find my way there."

Bjorn remained speechless during the feast and in the march. Yet in battle his bow had spoken with fire and truth. He had found his way as a warrior. His end had come.

She bent close. "To Valhalla," she said.

His body stilled.

Bjorn had lived in silence. He watched more than he spoke. His words were few, but they struck true.

In battle, he did not boast. He stood firm when others faltered. His bow sang until the end. His arrows found their mark.

She had spoken of choosing the ground with care. He had remained silent. It was his choice. He faced death and did not yield.

Ölrún closed her eyes and whispered the sacred incantations of Seiðr, the ancient magic she wielded as a Valkyrie. Her breath formed in the icy air. She called upon the spirits of the Valkyries to guide Bjorn's soul to Valhalla, hall of the slain. The snow held still. The earth murmured with her words.

Ölrún stayed still. Her thoughts lay heavy with his loss. She had not saved him. But she had done the only thing she could. Guide him to his rightful place. Valhalla would welcome him, as it welcomed all those who fought bravely.

She opened her eyes. The heaviness eased. The battle was over. She had honored him as best she could.

Ölrún stayed by him in the snow. She bowed her head and then rose. The others waited in silence. None spoke.

Together, they lifted him. They set him across his horse. His bow still at his side. The mount stamped but did not throw him. It bore its master home.

Ölrún took the reins. Her voice was low, steady. "We ride."

She led the riders home. Her heart still bore the loss of Bjorn, and the sting of the fight. The bitter winds howled around them, yet the air felt lighter. Behind her, her band of warriors rode in silence.

The gates stood open. The elders waited. A few children, their faces pinched with hunger but still full of hope, ran to the gates. The cheers of their small and pure voices filled the air. For the first time in weeks, they no longer lay in the icy grip of despair.

The elders stood in a line. Their eyes searched the riders. Ölrún slid from her horse. Her legs were weak from the long ride. The others followed. Hooves struck the frozen ground. Villagers gathered around them.

Elder Eiríkur stepped forward. His face was stern, but his eyes were soft. "Is it done?" he asked.

Ölrún nodded, her eyes drawn to the ground as she spoke. "The vættr is dead. We struck it down. But not all returned. Bjorn gave his life in the fight. His soul has been guided to Valhalla."

The horse bore Bjorn's body across the snow. His bow still hung at his side. The children's cheers fell off. The elders bowed their heads.

A hush lay over the crowd. Even the wind fell still. Elder Eiríkur set his hand upon his chest. "Bjorn was a good man," he said. "His death will be remembered."

They took him from the saddle and carried him into the hall. He was laid near the fire, among his people. Grief sat heavy in the room. The villagers stood silent. Their eyes turned to Ölrún.

Ölrún lifted her head. Her voice was firm. "The curse is broken. The famine will end. The fish will return. The crops will rise in spring."

Only then did the silence break. The villagers raised their voices. The sound broke the silence like a wave against the shore. They had endured much. Now they believed the dark had passed.

As the feast rose, Ölrún stood apart. Her mind carried the battle. Losing Bjorn cut deep. Yet she knew the farms would live. The land would heal in time.

Ylva stood at her side. "We did it," she said. "The farms endure."

Ölrún gave a slow nod. Her thoughts stayed with Bjorn. He was at rest. Still, he was gone.

The villagers sang and danced around the fire. Joy spread like a flame through dry grass. Even the elders eased their stance and joined the song. Food passed from hand to hand. Small bowls, but enough. The hall's warmth no longer came from fear. The curse had broken. The hunger would fade.

As the night wore on, the wind outside howled louder. But inside, the fire burned bright and cast long shadows across the walls of the mead hall. Ölrún could hear the laughter, the singing, and the clink of mugs, but she remained in her corner. Her thoughts were still far away. The battle may have been won, but the fight inside her was far from over. Other foes would come. Men. Beasts. Shadows.

Still, tonight, the village had peace. Tomorrow, there would be work to do. But for now, the curse was lifted, and the people would celebrate.

Ölrún sat apart as the village feasted. Their voices rose, but her mind was far away. The curse was ended, yet its peace was not hers to keep. She was a shadow of war, and shadows do not linger long.

CHAPTER 6

WHAT THE SEER SAW

Winter, Scandinavia, 1709

For more than a century, Ölrún Karlsson moved through the north like a shadow of war. She fought in battles chronicled by scribes and in skirmishes soon forgotten. She walked through fields black with blood. Steel meeting steel. Cutting down men and things not born of men. She led warbands. Her coming turned the tide. Time could not claim her. Death would not take her. She hunted what crept in the dark. Draugar clawing from graves. Beasts that reeked of Hel. Old things that had no place in Midgard. Tales spread of the red-haired warrior who did not age. Some called her Valkyrie. Some cursed her. All spoke her name.

The land she saved in 1602 grew strong, but she did not stay to see it. Ölrún was not made for peace. She rode from village to village. She answered calls. She chose her battles. She cut down the unnatural before it could root. She saw kings rise. She saw them fall. Weapons changed. Shields broke. Alliances shifted. She did not change. Men who once fought at her side grew old. She stayed the same. She knew their glances. Heard their whispers. Was she still mortal? Did Odin turn from her, or set her apart for more? No answer came.

In the winter of 1709, she rode to war again.

A horn gave its cry over the field. The wind swallowed the sound. Snow fell in thick curtains. Ice and blood slicked the ground. The fight had raged since dawn. Still, the foe came. The air stank of sweat, iron, and death. Ölrún's sword ran red. Her breath rose steadily in the frost. Warriors fought around her with grim fury. Some fell and froze in the snow. Others stood on. They knew surrender meant slaughter.

A massive warrior in chain black with gore swung his axe for her head. She ducked. The strike cut the air by her ear. Her sword drove into his ribs. His breath left in a wheeze. His eyes widened. He fell into the snow. She tore the blade free. A spear thrust towards her throat. She caught it with steel. The shock ran through her arm. She turned her wrist and knocked the shaft away. She slashed downward. Severed the fingers from the hand that held it. The enemy screamed. He clutched his ruined hand as she buried her sword in his chest.

Ölrún stepped over the fallen man. His eyes froze open in death. She turned and met the charge of another. Her blade cut his wool coat and split bone. He gasped, but the sound drowned in the surrounding clash. He crumpled. She turned before he struck the snow. She sought the next foe.

A warrior rushed with a battle-axe. Dirt and blood smeared his face. He swung with all his strength. Ölrún moved aside. Her sword cut through his ribs. He staggered. Eyes wide with shock. He dropped to his knees. A swift strike to the neck ended him.

All around her, men fell. Some under her blade. Others beneath the weapons of her allies. The battle swayed back and forth like the tide. Neither side broke. She caught glimpses of her warband. Warriors who had fought beside her for years. Erik, his face a mask of blood, drove his spear through a man's chest. Ingrid, swift and unyielding, carved a path through the enemy with twin blades. Torsten, a towering man who in earlier centuries would have been named berserker, roared as he lifted an enemy and broke his skull on the ice. Still, the foe pressed on.

Her arms ached, yet she did not fall back. She had fought past exhaustion before. She had battled for days without rest. Her body had gone beyond its limits. This was the same. She fought as always. Swift. Merciless. She cut down all who stood before her.

Nearby, Ingrid struck like a storm made flesh. Her twin swords rose and fell with a hard rhythm. Erik stood back-to-back with Torsten. Their blades flashed. They cut down foes on every side. The fight bent toward its turning point. They would drive the enemy back. Or they would fall.

Then Ölrún saw them.

A sudden shift in the battle caught her attention. A group of enemy soldiers broke away from the main fight. They retreated toward the treeline. Not in fear, but in purpose.

Ölrún narrowed her eyes. Something lay hidden.

She cut through the last warrior in her way and turned to follow. Erik and Ingrid noticed her movement and fell in beside her. Their breath rose white in the frozen air.

"They flee?" Erik asked. He wiped blood from his brow.

"No," Ölrún said. "They run toward something."

Torsten came after them. His frame loomed high. He roared. "Then we stop them."

Without another word, they moved. The remaining warriors of their band followed, leaving the main battle behind to pursue the men headed into the trees.

They passed beneath the first trees. The field fell away. The wind no longer howled. No steel rang. No voices cried. The silence stood heavy about them. It felt close. Unseen yet near.

Ölrún slowed her stride. She searched the dark between the trunks. Snow lay deep, broken only by the prints of the men ahead. The deeper they went, the thicker the air grew. The scent of iron lingered, but it was not only from the battlefield.

Beyond the fight, she saw three cloaked shapes. They passed quickly among the trees. They did not turn to strike. They fled to a hidden place. Steel flashed under their cloaks. Not like the others. A symbol burned into her mind. A black, twisted sigil carved into their bracers.

"Erik. With me." Her voice cut sharply. She drove forward at a run.

She struck through the last of the foe and left them in the snow. Erik kept pace. The three shapes slipped deeper into the wood.

Snow dragged at their boots. Ölrún drove herself onward. Her breath tore from her chest in the frost. Wind cried in the bare branches. Faint voices rode the gusts, the last sounds of the dying. Ahead, the figures darted between the trees. Their movements were impossibly fast.

"Not men," Erik growled at her side.

She knew it. Their steps made no mark in the snow. The air turned cold at their passing.

A whisper came with the wind. It was no voice of hers. Not of Erik.

"You follow shadows, Valkyrie."

Her stride broke. The shapes turned aside and were gone into the thicket.

"They lead us," Erik said.

"I don't care."

She went on. Her boots bit into the snow. The trees closed around her. The deeper they walked, the quieter it grew. The clash behind them died. Silence hung over them.

Then she saw her.

The fleeing men were gone. There was no sign of them, as if they had vanished. In the heart of the clearing stood a lone woman.

She wore heavy robes of dark blue. Her hands stayed inside the sleeves. Her hair hung white as bone. Fine as a cobweb. A hood lay on her head. Her eyes were pale and blind, yet they saw. She was old. Older than any crone Ölrún had known. Power still moved in her. She was a völva. One who bore the threads of fate.

She did not shiver. The wind passed her by. Her robes did not move.

Ölrún set her hand firm on her sword. "Who are you?"

The völva did not blink. She did not answer.

Wind shook the branches. A whisper came. It was not born of the storm.

It came from the völva.

"I have waited for you, Ölrún Karlsson."

Erik shifted at her side. His hands held the axe tight. "How does she know your name?"

Ölrún stepped closer. Her boots sank in the snow. "Then speak."

The völva opened her mouth. Her voice came thin, no more than a breath. She smiled. Her teeth shone too white for her age. Her clouded eyes turned toward what she alone saw.

"The Black Goat stirs. The Devil waits. Shadows fall on the western lands."

Ölrún stared at the völva. Her blood burned from the fight. Her mind caught on the words.

The völva stood still.

Watching.

Waiting.

The wind howled. The trees groaned.

Cold gripped her spine. It cut deeper than the winter air.

The völva raised a hand. Her fingers trembled as she thrust them toward Ölrún's chest.

"Midgard shakes, Valkyrie. You walked the path of war. Another road calls you now. The old lands will forget your name. Your fate waits across the sea."

The whisper ceased.

Eyes fell upon her from the dark. Not the völva. Not her band. Another gaze. Older than gods. Watching from beyond the veil.

Cold filled her veins. The words stayed. She did not yet grasp them, but she knew this: it was no trick.

It was a prophecy.

And prophecy was never ignored.

CHAPTER 7

THE CALL TO THE COLONIES

The völva's words stayed in her mind. They cut deep. She heard them again and again and could not drive them out. Their meaning lay hidden from her grasp.

"The Black Goat stirs. The Devil waits. Shadows fall on the western lands."

The words returned without end. Each return drove her toward the road she had not chosen. She asked why the völva spoke in riddles. If the woman saw the end, why keep it hidden?

Liv sat near the outskirts of the village, where the land sloped toward the sea. The morning air was crisp, saturated with the salt of distant waves. But the freshness did little to clear her thoughts. She clenched a small stone in her palm. She turned it absently between her fingers. The village behind her carried on as if nothing had changed. Children laughed. Men chopped wood. The distant clang of a blacksmith's hammer clanged. But for Liv, the world had shifted.

A rustle in the trees broke her daydream. A lone raven perched on a branch above. Its black eyes fixed on her. It called once. Then again. Then a third time.

Her heart beat hard. She narrowed her eyes.

The raven lifted its wings. It flew west toward the far sea. She watched until it was gone. The sound of its cry stayed with her.

Cold ran down her spine.

It was a sign. She had read omens before and knew this one. The völva had spoken of the western lands. Odin's bird called her west.

West.

The raven's cry stirred something deep in her mind. Not Vinland of the old sagas. Something new. The colonies men spoke of in the harbors.

Ölrún let out her breath and shut her eyes. No doubt touched her now. Her path lay across the sea. Darkness moved there. She would face it.

She rose to her feet and cast off her unease. The road ahead was hard. She would not go alone. Tonight, she would go where men gather and find those willing to join her.

She had a journey to prepare for.

The tavern near the wharf stood close and heavy with smoke. Heat came from the fire. Men drank ale. Sailors shouted. The air stank of salt and sweat. Ölrún sat in a corner. She gripped her own horn. She had not drunk. She thought about the words of the völva.

Flame roared in the hearth. Light spread across the tables. Men and women ate and spoke. Their talk held no meaning for her. She heard only the völva's words in her head.

The Black Goat stirs. The Devil waits. Shadows fall on the western lands.

The words lodged in her bones. They did not go.

The innkeeper came with a jug. He set it down. "Brännvin," he said.

Ölrún looked at him. "Have you nothing older?"

He frowned. He went to the back. He returned with a clay jug. "Mead. Few want it now."

Ölrún poured. The drink was thick and sharp on her tongue. She nodded. "It will do."

She turned the drinking horn in her hand. She stared into the golden liquid. Its surface rippled with the movement of the tavern. How many times had she sat in places like this? Surrounded by warriors. Warmed by fire and drink. Only to leave again when the next battle called.

But this time was different. The danger she felt creeping from across the sea was unlike any she had faced before.

A shadow crossed her table. She raised her head.

"You sit too still tonight," said Signe. She sat across from her. Thick braids hung heavy. Old scars lined her arms. She set down her own horn with a thud. "It does not suit you."

Ölrún raised her gaze. The tavern shook with talk and drinks. Her road lay elsewhere.

"I was given a sign," she said. "A warning from the völva."

Signe's face turned hard. She had fought at Ölrún's side for years. She had seen fate lean toward her.

"What did she say?"

Ölrún spoke the words. Each word felt heavy. Signe frowned, then rubbed a calloused hand over her jaw.

"The Black Goat..." Signe muttered. "That is a bad omen."

"It is more," Ölrún said. "It is a name. Old and patient. The völva spoke of the western lands. There the dark rises."

Signe exhaled and glanced over her shoulder. Others in the hall had noticed their hushed conversation. A few warriors leaned in.

Ölrún stood. Her voice carried through the tavern.

"I sail west."

The hall was hushed. Firelight showed their faces. Some eager. Some wary.

"The völva spoke of a great evil in the west," she said. "I have seen the signs. The raven flew west. I will not turn. I will meet what awaits. There is something coming, and I will face it before it spreads."

A murmur passed through the hall. Some looked away. Others sat firm.

Signe rose. She stood with her. "You will not go alone."

Ölrún looked across the tavern. "I need warriors. Not only men with steel. I need those who have faced the dark. This war is not like others."

Silence held. One voice rose. Then another. Then more.

"I go," said a woman with a sword hanging on her hip.

"And I," called a voice from the back.

A tall woman with dark braids wore a bow on her back. She gave a firm nod. "If you sail west, I stand. The raven may call you to battle. I will see the new land. I will take a new life there."

More answered. Warriors. Hunters. They had seen much. None turned aside. They knew better than to ignore an omen.

Her chest eased. She did not know what awaited across the sea. She would not face it alone. But she would not face it alone.

The docks stank of brine, damp wood, tar, and men who had long since grown numb to the scent of the sea. Merchants called at their stalls. Sailors reeled from alehouses. Gulls circled above. Their shrill cries were lost in the noise of trade and travel. Ölrún walked with a firm step. She drew her cloak close against the sea wind. The others followed her. Eyes turned away.

They needed a ship. A broad trader bound for the western lands.

They passed small craft not fit for the sea. They passed tall warships with guns and guards. They sought one between. Strong for the ocean yet plain enough to be ignored.

The threads of fate would guide her to the right ship. To the right destination. The seiðr had brought her this far, she thought.

Signe walked ahead. Her eyes moved over the crowd. "There." She pointed to a ship at the far berth. The Storm Hag. Her hull scarred and patched from old voyages. The crew moved with heavy steps. The captain stood on the plank. His hair gray. His eyes narrow. He spoke with the taxman.

"He looks worn. He wants coin," said Yrsa.

Ölrún gave a nod. "We make our offer."

They walked up with hard faces. The captain watched them. His coat hung in strips. A patch bore the name Jens Halvorsen. His voice came flat. "Your business?"

"We go west. To the American colonies."

He looked back at her. "Passengers?" His gaze flickered to their weapons, then back to Ölrún. "Or trouble?"

Signe smirked. "Passengers who can handle trouble. Should it come."

Jens exhaled. "I've got men for that."

"Not enough," said Ölrún. She pointed at the ship. "Storms come. Raiders wait. You lack men. We pay silver. We work. When war comes, we fight."

Jens stared long. His face showed the years at sea and war. He spat into the water. "Ten silver each."

Freydis scoffed. "Five."

"Eight," Jens said flatly. "And you work for your meals."

Ölrún did not look away. "Done."

The deal was struck. They would sail at dawn.

The Storm Hag strained against the sea. Her planks cracked. Days passed. Then weeks. The sea spread wide. The sky stayed closed. Cold lay in their bones, though spring had come.

She felt it long before she understood it.

A wrongness.

At first, the signs were small. A shadow longer than the man who cast it. The sound of boots on the deck when no one was there. The sea struck the hull out of tune with the waves.

Then came the dreams.

Each night the dreams returned. Fog closed around her. Trees leaned and bent. Shadows moved among them. The voices pressed against her mind. She heard their sound, though she did not know the tongue. A name came again and again.

She was not alone.

Signe woke one night with a sharp gasp. Her breath was ragged. Sweat slicked her forehead. Across the cramped sleeping quarters, Freydis lay awake and stared at the wooden beams above.

"You dreamed it also," Ölrún said.

"A forest of bones. A shape moved there." She rubbed her arms. "It looked at me. It waited," Freydis said.

She exhaled and rubbed her arms as if to chase away the chill.

"I felt it watching. Not like an animal. It waited."

Ölrún had no answer.

After that, the fear grew.

Men spoke in turn. They told of faces in the sea. They told of footsteps on the boards. A goat's cry rose on the wind. A sour smell came in the night and was gone by dawn.

Then a man was gone.

His name was Bjarke. A seasoned deckhand. Stronger than most. He had a wariness that kept men alive at sea. And yet, on the seventh morning, his bunk lay empty.

His boots stood by the bench. His coat hung on the peg. No struggle showed. No splash was heard in the night.

"He must've gone overboard," Jens said. But the words felt empty. Like a lie spoken not to deceive, but to ward off something worse.

None believed him.

Silence spread. Heavier than grief.

After Bjarke's disappearance, the ship itself seemed to turn against them. Ropes came loose. Shapes crossed the deck. The wind turned without warning and drove them off course.

One night, Ölrún stood at the rail. She looked out at the sea below. Wind roared across the water. A goat cried from the deep. A sound that did not belong to the waves.

A hollow call. A goat's cry.

It came from the deep. It struck through her flesh and stayed in her chest.

Yrsa came to her side. Her fists closed hard on the rail. "You hear it," she said.

Ölrún gave a nod. Her gut tightened.

"The men call the voyage cursed," said Yrsa. "They say we carry a doom. Or it waits on the far shore."

Ölrún did not answer.

She did not need to.

She already knew the truth.

The Black Goat stirs.

The Storm Hag strained forward. She cut through the gray sea. The sky never cleared. The crew didn't speak of it, but Ölrún could see it in their faces. The fear. The sleepless nights. The way they avoided looking too long into the dark waters below.

But Ölrún did not have the luxury of fear.

She spent the voyage watching her band. She judged them not only as fighters but as folk. They were bound for a foe beyond war of men. If they were to face it, she had to know their hearts.

Signe came to her at the bow one night. The sea spread endlessly before them.

"You wear that look," Signe said. She set her arm on the rail.

"What look?"

"The one that says you're trying to fight the gods themselves," Signe said. She gave a thin smile, though her eyes stayed hard.

Ölrún exhaled. She kept her eyes on the horizon. "I have fought many foes. Never have I felt fate so near."

"And yet, you march toward it like you always do."

"There is no other way."

Signe watched her in silence. "Then it's good that you do not walk alone."

They stood without a word. The sea beat low under them.

Another night the lantern burned low. Yrsa and Freydis sat cross-legged on the deck. They cast carved bones marked with runes. Freydis read them as if they spoke some truth.

Ölrún crouched beside them. "You still call on the runes," she said. "After so many winters?"

Freydis gave a short smile. "Aye. They speak more plain than men."

Yrsa set down her dice. "The marks hold truth, but I hold to my bow."

Freydis cast the bones. They struck wood and lay still. One showed the thorn. One showed the hail. One showed the yew.

Ölrún took one up. She knew the signs. Foes draw near. Death walks with them. The road west will change all who tread it.

Freydis gave a slow nod. "So it is. The marks speak. I believe."

Ölrún's voice was steady. "Tell me what you see."

Freydis sat in silence. Then she spoke. "The signs lie clouded. The gods give no word of victory or loss. Only passage."

"Passage where?"

Freydis met her eyes. "To a place we will not leave the same."

Cold settled over them. Ölrún set the bone down and rose. "Then we will be ready."

Freydis gave no word. Her eyes stayed on the bones. She sought what they hid.

Gudrun sat by the lantern. She ground dry herbs with hard strokes. The smell was bitter and sharp in the air. It fought against the salt of the sea.

Ölrún sat nearby. She didn't speak. She watched her hands move.

"I wonder how much healing can serve in what waits," said Gudrun. She kept her eyes on the bowl.

"It has served before," said Ölrún.

Gudrun let out a hard breath. "I mend wounds. The men fight once more. I close the cut. The blood runs again."

Ölrún met her eyes. "Yet you remain."

Gudrun raised her eyes. "Because some lives still matter."

"Then I hope you are right."

Ragna was the youngest. She wanted to prove herself. She held her tongue. She stood often at the rail. She kept her eyes on the sea. She watched for too long.

One night, Ölrún walked to her side.

"Do not give the sea your thoughts," she said.

"I watch the waves."

"You fear what awaits."

"I do."

"There is no shame in fear," Ölrún said. "But do not let it stop your blade when the time comes."

Ragna gave a nod. Her eyes showed doubt.

Hildr was the last. One night she stood with her at the stern. She gave voice to what Ölrún had known would come.

"You truly believe in this prophecy?" Hildr was the last. She gave voice to what Ölrún had known would come. "You say we sail to fight a foe not of this world?"

"I do."

"And what if you're wrong?"

Ölrún gave no pause. "Then we fight still. For a foe waits. You may not heed gods or signs. Yet you have felt it. We go toward it."

Hildr sighed. "Aye. I have felt it."

That was enough.

On the last night before landfall, the fog came.

It was thick and unnatural. It spread across the deck and hid all. The sound of the sea grew faint. The sailors muttered. They drew cloaks close against a cold that came from no wind.

WHISPERS IN THE PINES

Ölrún stood at the bow. She looked into the mist.

A sound rose across the sea. A goat cried low. The call came from the deep.

She let out her breath. It came slow. It came steady.

Tomorrow, they would reach land.

Tomorrow, they would step into the unknown.

The Black Goat stirred.

CHAPTER 8

THE TOWN OF WHISPERS

Newport, Rhode Island, 1710

The Storm Hag cut through the morning mist. Her sails hung limp as the ship slid into the harbor. Rhode Island. Land at last. Ölrún stood at the rail. The relief she had hoped for did not come.

Something was wrong.

The docks stretched before them. Unlike the noisy harbors of Europe, this place stood too still. Few people walked the waterfront. No gulls circled above. The air carried the scent of salt and damp wood, but underneath, something lingered. A scent she couldn't place, but instinctively distrusted.

Her warriors gathered behind her in silence. The Storm Hag creaked as the ship settled against the dock.

Signe came to her side. "This place is wrong."

Ölrún nodded. "Eyes are on us."

They were.

The dockmen did not come near. They stood apart. Their expressions were guarded. Their movements were stiff. Some pretended to be busy securing crates and barrels. They cast glances too often toward the newcomers. One man with a sea-dark face muttered to his mate. Then he turned and hurried inland.

Freydis ran a hand along her belt. Her dagger sat ready.

"They fear something."

Carvings scarred the posts along the dock. Some were old runes of ward, marks she knew. Others bent crooked. Spirals cut deep. Twisted shapes gouged into the grain. One showed a goat's head. Its eyes stood hollow. Its mouth gaped wide.

Yrsa frowned and laid her hand on the cut.

"Made not long ago."

A soft clack of wood struck the air along the dock.

Ölrún turned toward the sound.

At the pier's edge stood a woman. A hunched figure wrapped in a tattered shawl. Her face was half-hidden beneath heavy fabric. Her hands trembled as she clutched a string of wooden prayer beads. The carved symbols on them were worn smooth from years of use.

She stared at Ölrún.

Then she spoke with a voice faint as a breath.

"You should not have come."

The words clung to the thick air. They lay heavy as the mist.

Ölrún stepped from the gangplank to the planks.

"Why?"

The woman shuddered. Her fingers locked hard around the beads.

"He watches."

The dockmen slipped off. They wanted no part of her words.

Ölrún stepped closer. "Who watches?"

Her lips trembled. Her breath came short. Then she whispered.

"The Goat."

A gust tore through the docks. The rigging rattled.

Signe stepped closer. Her stance grew tighter.

"Who is this Goat?"

She shook her head fast. "He does not speak his name. Nor do they."

"They?"

Her eyes turned toward the houses beyond the docks.

"They keep apart. Yet they hear."

Ölrún looked that way. Wooden houses stood still along the road. Too many doors shut. Too many windows dark. The place felt like a grave.

Freydis spoke low. "This place is dying."

Ölrún turned back to her. "Speak what you know."

The woman swallowed hard. She drew a blackened token from her shawl and set it in Ölrún's palm. Her fingers shook as she did.

"Gooseberry Island," she said.

The name hung heavy in the air.

Ölrún looked at the token. A crude spiral cut its face. The same mark as on the posts.

She raised her gaze. Terror now filled the woman's eyes. Sudden. Sharp.

"I spoke too much." Her voice shook. "They know. They always know."

Ölrún watched her vanish.

Behind her, Gudrun whispered. "What have we stepped into?"

Ölrún clenched the token tight.

They had not stepped past the docks. Already the shadow of the Black Goat lay upon them.

Ölrún slid the token into her pouch. She faced her warriors.

"We move."

One by one, the others left the Storm Hag. Their boots struck the planks with a sound heavy and final. The town lay ahead, veiled in mist and unease.

As they went on, the streets came into view in broken pieces. Windows stood dark. Doors shut tight from within. A few people hurried through the narrow ways with heads low and eyes turned aside.

A town in retreat.

Gudrun spoke low. "A port should ring with life. Where are the merchants? The sailors? The cries of trade?

No smell of bread. No smoke of meat. No call of fishmongers. Only silence.

A few townspeople lingered near the houses. They cast quick glances toward the strangers and then looked away. Their shoulders bent inward. None turned their backs. Each feared what might walk behind them.

Yrsa set her hand near the hilt. "They fear us."

"No." Freydis searched the black doors. "They're afraid of something else."

The same cuts marked the houses. Fresh lines scored the wood. Spirals were cut into stone. The goat's head again. The same sign as on the token.

Signe stopped in front of a wooden sign nailed above a boarded-up tavern. It had once read *The Red Stag*, but black paint had been smeared over the words. A new sigil had been carved beneath it.

A spiral.

Astrid said, her tone flat. "A brand."

Hildr scowled. "Or a warning."

Ölrún's hand locked on the token. Gooseberry Island. The path pointed that way. Yet they needed words first.

A figure stood at the far end of the street. An old sailor in torn clothes. Broad of frame. Hardened by the sea. Fog veiled his legs. His eyes were dark.

He met their gaze and did not look away.

Ölrún lifted her hand to the others. She walked toward him. He did not move. He did not flinch.

"You seek something," he said before they spoke. His voice rasped like waves on stone.

Ölrún stopped before him.

"Gooseberry Island."

His mouth twitched but gave no smile. He pulled at his coat. "You do not want that place."

Signe crossed her arms. "Yet we will."

He breathed slow. "Then hear me first."

The street lay still. Only the far tide broke. The man shifted his stance and spoke.

"They came years ago. They called themselves Puritans." He gave a bitter laugh. "Not like the others.

They built no church. Took no trade. They kept apart on the island. They watched."

Ölrún frowned. "And now?"

"They take."

Wind struck the street. Shutters banged loose.

"Folk vanished," the sailor said. "First the drifters. Men no one missed. Then the children. Some returned." His jaw tightened. "They were not the same."

Gudrun pulled her cloak close. "And the others?"

His eyes turned darker. "Never seen again."

Silence.

Yrsa let out a hard breath. "And none fought them?"

He swept his hand at the empty street. "This is what is left of those who tried."

The Black Goat held this place. Unseen, yet the air bore its grip.

Ölrún held out the token from the old woman. "What does this mark mean?"

He stared for a long moment. Then muttered. "It marks their own."

Freydis scoffed. "Their own what?"

"Sacrifices."

Cold stillness fell.

Ölrún slid the token back into her pouch. "How do we reach the island?"

He studied her face and then looked past her to the warriors. His breath hissed through his nose. He shook his head as if mourning them already.

"Beyond the marsh lies an old dock," he said. "At low tide, the sand joins the island. Go if you must. But leave before nightfall. The sea comes fast."

Ölrún's voice stayed steady. "Why?"

The man swallowed. Then he spoke the same words the woman had whispered.

"Because He watches."

They went north along the coast. For two days the sea lay at their side. They passed villages that gave no welcome.

The wind carried the smell the sea. Salt and decay hung in the air. Marsh spread wide before them, dark and endless. Each step sank in wet earth. The path bent through reeds and still pools that held the gray sky.

Ölrún felt it at once. A breath touched her skin. Not the sea wind. Something other. A warning without a voice.

Signe walked at her side. Her eyes searched the horizon.

"This place is too still."

"It does not want us here," Yrsa said.

The path bent to the shore. An old dock leaned at the edge. Its beams sagged. Its posts stood black with tide and years. Beyond lay a thin bar of sand, half-hidden by fog. It led to an island set apart. An island men spoke of in whispers.

Gooseberry Island.

A mass of dark trees rose beyond the shore. Branches twisted upward like bones. No smoke marked a hearth. No sign of life stirred. Yet they knew eyes lay on them.

Ölrún let out a breath. She set her sword strap firm.

"We cross."

As they moved, a voice broke the mist.

"You shouldn't go there."

The group turned sharply.

WHISPERS IN THE PINES

A man stood a few paces away at the marsh edge. He was thin and wore patched clothes worn by many seasons. His hands bore calluses and dirt. His face was carved with age. His eyes were sharp. They knew.

He was no common townsman. He had waited for them.

Ölrún measured him with her eyes. "And yet we are."

The man let out a long breath and shook his head. "Then hear what awaits."

He spoke of what the others would not.

The settlers had come to Gooseberry Island nearly a hundred years past. Puritans, yet not the same as the rest. They raised no church. They welcomed no guests. They bent their knees to something older.

"They never called themselves a church," the man said. "They named themselves Keepers."

Ölrún looked at Signe. "Keepers of what?"

"A god that did not belong to the new land."

The air grew heavy.

He pointed to the cut signs on the posts. "Their mark. A warning. A vow. Cross the sand and you enter what never left."

Still, Ölrún did not bend. "How do we reach them?"

The man paused. Then, he drew a rusted key from his coat and held it in an open hand.

"On the northern edge of the island stands a house," he said. "Old. Near its fall. It once belonged to the last man who stood against them. This key will open it."

Freydis took the key. She turned it in her hand. "What waits inside?"

The man's eyes darkened.

"The beginning."

CHAPTER 9

THE HOUSE OF THE LOST

Gooseberry Island, Massachusetts, 1710

The sandbar lay before them. Wet with salt water. So narrow the sea could cover it within hours. It was the only path to the island.

Ölrún set her boot on the strip of sand. The wind ceased at her step. The air, the sea, the gulls, and even the world itself stilled.

She walked on.

The trees beyond the shore whispered.

Not with wind.

With another voice.

Ölrún exhaled and walked forward.

Her warriors came after her. Their hands held their weapons. Their eyes fixed on the dark edge of the trees.

By nightfall, they would stand upon the island.

And by then, the thing within would know they had come.

The house stood ahead. A ruin taken by years. Vines gripped its sinking timbers. Roots split the old wood.

Windows gaped. They were black and bare. The place had stood empty for years.

Ölrún tried the steps with her boot. The boards creaked but did not give. The others followed. They moved with care. Their eyes searched the overgrown clearing and its shadows.

She inserted the key into the lock. It fought her. Old metal bound with rust. Then it yielded with a hard click.

The door opened.

The air inside hung thick. It stank of rot and neglect.

Dust lay in layers. The floor bent and split where moisture had eaten the wood. Broken chairs and splintered boards lay where they had fallen. Forgotten.

A desk sagged by the wall. Its weight had broken it. Papers lay about. Their edges curled and darkened.

Freydis entered. Her step was wary.

"No one has dwelt here for years."

Yrsa knelt by a heap of books. She lifted one. The leather cracked. The binding nearly gone.

"They fled in haste," she said.

Signe went to a shelf of books. Many had fallen to dust. A few held shape. She drew one down. She frowned.

"Latin."

Ölrún crossed the room. She looked at the pages.

"Can you read it?"

Freydis took the book from her. The pages were brittle. The script slanted. She turned them slow. Her lips moved as she worked the words onto her own tongue.

At last, she spoke.

"It is no printed tome. The hand is of a man, not a press. It tells this: They gather in the black grove. The old rites endure, though the names are changed. The signs are plain. Something moves below. The door is shut, yet the ground is foul with its presence."

She lifted her eyes. "This was no common dwelling. It was their stronghold."

Gudrun bent by the hearth. She scraped the stone. A spiral showed. The same cut they had seen on the dock posts.

"They marked this place," she said.

Hildr stood over the shattered chair. "They kept something here. Someone sought to bury it."

Ölrún turned her gaze to the far end. A door hung open. Beyond it lay only darkness.

"We search the rest," she said. "What they hid, we will bring to light."

The house had been abandoned. But its secrets remained.

Ölrún went deeper. Her boots sank into the dust of years. The others came behind. Their steps were careful. Their breath held. The house was meant to be forgotten. Yet something stayed.

Wind slid through broken boards. Dust lifted. The old wood moaned.

Signe laid a hand on the shelf. "If there was worth here, they sought to erase it."

Ölrún scanned the wreckage. "Not everything."

She went to the desk. Parchment lay scattered. Ink bled into soft paper. Edges charred black. Burned in haste.

Freydis raised a page. The script ran thin and crooked. "This is no ledger. It is a record."

Yrsa frowned. "Of what?"

Freydis spoke low as she read.

He walks in the space between. The hollow-eyed beast stirs beneath the roots of the world. He is called forth in the grove of black trees, where the ground is thin and unclean. His voice does not echo, yet it is heard. The gate must not open. The gate must not open.

Stillness fell upon them.

Gudrun crouched beside the desk. She brushed aside the crumbling remains of another book. Beneath it, her fingers found something harder. She pulled free a wooden carving. Small enough to fit in a palm.

She turned it in the dim light. A goat's head, carved with crooked lines. Eyes cut hollow.

She shivered and gave it to Ölrún. "Made with belief," she said.

Ölrún held it. She felt the mark of faith upon it.

A sound came from the rear of the house.

The warriors stiffened. Hands found hilts.

Signe raised her hand toward the open door. "It waits there."

Ölrún went first. The others followed.

The door stood ajar. Darkness waited beyond. The air smelled of damp earth. And of something older.

She pushed it wide and entered.

The floor ended at a cut in the earth.

The floor ended at a cut in the earth.

Symbols cut deep into the soil and stone. Some painted in dried blood. Bones lay at the bottom. Beast and man alike. Some too broken to tell.

Yrsa drew breath. "This was no home."

It was a temple," said Freydis.

Ölrún crouched at the edge. She stared into the black earth.

The ground lay wrong beneath her.

Too dark.

Too deep.

As if touched by what should not be here.

A whisper drifted through the still air. Not a voice of men.

Freydis set her hand to her brow. "The earth is foul," she said.

Hildr spoke steadily. "Then we burn it."

Hildr's voice was steady. "Then we should burn it."

Ölrún rose. Shadows closed in. The silence no longer lay empty. The house listened.

"Not the end," she said. "The beginning."

The Keepers were still here.

They had only begun to uncover the truth.

Night had fallen on Gooseberry Island. A thin crescent hid behind the clouds. The torches in their hands gave the only glow.

The ruins stood before them. A husk that should not remain. They had seen the pit. They had read the records. They had held what was left behind decayed walls. "This place should not stand."

Hildr moved ahead. Her torch cast long shadows on the rotted boards. "This place must fall."

Ölrún nodded. "Burn it."

Hildr flung the torch into the dry wood. The flames caught.

For a moment, it burned like true fire.

Then it changed.

Flame ran across the planks. Too fast. Sideways. It spread but did not eat the wood. The fire turned blue. It writhed like a serpent.

Freydis stepped back. "This is no fire."

The flames coiled like things alive. The board stayed whole. No smoke rose. The air grew close. Hard to breathe.

Then the ground shifted.

Yrsa's breath caught. "Look."

A shape slid through the soil.

One at first. Dark and thin. It wound through the grass to the stones. Then another. Then more.

Serpents.

WHISPERS IN THE PINES

They poured from the earth beneath. From the broken boards. From the pit.

Their bodies shone in the blue light. Scales dark as deep water. Some no thicker than rope. Others vast, coiling in ways no eye could follow.

One great serpent rose from the pit. Its body climbed higher than it should. Its jaws stayed shut. Still, Ölrún felt something.

A voice.

Not spoken. Not of men.

It struck her skull. It rang in her bones.

"You do not understand. You do not belong."

Ölrún drew a hard breath. The fire burned on. The house stood unmarked.

Then the flames died at once.

The serpents vanished.

No retreat. No remains. One moment they writhed. The next, the ground lay still.

The house remained standing. Untouched. The wood was whole as it had been before they tried to burn it.

The only sign was silence.

Signe exhaled sharply. "We leave."

Ölrún nodded. They could not destroy this place. Yet something had marked them.

She turned toward the dark trees. Her hand closed on her blade. The village waited.

And now, it knew they were coming.

CHAPTER 10

THE BLACK GROVE

The path to the village cut through the island's thick interior. The trees stood close. Branches grew mangled and reached upward. The air grew colder the farther they walked. No wind stirred the leaves.

The warriors walked in silence. Their breath showed in the night air. Unease clung to them, but Ölrún went on. There was no turning back.

In the distance, water lapped against the shore, slow and steady. But beneath it, another sound drifted through the trees.

A hum.

Low. Distant.

It shook the ground.

Gudrun slowed her steps. "That is no wind."

Yrsa turned her head. "It comes from the grove."

Ölrún knew of the place. She remembered the words in the Latin journal.

The Black Grove.

The Keepers of the Black Goat did not worship in the village. They gathered deeper in the forest. In the grove where the oldest trees stood. Roots knotted deep in the island soil.

Signe murmured, "We should not go near it."

The hum changed. It became a chant.

Freydis drew in a sharp breath. "They pray already."

Ölrún raised her hand for silence. She stepped from the path toward the trees. The others hesitated but followed.

The deeper they went, the thicker the air grew. A smell hung in the leaves. Not rot. Not decay. Metallic. Wet. Old.

The hum grew louder.

The trees thinned.

Beyond the branches, the Black Grove opened before them.

They stopped at the edge, half-hidden behind the trunks.

At the clearing's center stood a great stone altar. Its surface was slick with dark stain. The stain pooled at the edges and dripped into the earth.

Spirals were carved deep into the rock. Sharper than those on the docks.

Figures stood in a circle. Heads bowed. Hands raised in slow rhythm. Robes dark as the grove. Faces hidden under hoods.

The chant was not English. Not any tongue Ölrún knew.

A presence touched her mind. She understood.

Freydis gripped her dagger. "They are not alone."

Ölrún held her breath. Beyond the altar, at the roots of the trees, something moved.

It was not a man.

Not a beast.

Smoke thickened at the roots. From it came a shape. Not steady. Not whole. It rose, broke, took form, and broke again. Horns flickered.

Dark as night.

A goat's shape, yet not of flesh.

A spirit of the wood.

A hunger that poisoned the ground.

The chant rose.

The goat-shape turned.

Ölrún lifted her sword and strode forward.

Her warriors moved with her.

The cloaked ones raised their hands.

The smoke drew them back.

One by one they vanished into the dark, as if the Grove itself had swallowed them.

Beyond the roots, the spirit writhed, but it did not cross the trees.

It did not need to. They had been seen.

They had been marked.

The village waited.

CHAPTER 11

THE SILENT VILLAGE

The warriors walked on in silence.

The Black Grove lay behind them. Yet what they had seen stayed with them. The goat-shape in the smoke. The chant that had crawled through their bones. The shapes had vanished when they charged. Gone like breath on cold air. Still, the sense of it followed.

The village lay ahead.

The path narrowed. Trees stood close, then gave way. Wooden houses rose in rows. Their roofs dark with age. A dirt road cut through the settlement, ending at a bare space where an unlit bonfire stood.

It looked like any Puritan village. Yet something was wrong.

Nothing moved.

No voices.

No livestock.

No hammers.

The daily sounds were gone. The air lay still.

Freydis spoke. "Where are they?"

Ölrún looked at the windows.

Dark.

Some closed with cloth.

Others gaped. Hollow. Like empty eyes.

But Ölrún knew they watched.

Signe stepped forward. Her hand lay on her blade.

"They know we are here."

Gudrun shivered. "They have been waiting."

Ölrún went on. Her warriors followed. Each footstep struck hard on the earth. The houses were not empty. Smoke clung to the air. The fires had been put out recently. The path lay clear.

No ruin.

No fight.

Only silence.

Only absence.

They passed a well. The stone rim bore the same spirals seen at the ruins. Cut deep. Carved with devotion.

A single wooden cross stood near a house. It was not true. The wood bent in a way no man could shape. A sign of the Goat's touch.

Ragna shifted her weight. "They watch."

Ölrún felt it too.

They were not alone.

Then the village changed.

A door opened. Its sound carried through the silence.

An old man stepped onto the street. His face was lined. His eyes gave nothing. He wore dark clothes. His hands were folded as if in prayer.

Another door opened.

Then another.

The villagers emerged.

Men, women, and children came forth. Onto porches. Into the street. Along the dirt paths. They did not move. They did not speak. They only watched.

A child clutched his mother's skirt. He peered out. His eyes were too solemn for one so young.

The old man walked forward. The others stayed. They watched.

Ölrún stood still.

The man halted a few paces away. He tilted his head as if to study her. His voice was low. Steady. Certain.

"You have come at last."

Ölrún's hand closed on her sword hilt.

The man smiled. Not with warmth. With certainty.

"You were expected."

The villagers did not move. Their faces were blank.

Signe shifted beside her. "They are too quiet."

Gudrun's hand brushed her satchel, seeking a charm.

The elder's eyes were certain, as if he had seen this moment long before. The villagers behind him stood without changing.

Ölrún studied him. His certainty unsettled her.

He was not afraid.

None of them were.

Ölrún exhaled. Her voice was even.

"Then you know why we are here."

She did not lower her guard.

The elder folded his hands.

"We have always known."

The warriors stood tense. Hands near weapons. The villagers did not move.

The elder gestured toward the square.

"You have come far," he said. "There is much to speak. Come. Let us not stand as strangers under the open sky."

Ölrún did not move. "What do you call yourselves?"

The man smiled again. Thin. Certain.

"We are those who keep the old ways," he said. "Those who listen."

Gudrun whispered, "They are Keepers."

The elder's face did not change. A flicker passed through his eyes. Amusement at being named.

"You are tired," he said. "Come. Rest. Eat. Then we shall speak of the things you have come to know."

A trap.

Ölrún felt it, but they had little choice. The village watched. The forest watched. The Goat waited.

They would go inside. They would listen. They would not lower their guard.

They followed the elder through the village. The houses stood too well-kept for such an isolated place. This place thrived while others starved. The faint smell of food carried on the air. An insult to the starving lands elsewhere.

The hall stood at the village's heart. Long. Dark beams. A high roof. Inside, the air was thick with burning tallow, fresh-cut herbs, and something else. Something metallic.

The villagers stayed outside. They did not follow. They watched.

A long table was set. Food lay untouched. Bread. Roasted meat. Bowls of stew. The elder gestured to the benches.

"Eat," he said. "There is no need for swords here."

Freydis gave a short laugh. "You expect us to believe that?"

The elder smiled. "No."

Ölrún stayed standing. "You speak as though this tale was written long before we came."

The elder poured a cup. Dark liquid. He drank slowly, then spoke.

"There are many stories. Ours is older than most."

Ölrún held his gaze. "Tell it."

The elder set his cup down. His hands were folded on the table. His eyes shone, pleased to speak.

"This land is old," he said. "Older than the men who claimed it. Older than the tribes who walked here Before any foot touched the soil. Before any tree rose. It was claimed."

His voice carried rhythm. A sermon. A hymn.

"The God of the colonies is new," he said. "We remember the one before. The one that has always been. The Ancient One. What lies beneath."

His fingers tapped slowly on the wood.

"We are not like other villages. We do not struggle. We do not starve. We are blessed, for we do not deny Him."

Ölrún's stomach tightened. "The Black Goat."

The elder smiled at the name.

"We do not call Him that," he said.

"What do you call Him?" Signe asked.

The elder's smile did not fade. He gave no name.

He leaned forward.

"You speak the name of strangers," he said. "His true name is not for your tongue. To speak it is to bind Him. Only we may speak it."

Ölrún did not look away.

"You have seen His signs. The spirals. The ones taken. You felt it in your bones," he said. "The world crumbles, blind to what breaks through."

Freydis gripped her blade. "You speak in riddles, old man."

He chuckled. "Then I will speak plainly."

His gaze darkened.

"We made a covenant. A pact older than the stone. We do not fear famine. We do not fear war. We do not fear the god of men. We serve the Old One of the Grove. He does not belong to them."

Gudrun's expression tightened.

"And the sacrifices?"

The elder tilted his head.

"The land remembers," he said. "The land keeps what is given."

The warriors glanced at one another.

Ölrún's voice was steady. "Who do you sacrifice?"

The elder smiled.

"The chosen."

The air grew heavy.

Yrsa's voice was low. "And have you chosen tonight?"

The elder lifted his cup. He drank slow. He set it down. His fingers traced the rim. Then he spoke.

"You misunderstand."

He lifted his gaze.

"The choosing is already done."

The door opened behind them.

A figure stood in the doorway.

A figure stood in the doorway. A woman from the village. Plain clothes. Her face smooth. Her eyes dark. Black as the Grove.

Her lips parted. The voice was not human.

"He stirs."

The candles shook.

Beyond the walls came a sound. Low. A bleating. Distant in the trees.

Ölrún's hand found the sword hilt.

The sacrifice had already been chosen.

Ölrún said, "How do you choose?"

The elder's thin fingers touched the rim of the table. His face remained expressionless. His words cut sharply.

"The Old One does not ask," he said. "He takes. When the land hungers, we give."

Ölrún faced him. "How do you know the hour?"

The elder smiled. Pleased by the question.

"The land speaks," he said. "The wind bears His word. The fields fail. The storms come before their season. They do not pass. The beasts are born crooked, shaped against their kind."

Gudrun spoke. "And the people?"

The elder did not look away. "They change."

Silence fell upon the hall.

Yrsa exhaled. "You sacrifice them."

The elder tilted his head. The elder tilted his head.

"Not we. The land chooses."

Freydis gave a hard laugh. "So you tell yourselves."

The elder's hand closed on the cup.

"There are nights when the veil grows thin," he said. "When the Old One moves in smoke and root. When the stars stand strange. Then an offering must be given."

Ölrún said, "And now?"

The elder's smile widened.

"The time has come."

CHAPTER 12

A WARRIOR'S SACRIFICE

The warriors did not wait for more words. The elder had spoken enough. His tale confirmed what they feared. They left the village before the mask of welcome could turn to steel.

The Black Grove rose before them. Trees stood close. Dark and still. Mist clung to their feet as they entered the clearing. The air grew close. The land looked upon them.

A stone altar stood at the center of the Grove.

Its face ran dark with old blood. Deep cuts carried it into the soil. A girl lay upon the stone. She was only fifteen.

Her hair hung in knots. Ropes bound her hands and feet. A white robe lay loosely on her thin frame. Dirt marked her face. Her eyes shone wet, though no tears fell. Her lips moved. Her breath spoke words too soft to catch.

A figure stood above her.

A man in a crimson robe. His face was hidden. A mask shaped like a black goat's head.

He lifted a broadaxe. The edge bore old blood.

Ölrún stepped forward. Yrsa was faster.

She drew and released. The shaft struck before the axe could fall.

The arrow struck his shoulder. He staggered. The axe fell. Its blade bit earth beside the girl's head.

She screamed.

The mists stirred. From the shadows stepped more robed figures. The circle closed. Faces still hidden. Heads bent.

The Keepers had been torn from the dark. Their rite was broken.

Ölrún strode before the girl. Her sword caught the red glow from the altar.

"It ends now."

The priest of the Goat still stood. Blood ran from his shoulder. The goat-mask hid his face. He raised his head.

The priest's voice cut across the Grove. "The Old One waits. You were summoned. Yet you should not have come."

The Keepers did not strike at once. They stood in their circle. Waiting.

Waiting for the Old One to answer.

The ground shook.

The wind gave voice.

Ölrún did not turn. She had known it would come.

The Old One stirred. Smoke rose from the roots. Horns bent in the dark.

The circle held. The robed ones bowed their heads. They gave ear to the Grove.

The air grew close. The ground shook with a sound not of men. It entered the bone.

The priest raised his sound arm. His voice rang clear. Blood trailed down his arm.

"The sacrifice must be made," he said. His tone was steady. No plea. No fear. Only faith.

Ölrún said, "The girl will not die here."

The priest tilted his head.

"No," he said. "She will not."

The wind rose.

Then the Keepers moved.

They did not cry out. They did not shout. They came as one.

The clash began at once.

Signe met the first with steel. Her strike bit true. The robe split. Flesh parted. The shadow fled, and the body fell.

Freydis swung her axe. The edge split cloth and bone. A shadow slipped out as the body fell.

Yrsa threw her bow aside. She took steel in both hands. One cut across a throat. Blood leapt. The shadow within tore free and fled into the dark.

The warriors held the line. The Keepers pressed near. They struck as men, yet when steel found them they showed no fear. Flesh fell. Their spirits tore loose. Dark mist slipped toward the roots.

No cries left their mouths. Blades cut them through, yet they did not fall back. Even as blood poured, their hands seized and pulled. They tried to drag the living down into the soil.

Two rose against Ragna. She struck one down. Cloth tore. Flesh fell. Its shadow hissed and slid toward the roots.

Ölrún saw it slip. She knew then. They were bound to the Old One. She spoke a hard stave of seiðr. The word cut through the air. The roots shuddered. The shade halted. Across the Grove other shadows checked and hung. None could vanish.

The second robed one seized Ragna's arms. Grip of iron. He dragged her to the altar.

"Ragna!" Ölrún cried out. She drove forward. More robed figures rose from the mist and blocked her path. She cut one down. The body fell. No shadow fled. Her binding held. Still, the altar lay beyond her reach.

The priest raised his arm. His voice carried through the mist.

"The Old One has chosen," he said. "The pact is kept."

Ragna fought with all her strength. She kicked, struck, and clawed. One hand bound. One arm held fast. She could not break free.

The robed ones dragged her to the altar. They forced her hard against the stone, blackened with old blood.

Ölrún cried out. She cut down a hooded foe. Its body fell and did not rise.

Another stepped forward.

More came.

The priest bent over Ragna. Blood fell from his wound onto her face.

The goat-mask tilted. A voice not his own spoke. "You will take her place."

Ölrún struck again. The ground heaved under her feet. Shadows clutched at her legs.

The Keepers did not seek victory.

They needed only to hold her back.

Ragna cried out.

The Old One waited.

The wind roared through the Grove. The trees stood stiff. The earth shook with a power older than stone.

She struck again. Another robe split. Flesh fell. The shade fled to the roots. More seized her arms. They held her at the altar.

The priest did not falter.

Ragna fought on the stone. She kicked. She struck. She clawed. The hands did not release her. Her cry tore across the clearing. None came.

None but Ölrún.

The priest raised his arm. Blood slid from his wound onto Ragna's bound sleeve, streaking the cloth. His lips shaped words not meant for men. The voice that followed was not his own, but the Old One's.

The wind fell still.

The air held. No breath moved.

The forest gave a long breath.

Then it came.

Black coils rose from the ground. Not smoke. Not mist. Limbs of shadow reached for the stone. The Keepers stood unmoved. They bowed their heads in honor as the dark gathered.

Ölrún cut through another of the hooded ones. Its body broke. She was still too far.

The priest's hand clamped on Ragna's throat.

She gasped. No breath entered.

The coils gathered upon her. They sank into her chest. They entered her mouth. They burned her flesh.

She grew still. Her were eyes wide. Her mouth opened in silence.

Then

The darkness shifted. Not smoke. Not mist. A living beast.

The black limbs wound around her. They raised her from the stone. Her head fell back. Her arms hung loose. She hung in the air, caught in the shroud of the Old One.

The dark drew tight. The coil bent inward. Out of the mist stood a shape. A being wrought of shadow.

A goat.

Yet not a goat. A spirit wearing a beast's skin.

Horns curled sharply. The body heaved and wavered, as if no flesh could bind it. The eyes were blank.

It bent close above her. Breath poured cold from a mouth that was not a mouth.

Then

It crushed her.

The black limbs fell inward. They dragged her down into the roots. Flesh fell.

In one breath she had been there.

The next she was gone.

The altar stood bare.

Only the blood remained.

Ölrún screamed.

Ölrún cried out. The cry was not of woman or bird. It was the sound of wrath and grief made one. A storm was unleased. It was the birth of something terrible.

The Keepers moved then. Too late.

She fell upon them as a storm upon trees. Steel swung. Bodies fell.

She did not fight. She broke all before her.

She destroyed.

Signe. Yrsa. Freydis. Gudrun. They had no time to act. Ölrún was already among the Keepers.

The priest lifted his arms. His voice rang across the Grove.

"She was given freely," he said.

The Ancient One had claimed her soul.

Ölrún struck the last of them. Their bodies broke. She did not halt.

She strode to the altar. To the priest. To the Old One that had taken Ragna.

The Old One's breath hung over the stone. The black veil coiled and folded. Horns rose from the mist. The shape moved. Half here. Half gone.

Ölrún lifted her sword. She struck.

The steel passed through.

 Nothing.

The dark split and closed again. No wound showed. The Old One did not turn. No notice. No care.

It had taken what it sought.

Her rage meant nothing to it.

Ölrún drew a harsh breath. Her fury sought flesh.

Something that could bleed.

Her eyes found the priest. He alone had not fled. His crimson robe clung wet. His hands hung empty. The goat-mask stared. He did not move.

He only watched.

Ölrún stepped forward. She raised her blade high. The warriors cried out behind her, but her wrath was her own.

The circle broke. The Grove trembled.

The last of the Keepers scattered into the trees.

The warriors held silent.

Their weapons spoke. They struck, grim and without mercy.

Some escaped into the woods. Those who lagged stumbled. They raised their hands. They begged for mercy.

None were spared.

Not this time.

Only the priest remained.

He was Ölrún's.

She charged and struck.

Steel bit through flesh and bone.

The priest's head fell to the ground.

Blood poured over the stone. The priest's body sagged. His arms hung loose.

The goat-mask slid free of his head and struck the dirt. Beneath it, there was no human face. Only a smear of shadow. It bled away into the roots.

Ölrún roared. She lifted the mask. She held it high before the fleeing figures. The carved horns caught the dim glow. The hollow mouth grinned. A whisper of dark laughter moved through the air.

Ölrún lowered the blade. The severed head hung in her grasp. The Grove was soundless but for her breath.

She did not falter. She did not weep.

She swore to tear their world apart.

When the dead lay at her feet. When the Grove ran red. Ölrún did not stop.

She turned toward the village.

The Old One had taken from her.

Now, she would take all.

She pressed the mask to her face. The wood was cold. The smell of iron clung to it. Her voice thundered through the trees. "I am coming for you. And Hel comes with me."

HEL'S COMING WITH ME

Ölrún and her warriors left the Grove and pressed into the village. Her face lay hidden behind the black goat-mask, its wood hard against her skin. The sockets stared empty into the dark.

Signe looked at her. "Why wear their mark?"

Ölrún raised the mask in one hand. Her voice was iron. "They bowed to this face. Now they will fear it."

She pressed the mask back in place. The horns stood tall.

She turned to her warriors. "Enough hiding. We end this now."

Torches lit their path.

The village was no longer silent.

Screams rang between the houses. The warriors cut down those who had not escaped. The villagers who had stood resilient, who had believed themselves untouchable, now scattered like rats in the dark.

They had taken from her.

She would take everything from them.

She wore the black goat mask of the fallen priest.

She hurled a torch into the nearest home. Flames climbed the beams. The fire spread with unnatural speed. It leapt from roof to wall as if the land itself turned against them.

Freydis dragged a man from a doorway. Terror twisted his face. His hands lifted in prayer. She cut his throat before he could finish.

Signe and Yrsa gave chase. Their blades caught the firelight as they struck.

Gudrun and Astrid set fire to the meeting hall. It had stood at the village's heart. Now it burned.

The sky filled with smoke.

Flames devoured the village.

The fire burned for three days.

When it died, nothing remained but charred wood and blackened earth. No stone was left untouched. No body was buried. The wind carried only smoke and ruin.

Not all had perished.

Some had fled before the flames reached them. They vanished into the night. They fled into the forests, onto ships, and into hidden places in the colonies.

Some made it.

But others, Ölrún would not let escape.

She hunted them through the trees, through the marsh, through the ruins of what had once been their sanctuary.

They had lived untouched for too long.

They had thrived while others suffered.

They had believed themselves protected.

Now, they would learn what it meant to be hunted.

And Ölrún Karlsson would not stop.

Not tonight.

She would chase them across New England.

And she would end them all.

1711 – The First Whisperings

The first rumors began in Massachusetts Bay. A farming settlement found three men hung from an ancient tree. Their throats were slit. Their robes were soaked with blood.

A woman was seen leaving the village before dawn.

Her hair was red as fire.

Face hidden by a black goat mask.

Her cloak was dark with ash.

She spoke to no one. She asked for no shelter. No food. No rest.

She was gone before the sun touched the earth.

The villagers prayed she would not return.

1713 – The Terrors of the Woods

A merchant in Providence whispered of a hidden settlement in the woods. At dusk he passed through the trees and saw a dozen figures kneeling before a carved symbol on the rocks.

He fled before they saw him.

But someone else had found them.

Days later, the settlement was empty.

The houses stood abandoned. Doors swayed in the wind.

Fire pits lay cold. Ash untouched for days.

In the center, carved deep into the beams of the meeting hall, were words in a tongue none could read.

Outside, nailed to a tree, hung the body of a man in a crimson robe.

His mask was shattered.

His eyes were carved out.

His throat was cut so deep that only the spine held the head.

A child from a nearby village saw the woman who did it.

She stood among the trees. She watched. She waited. Her sword dripped blood.

The child blinked. She was gone.

1715 – The Waters of the Susquehanna

The trail led her deep into Pennsylvania. Whispers told of a cell hiding in the river valleys. For three days she tracked them through dense woods. Settlements watched her pass but asked no questions.

On the fourth morning, she found their camp abandoned. Ash lay cold. Belongings scattered. Fear hung in the air. They had fled in the night. Warned by an unseen hand.

She knelt by the river to drink and to fill her water-skin. Movement caught her eye. Across the slow water sat a figure on a log. Small and wiry. Its body covered in pale hair. Long arms, narrow chest. A face more beast than man, yet not without thought. In its hand was an apple. It bit slowly and steady.

Their eyes met across the water. Recognition passed. Recognition passed. Predator to guardian. She hunted men. It watched the wild. The creature showed no fear. Only mild wonder at the red-haired woman who walked its ground. It bit the apple once more. It stepped into the reeds. The water stirred, and it was gone. Ölrún rose and went downstream. The trail grew cold. But her work remained.

1718 – The Tunnels Beneath Boston

Sailors told of a brotherhood that met beneath Boston's streets. No lanterns burned. No prayers rose to any god but one.

Men who went into the tunnels at night did not always return.

One evening, a dozen went below.

By morning, only the red-haired woman wearing a black wooden goat mask emerged.

Her boots marked blood across the cobblestones.

Her sword was notched with use.

She spoke no words.

The tunnels never saw another gathering again.

1724 – The Last Keepers of Salem

The last survivors of the Keepers of the Black Goat gathered in secret. They had lost too many.

Their settlements had burned.

Their priests had been slain.

Their altars had been defiled.

And the red-haired huntress in the black goat mask had never stopped.

She chased them from Rhode Island to Connecticut. From the wild frontier to the cobbled ports. They hid among Puritans, Quakers, traders, beggars. She found them all.

It was said that when she entered a town, some vanished by dawn.

It was said that she did not sleep.

That her blade did not dull.

That when the moon was high, the trees whispered her name.

She did not age.

And still she hunted.

The last Keepers of Salem prepared a last rite. Their last hope to break the cycle. To rid themselves of the woman who had become their curse.

But they did not know.

Ölrún Karlsson was already there.

CHAPTER 14

THE RED-HAIRED
HUNTRESS

Salem, 1724

The tavern was war. It was filled with the scent of old wood, spiced cider, and damp wool coats. The fire in the hearth burned low. Shadows leapt along the stone wall.

The room held little sound for a tavern. Men bent over their cups. Their voices came in mummers. Their eyes went again and again to the door.

Thomas Crowe saw it at once.

He had sat in many taverns before. He had passed through ports. He had walked in towns where strangers found no welcome. Yet this silence came not from distrust.

It came from fear.

He set both hands on the tankard. Heat ran through his fingers. Outside, the wind howled through the street. Shutters beat hard against the walls.

At the next bench, two men spoke low in haste.

"She walked in Portsmouth three nights ago," said one.

The other gave a sharp breath. "Then she comes."

Thomas frowned. He had heard whispers of such a woman before. A huntress who moved in shadow. The mask of the Black Goat. Hair the color of fire. She left a trail of bodies in her path.

An old man spoke by the fire. He did not lift his face.

"If she comes, then the hour is already lost."

The men grew still.

Thomas bent forward. His need to know overcame him. "Who?" he said.

The three raised their faces as one.

Cold crept along his spine.

The old man searched his face. He lifted his mug. He drank slow. "You are not from this place."

Thomas shook his head. "I ride the roads between colonies. I sell books. I keep ledgers."

The old man gave a nod. He beckoned him near.

"The tales say she crossed the sea from the Old World," the old man said. His voice rasped with age. "She followed a thing that should not be followed."

Thomas frowned. "Who is she?"

The old man's mouth closed hard.

"The Red-Haired Huntress."

A heaviness sank into Thomas' chest. He had heard her name before. Always a whisper. Always a warning.

"Some call her not of this world," the old man said. "They say she eats no food. She takes no rest. She grows no older."

Thomas gave a harsh laugh. "A ghost tale."

The old man did not laugh.

"Have you seen a ghost that leaves corpses in its path?" he asked.

The men at the bench spoke no words. One traced the cross on his breast.

Thomas leaned away. "You believe it?"

The old man's eyes held steady.

"She has hunted them for many winters. From Rhode Island to Connecticut. From Boston to the edge of the wild." His fingers traced the rim of his cup. "She burned villages. She tore men from their doors. She nailed the dead to trees for all to see."

Thomas frowned. "Why?"

The old man's mouth bent in a grim shape.

"She hunts the servants of the Black Goat."

Thomas drew breath as if struck.

There stood the name again.

He had heard it before. None spoke of it in the open. It lived as a rumor. It clung as dread. Men in crimson robes. Altars in the trees.

The old man watched him close. "You have heard the name before."

Thomas sat still.

He had heard it.

Years past, on a road outside Providence, he had stopped for a night in a village that felt wrong. He left before dawn. Two weeks later, the village lay in ash.

No man spoke of what had come.

Now he sat again with the name in his ears.

He let out his breath. "Where did she walk last?"

The old man looked to the door. He waited for it to break wide.

"Nearer than your heart would wish."

The wind howled outside.

Someone in the tavern shifted uneasily.

Then the old man spoke.

"If you see her keep your tongue still."

Thomas swallowed.

"Why?"

The old man met his eyes. His face showed no mercy.

"If you see her, then death has walked before you."

The fire and flared then fell.

Outside, the wind bore the sound of steps.

Cold filled the tavern.

Thomas closed his hands on the tankard. He no longer felt the warmth of the cider.

The old man held his breath. His eyes went once more to the door.

The men at the bench drew back from Thomas. They had not seen him before. Now they looked at him differently.

With suspicion.

With recognition.

The wind struck the shutters. A gust tore through the rafters. A long creak rose from the beams.

Then

A single blow rang against the wooden wall outside.

A sharp impact.

It came not from the wind.

The tavern keeper stood stiff.

The men at the bench sat rigid. Their faces pale.

Thomas turned his head to the window.

Through warped glass he saw firelight move in the fog.

Something waited outside.

He rose to his feet. No one in the tavern moved to stop him.

The old man exhaled. "You do not want to see her."

Thomas set his hand on the door.

He thrust it wide.

The wind struck him first.

Cold.

Sharp.

Full of smoke and iron.

The street lay empty. No soul walked between the houses. Only the tavern torches gave light. Their glow threw long shadows over the dirt road.

His eyes found it.

The mark.

A spiral cut deep into the tavern wall beside the door.

Not carved as the Keepers carved it.

Not in honor.

This one lay ragged.

The edges were torn by a blade.

A warning.

Or a promise.

His breath broke. He knew the meaning.

She had stood here.

She might stand here still.

She knew him.

His gut turned. A darker truth dawned on him.

She hunted the last of them.

His name lay among theirs.

The wind rose and tore along the street.

Cold drove through the open door.

The old man stood behind him.

His eyes unreadable.

"She knows you."

Thomas swallowed.

He needed to ride.

To his young son. To Phineas.

CHAPTER 15

THE PRICE OF SURVIVAL

Thomas turned from the spiral carved into the tavern wall. His pulse struck like a drum.

She had stood here.

She knew his name.

His hands shook as he pulled his coat tight and stepped into the night. The streets of Salem lay still, yet not empty. Behind shutters and behind doors, he felt eyes upon him.

All men knew the stories.

They had seen the bodies.

They had heard the whispers.

No hand would aid him.

He walked with haste. He forced his eyes forward. The wind bore a far sound.

A creak.

A shape that shifted among the trees.

The docks lay close. The ships for New York would not leave until dawn. If he held his wits, if he moved with speed, he could take his son and vanish before first light.

His boots struck the wooden steps of his boarding house. He thrust the door wide.

The fire had sunk low in the hearth. The air within lay still.

Too still.

He knew before his eyes found it.

A spiral lay carved into his door.

Not jagged like the tavern mark. This one lay carefully and sure.

A mark not set to terrify but to warn.

She had stood here.

And she had spared him.

For now.

His hand closed hard on the knob. He thrust the door open.

The room was not empty.

She stood by the hearth with her back to him. Her red hair caught the last glow of the embers.

Her cloak hung damp from the mist. Her boots left dirt across the floor. Her sword hung loose at her side, yet he knew it meant nothing.

Thomas held his tongue.

Ölrún Karlsson turned.

She removed the goat mask.

Her eyes were cold. Sharp. Unyielding.

She had not aged since the first tale he heard of her.

Or not in a way that years could mark.

She studied him for a long moment.

Then she spoke.

"You are not a believer."

His throat dried. "No."

She stepped forth. "Yet you have seen."

Thomas clenched his fists. "I have."

Another step.

"You know what they are."

It was no question.

He let his breath go. "Yes."

Silence stretched between them.

Ölrún's hand touched the hilt of her sword, yet she did not draw.

"You do not belong to them," she said. "Not fully. Yet you bear their sickness."

Thomas felt his gut twist. "I was born into it. I did not choose."

Her voice held steady. "Nor did the ones they gave to their god."

He swallowed hard. "I never took part in it."

Ölrún tilted her head and watched him.

She measured.

She judged.

"Then prove it."

Thomas drew a short breath.

"How?"

Her grip tightened on the hilt.

"Leave."

He blinked.

She stepped closer. Her presence bore down on his ribs like iron.

"Disappear," she said. "Take your son. Burn your past. Speak never again the name of the Black Goat."

Thomas let out a sharp breath. "If I do…"

Her eyes burned into him.

"Then I will not kill you."

A heavy silence.

Thomas let out a slow breath. "And if I stay?"

Ölrún did not blink.

"Then I will not have to seek you."

He felt it then. The burden of the moment.

She had given her judgment.

Now he must make his.

Thomas found no sleep that night.

By sunrise he had gathered what little he owned.

By midday, he and Phineas boarded a ship bound for Philadelphia.

He never told his son why they had fled.

Yet he did not forget.

The Black Goat still whispered in his mind.

Though he left the cult's heart, he still bore the old words and the old rites.

So did Phineas.

Years later, when Phineas grew into a man with ambition in his blood, he remembered.

He remembered the power his father had cast aside.

And in 1935, he called it forth once more.

CHAPTER 16

THE INK AND THE QUILL

Burlington, New Jersey, 1735

The Blue Anchor Tavern sat near the riverfront in Burlington, its beams darkened by years of damp air and smoke. The place had seen better days, but it remained the heart of town. A place where men gathered to drink, trade gossip, and escape their wives for a few hours.

The usual crowd filled the room that night. Boatmen. Dockhands. Traders. Farmers. They nursed their drinks. Their talk rose and fell in a steady hum.

By the bar, Phineas Crowe leaned back in his chair. He rolled a coin between his fingers.

He was young. Sharp-eyed. Restless. His clothes marked him as someone who wished he were elsewhere. He had his father's broad shoulders, but none of his patience.

He had no wish to waste his life in Leeds Point. He had not yet learned where he was meant to go.

At the bar, Josiah Moore wiped his mouth with the back of his hand. He leaned toward Phineas.

"You ought to work for Franklin in Philadelphia," he said, with a raised drink.

Phineas raised an eyebrow. "Franklin?"

Moore nodded. "Ben Franklin's almanac. He seeks apprentices. Pays well."

Phineas frowned. "Franklin has an almanac?"

Another man, Edgar Price, chuckled into his glass.

"Of course. Started it three years ago. *Poor Richard's Almanac*. Sells better than any thought."

Phineas set down his coin. "And what of *The American Almanack*?"

Moore exhaled and shook his head. "It fell out of favor. Folk do not trust the Leeds name now."

Phineas frowned. Everyone knew of Daniel Leeds.

Phineas frowned. All knew the name Daniel Leeds. It still carried weight, but not the kind a man sought.

Price leaned closer. "You know how it began?"

Phineas gave him a hard look. "Do I seem the sort to fret over old almanacs?"

Moore chuckled and shook his head. "You should. Leeds was once the most popular almanac man in the colonies."

Price nodded. "And he might still be, had the Quakers not hated him."

Phineas scoffed. "Why? Did he write storms too fierce for them?"

Moore smirked. Price took a slow sip before he spoke.

"Worse. He wrote of things they despised."

"Back in the 1680s, Daniel Leeds printed an almanac. A strong one. But the Quakers said his words were unfit. The signs and names he used were too pagan."

Phineas snorted. "Pagan?"

Moore nodded. "Aye. Leeds even made a public apology, yet they ordered all copies destroyed. Burned. Banned. Gone."

Phineas tilted his head. "And he let them?"

Price smirked. "Not so. He grew bitter. Broke with the Quakers and kept publishing. That is when it worsened."

Moore leaned in. "In 1688 he published *The Temple of Wisdom*."

Phineas rolled his eyes. "Harmless enough."

Moore shook his head. "It was not."

Price chuckled. "It spoke of angels, astrology, and devils."

Phineas raised an eyebrow.

"Much of it drew from Jacob Boehme," Price said. "A German mystic bound to sin and redemption."

"That angered the Quakers all the more," Moore said.

Phineas scoffed. "Because of angels?"

"No," Price said. "Because of what else he wrote."

"What else?"

"1699 *The Trumpet Sounded Out of the Wilderness of America*," Moore said.

Phineas frowned. "What kind of title is that?"

Price smirked. "A blasphemous one."

Moore nodded. "He kept pressing on. By the time he defended the English crown, that was the final nail in his coffin."

"The Quakers do not suffer loyalists," Price muttered.

Phineas tapped the table. "So he was cast out. Yet he kept printing."

Moore raised his glass. "Aye. In 1716 he gave the almanac to his son, Titus."

"It did not help," Price said. "The quarrels went on."

Moore looked at Phineas. "You ever seen the Leeds crest?"

Phineas shrugged. "No."

Moore smirked. "Wyverns."

Phineas blinked.

"Two of them," Price said. "Big. Winged. Dragons. Not the mark of Christ."

Phineas looked between them. "You mean the Quakers ruined him over dragons?"

Moore shook his head. "Not only that. They already thought him a heretic. The crest was fuel for their fire."

Price chuckled. "And now Franklin seeks to wipe the Leeds name from almanacs altogether."

Phineas leaned back in his chair and thought.

An old almanac man turned enemy of the Quakers. His son struggles to keep the name alive. And now Franklin in Philadelphia, one of the most ambitious men in the colonies, setting up shop to bury them.

It was a war.

Not with swords, but with words.

Phineas liked that.

Moore nudged his arm. "So. Will you take the work?"

Phineas rolled his coin between his fingers. He thought.

At last, he smirked.

"Well," he said, "a man must make a name for himself somehow."

Philadelphia, 1735

The tavern smelled of ale, pipe smoke, and damp wool. The air hummed with the voices of merchants, dockmen, and printers. They spoke of trade, politics, and scandal.

Phineas Crowe sat across from Benjamin Franklin. An untouched tankard rested before him.

Franklin was already well known, though still young. He leaned back in his chair, a sly smile on his lips. He enjoyed the game of influence and played it well.

"I value a man eager to work," Franklin said, and raised his drink. "Ambition serves a man well."

Phineas gave a thin smile. "So I hear."

Franklin chuckled. "I'll speak plainly with you, Mr. Crowe. My almanac grows faster than I thought. You know the name. *Poor Richard's Almanack.*"

Phineas nodded. "I've heard of it."

"Good," Franklin said, and set down his drink. "Then you've heard of Titus Leeds."

Phineas shrugged. "A little. Son of Daniel Leeds. Still prints *The American Almanack.*"

Franklin smiled. "Still he prints, though I wrote him dead in 1733."

Phineas tilted his head. "You wrote him dead?"

"I foretold his death in 1733. Wrote it plain. The readers laughed, but they remembered."

Phineas frowned.

Franklin leaned forward. His voice carried the same wit that made his writing famous.

"In 1733 I wrote a prediction," Franklin said. "I said Titus Leeds would die that year."

Phineas laughed and shook his head. "And folk believed it?"

Franklin spread his hands. "They were entertained."

Phineas scoffed. "So it was a joke?"

"A profitable joke," Franklin said. "Readers bought my next issue to see what I would say of Leeds' ghost."

Phineas blinked. "Wait. He still lives?"

Franklin chuckled. "He lives still. That is the best part."

Phineas listened as Franklin went on. His voice was rich with amusement.

"Titus took offense. Called me a liar in his almanac. Said I was a false predictor. A fair charge, since he still draws breath."

Franklin's grin sharpened.

"So, I answered him. I wrote Leeds had died indeed, and the one printing his almanac was his ghost."

Phineas chuckled. It was cunning. A way to stir curiosity. To keep readers buying.

Franklin's eyes gleamed. "Here's the best of it. As his name weakens, my almanac gains ground. His sales fall. And when he does die, my words will stand true."

Phineas' smirk faded.

Franklin leaned back and drank deeply.

"Then my prediction becomes true."

A slow thought settled on Phineas.

Franklin was not only a writer. He was a manipulator.

He knew that the truth was not what mattered most.

What mattered was belief.

Phineas liked him more each passing moment.

Franklin set down his drink. "I need hands. I hired one lad, Silas Thorne. Clever, good with ink and quill.

But I need another. A sharp mind. A man who knows the worth of words."

His gaze fixed on Phineas.

"Are you that man?"

Phineas was ambitious. He wanted more than his town. More than an ordinary life.

Franklin had just shown him the power of shaping a tale.

Phineas smirked.

"A man must make a living."

Franklin grinned and held out his hand.

Phineas clasped it.

CHAPTER 17

WAR OF THE ALMANACS

Phineas Crowe kept to the print shop. Ink marked his hands. His mind held a hunger for what might be. He learned Franklin's lessons fast. He learned how words bend men and make them move.

He was not alone.

Silas Thorne had begun months earlier.

Franklin favored Silas.

Silas fit the mold. Sharp. Diligent. Dependable. His typesetting was set clean. His columns held true. He spoke with the small reserve a tradesman keeps.

He stood like the model the master would point to.

Phineas hated him.

The shop was hot. Paper, ink, and sweat filled the air. The steady rhythm of the press clanked in the background. Apprentices worked at the tables. They arranged type and bound pages in silence or low talk.

Franklin stood near the front. He reviewed the next *Poor Richard's Almanack* and sent for Silas and Phineas to show him their work.

Phineas watched in frustration as Franklin nodded at Silas' pages.

"Good work, Silas," Franklin said and touched the paper. "Your type holds. The columns read true."

Silas dipped his head. A thin smile. "Thank you, sir."

Franklin turned to Phineas' sheets. He read with a face that gave little away.

Phineas braced himself.

"This is good," Franklin said. "Not as sharp as it can be."

Phineas bit the inside of his cheek. "Where does it fail?"

Franklin pointed. "Your letters sit too tight. Here they seem fair. Once set, men will frown and turn away."

Phineas nodded, but heat burned in his chest.

Franklin moved on and dismissed them.

Phineas saw a flicker of amusement in Silas' eyes as they turned back to their stations.

"Tight spacing," Silas said, low. "A shame."

Phineas clenched his jaw. He wanted to drive his fist into Silas' smug face.

That night, Phineas sat in the tavern corner. With a drink before him, he turned a coin in his fingers and thought.

The fire did not ease the bitterness in his belly.

He had worked just as hard as Silas.

He had spent just as many hours setting type. Writing lines. Reading Franklin's lessons.

Yet Franklin favored Silas.

Phineas wanted more than apprentice work.

He wanted influence.

A man men would hear.

How did a man win influence? Franklin had shown him that words could shape public opinion. They can lift a man or drown him.

How does a man stand apart?

He needed more.

His father's voice came back. Low. Wary. A warning from the past.

The Keepers. The Black Goat. Old rites.

His father had walked away. Had he truly left it?

Phineas breathed and tapped his cup.

He had spent his life blind to that part of his past.

Now, in the dim tavern, men talked and did not see him. He wondered.

What if the old ways held power?

What if they could make him more than just Franklin's second apprentice?

What if they could make him something greater?

He watched the men closely. How they reacted. How they believed without question when a story was told right.

Franklin had shown that words hold power.

How far might power through words reach?

He set a test.

The shop fed the town news. Some true. Some sharpened. Some bent to sell another sheet.

Phineas picked a small rumor. Something insignificant. A ship arrived late. A few crates were gone from its cargo.

He rewrote the details. Shifting blame. Added uncertainty. Crafted a narrative that hinted at scandal without outright stating it.

Then he let it loose.

A week passed. Men in the market spoke of it as truth.

A ship gone. Or robbed. Merchants had lied, said some.

None of it was checked. None needed to be.

Phineas smiled.

His taste for shaping talk grew. So did his eye for old things.

One evening by the docks, he found a small shop set between warehouses.

The sign above the door read: *Aldous Blackwell. Books & Curiosities.*

Inside, the shop smelled of old paper and candle wax. Shelves rose thick with books older than living memory.

The keeper, Aldous Blackwell, was thin and sharp. His eyes remained still. His waistcoat was dark. Ink stained his fingers.

Phineas ran his hands along the worn spines. Some were ordinary. Some were not.

He drew one free.

The Hidden World of Spirits & Demons.

Aldous watched.

"You read such things?"

Phineas smirked. "I enjoy knowing what others do not."

Aldous nodded. "Then you may want something rarer."

He went behind the counter and took a volume from a locked case.

The cover had rubbed thin. The pages time-worn.

The Keepers of the Old Ways.

Phineas froze.

The title put a chill in his bones.

"You know this?" Aldous asked.

Phineas swallowed. He had never spoken of his father's past. Yet here it was.

This proved the Keepers were not only tales.

He took the book.

That night he read from the first page to the last.

Nights later, he sat in the tavern. A drink in hand. A coin in his fingers. Dark knowledge in his mind.

He read more from Blackwell's shelves.

The pages spoke of spells. Of rites. Of things buried under history.

The change came when Titus Leeds entered the tavern.

Phineas saw him at once.

Titus was larger than Franklin. More imposing. His presence was commanding. He walked as a man who expected the world to bend to his weight.

Two men walked with him. His voice cut through the noise.

Phineas did not rise.

He listened.

Titus laughed and struck his tankard down.

"Franklin thinks he has won," Titus said. "He has not. He plays at trade like a boy."

One man smirked. "You still sell well?"

Titus nodded. "We sell. We were among the first to print here. Soon I will drive his small sheet from the stalls."

Phineas leaned forward.

A man chuckled. "How will you do it?"

Titus drank slow.

"I go to my kin," he said. "Leeds Point."

Phineas felt his gut close.

Leeds Point.

The name sounded like an echo from another life.

It lay some sixty miles away.

A place tied to Daniel Leeds. To the old ways. To the things the Quakers had tried to erase.

Titus was going there.

Phineas sat and stared into his cup.

Maybe it meant nothing.

Maybe it meant everything.

His fingers closed on the cup.

Perhaps it was time he rode to Leeds Point.

The road to Leeds Point took two days by horse. The track ran through pines and low marsh.

Phineas rode alone. He kept to lanes and avoided talk in villages.

Leeds Point was quaint. A place that time had not yet bothered.

It seemed ordinary.

Phineas knew otherwise.

The Pine Barren Inn sat dark. Pipe smoke filled the room. Fishermen, traders, and travelers made up the crowd.

Phineas sat at the bar and ordered a drink. He drew *The Keepers of the Old Ways* from his satchel.

He hadn't meant to draw attention.

But someone noticed.

A man came and took the stool beside him. Older. Lean. Eyes like a hawk. Cloth worn, but he carried a weight.

He pointed at the book.

"Not the sort of book most men carry," he said.

Phineas smiled thinly. "Most men are not me."

The man watched him. "Where found?"

Phineas chose his words. "Philadelphia. A bookseller."

The man nodded. "Then you do not know what you hold."

Phineas raised an eyebrow. "And you know?"

The man leaned close. "It is not mere words. It is knowledge. Power. Influence."

Phineas took a slow sip.

"Go on."

The man did not change his expression. "The Old Ways were never lost. Men learned to hide them."

Phineas let out a breath.

He had come to spy on Titus.

But perhaps there was something more valuable to be learned.

"Tell me. What do you know?" he asked.

The man named himself Jonah Fisk.

No priest. No scholar. But he had seen things.

"The Keepers knew what men forgot," Jonah said. "Power is not given. It is taken."

Phineas listened.

"This world," Jonah said, "bends to those who dare to control it."

Phineas thought of Franklin. How one sharp lie had cut at Titus' trade.

Jonah saw the look on him and smirked.

"You have tasted it," he said. "Have you not?"

Phineas said nothing.

He need not answer.

Jonah leaned closer. "The Old Ways hold. A clever, bold man can rise above the rest."

Phineas sat and thought.

He came to protect his place in the press.

Now he wondered for the first time.

Did he think too small?

Later that night, Phineas stepped out of the tavern. The drink warm in his blood.

Then he saw the man.

Titus Leeds.

He walked across the square. His broad shape showed in the lantern glow.

Phineas paused.

Then he followed.

Titus went into a smaller tavern where men kept talk low.

Phineas slipped in unseen.

Titus was not alone.

Across from him sat another man.

Japheth Leeds.

Unlike Titus, Japheth was lean and spoke little. His clothing was simple. His posture relaxed but cautious. He wasn't in the almanac business. He was an oysterman.

Phineas listened.

The brothers spoke of kin and of trade.

Titus' voice grew sharp.

"Franklin thinks he has won," he muttered. "I have a plan to ruin him."

Phineas' stomach twisted.

Japheth sighed. "I do not want to hear this."

Titus scoffed. "Come now. You cannot steer oysters forever. There is room in the family trade."

Japheth shook his head. "I told you. I do not care."

Titus leaned and frowned. "Suit yourself. Mark me, Japheth. Franklin will rue the day he crossed me."

Phineas knew then.

If Titus won, Franklin would fall.

And Phineas with him.

He must act. Soon.

In his small room above the tavern, Phineas stared at the candle.

Titus held a plan.

A plan to ruin Franklin.

Phineas must learn what it was.

His fingers touched the book beside him

The Keepers of the Old Ways.

Jonah Fisk's words remained with him.

Power is not given. It is taken.

Phineas leaned back and smirked slowly.

Perhaps the time had come to take for himself.

CHAPTER 18

AMIGO THE DEVIL

The room above the tavern was dim. The candle's glow was weak against the dark.

Phineas Crowe sat at a wooden desk. The chair creaked as he leaned forward. The air smelled of paper, wax, and damp wood. The scent of ale crept through the floorboards from the tavern below.

His eyes moved over the yellowed pages. *The Keepers of the Old Ways* had been enlightening. But tonight, his hand rested on another book. Darker by far.

Daemonologia Arcana.

The book carried weight. Not only in its cracked leather binding, but in what it held. The pages were aged and brittle. Foxed by time. Heavily annotated by hands long dead.

He turned the worn pages with care as he scanned the names of forgotten creatures. He stopped at one.

He leaned closer. His fingers tightened on the parchment. He thought of Aldous Blackwell's shop in Philadelphia. The old man had given him a look. Knowing.

As if he knew Phineas was not merely curious, but ready to act.

Phineas turned the pages. He skimmed the names of entities. Each name fouler than the last. He had heard whispers of these things before. Half-referenced in Franklin's printing shop. Dismissed as nonsense from European superstition.

This was not superstition.

This was a ledger of the forgotten.

Then he found it on a page stained with ink and fingerprints.

A heading nearly buried in scrawled notes:

The Book of Azraelion.

His breath slowed as he read.

Azraelion. Harbinger of Lies. Demon of Twisted Fates. A shadow born of deception. Summoned by cunning.

His pulse quickened. He forced another slow exhale.

The illustration showed through the faded ink. The details struck him clearly. Cloven feet. Broad and heavy like those of a beast. Hooves cut deep as if made for harsh ground. Tufts of coarse black hair lay thick across the shoulders and spine. The eyes burned red. The glow bled like embers torn from a fire. The face was long, like a horse. Twisted. Cruel. Two black horns rose from the brow. They arched sharply against the faded page. The gaze beneath them was cunning. It carried intent. The legs bent wrong. Twisted like a goat. Long as a stallion. From its back spread vast wings. Bat-like. Veined. Leathery. A barbed tail coiled behind it like a whip ready to strike. The demon stood six feet tall. A figure of power. A figure of lies. Phineas thought of the wyverns carved in the Leeds crest.

Dragon-winged. Fierce. A shadow of the same form.

Phineas let out a sharp breath.

Beneath it, a passage tightened his gut:

Azraelion comes not by reverence but by belief. He needs no worship. Only a tale worth repeating. A deception so deep, so convincing, that the world itself bends to make it true.

Phineas leaned back.

The meaning settled over him like a shadow.

A story.

A lie so bold, so monstrous, so outrageous that people would believe it simply because it was too wild to deny.

His mind raced.

He could forge a legend.

A Devil born of Leeds blood.

Not Daniel. Not Titus. Not Japheth. Not any by name.

No. The child would come from a nameless mother. A cursed woman.

A woman known only as Mother Leeds.

He could print the story. Plant the seed. Stoke superstition.

And when belief took root, Azraelion would live.

His fingers trembled as he traced the name again.

Then he saw a note in the margin.

A warning.

In a hand not his own, faded with age.

WHISPERS IN THE PINES

Be careful which tale you tell.

Unease stirred within him.

For the first time since opening the book, he felt hesitation.

He cast it aside.

Only superstition.

Men had written warnings for centuries. He had seen Franklin invent ghosts. Turn lies into tools. Bend the truth until people swore it had always been.

This was no different. He shut the book and exhaled.

It was only a story.

It was only a story. He would make it the greatest ever told.

The next morning, the market at Leeds Point bustled. Stalls lined the dirt road. Baskets brimming with apples, potatoes, salted meats, and oysters from the bay. The scent of fresh bread and damp earth hung thick in the cool air.

Japheth Leeds walked between the stalls with a basket. He worked the bay, but when not oystering, he came for supplies.

He was not a businessman like his brother, nor a man of politics or the press. He kept to himself, worked hard, and let the world spin as it would.

So, the stranger caught him off guard.

A younger man stepped close, carried by arrogance.

Japheth had never seen him, yet the man looked at him as if he knew.

"You must be Japheth Leeds," Phineas said, voice light but edged with something sharper.

Japheth frowned. "Who's asking?"

Phineas smirked. "A man who keeps count of failures."

Japheth stiffened. "Excuse me?"

Phineas lifted an apple from a stall. He turned it in his hand as he spoke.

"I hear you take no part in the family trade," he said. "Your brother? He'll be finished soon. Franklin has him where he wants him."

Japheth stiffened.

"You know nothing about my family."

Phineas laughed, as if Japheth were a fool.

"Your father was a failure. A bitter man who thought himself a scholar. The Quakers turned against him, dragged his name through the dirt." He stepped closer and lowered his voice. "Your brother clings to his almanac like a drowning man. Soon he'll be swept away with the rest of you."

Japheth's fists clenched.

Phineas leaned closer.

"I'm working on something," he said low. "Something to end your family once and for all."

He bit the apple, turned, and walked away.

Japheth stood frozen. Anger burned beneath his skin.

Who was that man?

He did not know.

But something about him felt wrong.

Even as he finished his shopping and went home, the words lingered.

CHAPTER 19

THE SUMMONING OF AZRAELION

Candlelight flickered against the rough wooden walls of Phineas Crowe's rented room. The window was shut. Yet the air felt colder than it should.

Before him lay *Daemonologia Arcana*. The brittle pages spread open to *The Book of Azraelion*.

His breath remained steady. He had spent the evening in preparation.

A circle of chalk marked the floor. Symbols matched the book's instructions. At the edges, he set tallow candles. Their flames burned low. Wax pooled onto the boards. A copper bowl sat at the center. It held herbs mixed with drops of his own blood.

The text was clear.

Azraelion does not require worship. Only belief. To summon him is to speak a truth that does not yet exist.

Phineas smirked at the line.

What was truth anyway?

He rolled his shoulders. He lifted the book and read aloud.

The words were older than the colonies. Older than his tongue. They tasted strange in his mouth. They felt wrong. They were not meant to be spoken aloud.

The candle flames trembled.

He read on.

The wind outside stopped. The tavern below fell silent. No voices. No clink of tankards.

Sweat beaded at his temple.

His fingers tightened on the book.

He spoke the final words.

And then…

Nothing.

No black smoke rose from the floor.

No whisper crept into his mind.

No shadowy form forced its way into the room.

Only silence.

Phineas blinked. Then he laughed.

He laughed at himself. At the foolishness of it all. He had expected too much.

What had he thought would happen?

That some ancient beast with hooves and wings would appear in his room? That he would command it like a lord of Hell?

He shook his head. He kicked at the chalk circle. The symbols smeared.

"Damn fool," he muttered. He snuffed a candle with his fingers.

He grabbed his satchel. He stuffed *Daemonologia Arcana* inside. He blew out the rest of the candles.

Tomorrow he would return to Philadelphia.

The press was where real power lay.

He had wasted enough time chasing shadows.

Early the next morning, Phineas packed his bags and left the tavern room.

If he had stayed a moment longer, he might have noticed it.

A whisper. Faint. Distant. Barely there.

A breeze stirred the ashes in the copper bowl.

A dark presence coiled in the space beyond sight.

Waiting.

Phineas Crowe returned to Philadelphia with a story burning in his mind. Ambition trailed close behind. The summoning had failed. Or so he thought. Yet the story it birthed was another matter.

In the print shop, he sat alone at a worktable. The press stood silent. The others were gone. Candles burned low as he dipped his quill and wrote.

In the woods of New Jersey, where the pines grow thick and dark, there lives a creature born of curses and shadows…

He smiled as he wrote. The words came easily now. He did not need to believe them. He only needed to make them believable.

Mother Leeds, a woman worn by twelve children, cried out in anger when she learned she was with child once more. "Let it be the Devil!" she cursed. And so it was.

The babe was born twisted and monstrous. Hooves. A tail. Leathery wings. Eyes that burned like embers. It gave a terrible cry, spread its wings, and fled up the chimney. It vanished into the Pine Barrens.

He slipped it into Franklin's next batch of pamphlets. Not as an article. Hidden between satire and rural curiosities.

A small tale. A local legend.

A harmless fiction.

Or so he told himself.

A week later, while eating breakfast in the shop, Phineas overheard two pressmen talking near the rear window.

One of them, Henry, held a letter that had arrived from New Jersey.

"A man in Leeds Point swears something tore through his chicken coop," Henry said. "Feathers scattered. Boards smashed as if struck by a ram."

The other man laughed. "A bear, maybe."

Henry shook his head. "No. He said it had hooves. And wings. Left tracks in the mud."

Phineas stopped chewing.

The description was familiar. Too familiar.

Another day passed.

Another report came from a dockworker. A sailor said he saw something fly low across the pines. It screeched like no bird he had ever heard.

At first, Phineas thought it was a coincidence. A shared dream. An echo of his printed tale.

But the sightings spread. First to Burlington. Then downriver to Egg Harbor. He no longer slept well at night.

People were not only repeating the story.

They were living it.

Every version that returned to him matched the creature he had described. Down to the last hoof. Down to the last wing.

He had invented it. He was sure.

But now…

He was no longer sure.

Days passed. Then a week.

The sightings did not stop.

Phineas Crowe sat alone at his desk in the back of Franklin's shop. Evening light slipped through warped glass. His quill lay untouched beside an empty page. He had written nothing all day.

The latest report had arrived that morning:

A man near Bass River claimed he saw a creature in the fog outside his barn. Red eyes glowed. Hooves left scorched marks in the soil.

Another claimed he saw it fly over a churchyard at dawn.

A man in Mays Landing swore it had followed him through the pines.

Every story carried the same details.

The same ones Phineas had invented.

Hadn't he?

He opened *Daemonologia Arcana* again. The pages felt heavier. Less like curiosity. More like something watching him.

He turned to the chapter he had not dared revisit since that night.

The Book of Azraelion.

There, scrawled in the margin, was the warning again.

He does not demand worship, only a story. Be careful which tale you tell.

He ran his fingers over the ink.

It had smudged. As if someone, perhaps him, had touched it with wet hands.

A shiver ran down his spine.

Had he summoned it?

No.

There had been no flash of light. No shadow. No voice.

Only silence.

He had left the room.

Returned to Philadelphia.

Printed a story to amuse and provoke.

And now...

The story was everywhere.

Could belief alone be enough?

He thought of Franklin's trick with Titus Leeds.

A man declared dead in print. Repeated until people believed it. Even when Leeds himself responded, Franklin claimed he was a ghost.

The lie had crushed the truth.

Could this be the same?

Phineas looked around the shop.

No rituals. No circle. Just words.

But words were enough.

He whispered so low he barely heard it. "Did I create you?"

There was no reply.

But when he looked up, he thought he saw something in the glass. A dark shape. Tall. Still. Standing in the street beyond.

He blinked. It was gone.

Titus Leeds was not a man given to fear. He had spent years fighting Franklin's attacks, defending his name and his almanac.

But something was different now.

People no longer mocked him as before. They did not argue about his predictions. They no longer scoffed at his replies to Franklin's tricks.

Instead, they whispered behind his back.

His name was tarnished.

Not from Franklin's false obituaries, but from something stranger.

When he traveled to the press in Burlington, printers hesitated before shaking his hand.

When he stopped at a tavern for a meal, he caught whispers about the Devil loose in the Pines.

More than once, he noticed that when people said "Leeds," they no longer meant him alone.

They meant Mother Leeds.

The nameless woman in the tale.

The cursed mother of a cursed child.

And the monster that bore his family's name.

Titus laughed the first time he heard it. He dismissed it as drunken superstition. Nothing more than Franklin's men playing a new game.

But then the stories spread.

And they grew worse.

CHAPTER 20

BLOOD ON THE SNOW

Leeds Point, New Jersey

December 1735

The first body lay in the snow.

Levi Barlow, a farmhand, went to check the horses in the predawn dark. The sun had not risen. The world stood blue with cold.

His employer found him two hours later. The body was torn open. The throat ripped as if by jagged teeth.

The second victim was a woman traveling by carriage.

She was found alive, but barely. The driver had been thrown from the cart. His skull cracked on a rock. The woman, Elizabeth Hayworth, was pinned under the overturned carriage. She was unconscious when found.

When she awoke, her eyes were wild with terror.

"It came from the trees," she rasped. Her fingers clutched the healer's wrist. "It watched. Its eyes burned red through the dark."

She refused to say more.

The third was worse.

A boy, Daniel Mercer, vanished from his family's cabin one night.

His mother swore she had seen him curled by the fire when she went to bed. But when she woke, the door stood open. Snow drifted inside.

Daniel was gone.

A search party went into the woods. Torches in hand. They called his name.

They found small footprints in the snow. They led into the pines.

But they did not find Daniel.

Instead, they found hoofprints.

Too large for a deer.

Leading in circles.

And nothing else.

Within weeks, Leeds Point was gripped in fear. People refused to travel alone at night. The road between the villages went dead. No wheels. No voices. Only silence.

In the market, people spoke in hushed voices of the Devil.

And always it returned to the same cursed name.

Leeds.

Titus tried to fight it.

He printed a rebuttal in the Leeds Almanack. A short column. He called the stories superstition. Rumors spread by fools and liars.

But it did not matter.

People were already afraid.

And fear moved faster than truth.

Benjamin Franklin did not believe in devils.

But he did believe in the power of a well-told lie.

The first time he heard whispers of the Devil of the Pines, he was drinking with associates in a Philadelphia tavern.

A merchant Franklin barely knew retold the tale in full dramatic detail.

"Flew up the chimney, they say," the man muttered. He leaned in as if sharing a great secret. "Straight into the Barrens. Wings like a bat. Hooves like a beast of Hell."

Franklin sipped his drink and listened.

When another man laughed, Franklin spoke up and played along.

"Ah," he said. "Tell me, gentlemen. What family bore this cursed child?"

The men exchanged glances.

"Leeds," one of them said. "The name is Leeds."

Franklin smirked.

He did not have to say more.

Titus Leeds had been his rival in the almanac trade for years. Franklin had printed a joke about his death. He had turned the man into a ghost and watched him scramble to prove he lived.

And now…

The man's family name was tied to the Devil itself.

And Franklin had not lifted a finger.

He found it amusing.

A ridiculous piece of folklore. A silly distraction for the masses.

If Phineas had spread it, that only proved the boy had promise.

Maybe he should have been a writer instead of a printer.

Phineas Crowe sat at his desk in the shop. His fingers hovered over the quill.

He could not focus.

The latest news from New Jersey was worse than before.

A woman had survived an attack. A child had vanished. People now feared the thing he had created.

At first, it had been entertaining.

He had chuckled at the irony. Titus Leeds struggled to keep his business alive while a foolish tale of a curse rotted his name faster than Franklin ever could.

But now?

Now it no longer felt like a joke.

The details people repeated were too close to what he had written.

The glowing red eyes. The hooves. The wings.

The blood.

The tale should have stayed that. A story.

But something in his gut told him otherwise.

Phineas leaned back in his chair and ran a hand over his face.

Had he summoned something after all?

No.

He had felt nothing that night.

But what if belief alone was enough?

He thought of the words in *Daemonologia Arcana*.

He does not demand worship, only a story. Be careful which tale you tell.

His hands turned cold.

What had he done?

CHAPTER 21

THE PUKWUDGIE CONFLICT

Night swallowed Leeds Point. Stars hid behind thick clouds. A cold wind cut through the trees. The air stilled. Then it came.

Azraelion rose from the ground behind the tavern.

Hooves sank into frozen soil. Eyes burned red, unblinking. It stood six feet tall. Goat-like legs bent sharply beneath it. Shoulders hunched under coarse black hair. Its tail twitched.

Barbed.

Slow.

Deliberate.

Its face stretched long. Horse-like, but wrong. Two black horns rose high. The snout flared. It drew in the night air. Wings unfurled.

Wide.

Leathery.

Strong.

Each beat stirred dust from the ground.

Then it screamed.

A sound sharp enough to rattle windows. A cry no beast should make. It snapped its wings once and rose.

Over rooftops.

Over fields.

Toward the black sea of trees.

Toward the Pine Barrens.

The Pine Barrens stretched for miles. Pines tangled with brambles. The forest floor stayed soft and cold. Even in winter, the trees whispered. Men feared the Barrens. No path stayed clear. No map marked every clearing. The woods shifted.

Azraelion landed in a dead clearing. Ash lay thick on the ground. A pine split down the middle. Decay crept through its bark. The demon walked forward. Slow and sure. Each hoof left scorched prints.

Eyes watched from the trees. Not men. Not beasts. Something else.

Tiny.

Wide-eyed.

Gray-skinned.

Hairless.

Crouched low to the ground. Teeth clicked in warning.

Pukwudgies.

The small creatures lived in these woods. They hated humans. They hated anything new. They felt the wrongness of Azraelion.

One stepped into the clearing. It hissed. Sharp claws caught the moonlight. Azraelion stared. It did not move. The air grew heavy.

A second Pukwudgie leapt from a branch.

Then a third.

They circled the demon. Claws bared. Backs arched.

Azraelion stood still. Then it lashed out. Its tail struck one. The Pukwudgie flew back. Limp.

The others screamed. They rushed in. Azraelion moved fast. Faster than they expected. It split one with its hooves. Tore another with its teeth.

It screeched again.

The sound carried for miles. The rest fled. They vanished into the trees. The demon stood alone. Blood steamed on its fur.

It turned its eyes north. Toward the nearest village. Then it walked into the trees. The Barrens swallowed it whole.

Azraelion was not born. He was spoken into existence. Summoned by a lie so strong, reality bent to make it true.

But he did not belong. Not to this world. Not to this time. Not even to himself.

He stood in the cold pine woods. The air burned in his lungs, though he did not breathe.

He hungered.

Not for food.

For meaning.

For belief.

He wandered. Claws scraped tree bark. Eyes glowed through the fog. Every step left ash where snow should have lain.

He did not know why he was here. Only that he had been called. Now he must remain. From the moment he landed in the Barrens, they felt it.

The Pukwudgies lived by instinct.

By balance.

The forest spoke to them.

Now the forest screamed.

Azraelion was not a creature of these woods.

Not born of the earth.

He was wrong. An echo of a story.

A thing that should never have drawn breath.

The Pukwudgies attacked not to win. Only to push it back. Darts struck his hide. Quills bounced from his limbs. Azraelion barely noticed.

One swipe of his tail scattered them. A shriek from his maw sent them fleeing into the trees. They knew then. This was not a thing they could kill. This was a thing they must warn others about.

Azraelion haunted the Barrens. Not to hunt for food. To anchor himself. He lingered at the edges of villages. Peered through trees at the glow of fires. Waited. Not with a plan. But because he knew someone would speak his name again. And when they did, he would grow stronger.

The Pukwudgies withdrew into the thickest parts of the Pine Barrens. Their quills had failed. Their darts bounced off Azraelion's hide. Their claws did nothing.

They knew they faced something unnatural. Born outside the world they knew. He did not bleed like a beast or move like a man. He walked as if the forest held no claim on him. Every step scorched the ground.

The creatures slipped into hollow trees. Into old fox dens. Into narrow tunnels beneath the roots. None returned to the clearing. None dared follow him. The forest had been theirs for generations. Now it felt different. Now it listened to something else.

They waited in the deep places. Whispered to one another without a sound. And if nothing stopped the demon, they would find the one who could.

Three nights later, Elias Martin woke to a terrible sound. Wood splintered. Something high and sharp screeched through the wind.

He stepped outside with a lantern in hand. The flame guttered against the cold. Snow lay thin. The sky hung overcast.

No stars.

No moon.

The sheep pen stood beyond the fence.

Elias knew something was wrong before he saw it.

He crossed the yard. The wooden gate lay broken open. One hinge snapped clean off.

Blood streaked the snow in thick lines. Sheep lay scattered. Torn open. Steam rose in the cold. Some were crushed. Others looked as if something had ripped them apart from within.

The air stank of iron.

Of smoke.

Of something worse.

Then he saw it.

In the far pasture, at the edge of the woods, a figure stood among the trees. Tall. Taller than a man. Covered in coarse black hair. Long legs, jointed like a horse. Wings folded along its back.

Its face stretched long and narrow. Two red eyes burned through the dark. It did not move.

Elias could not speak. Could not run. The creature stared at him. Moments dragged like hours.

Then it turned.

Without a sound it walked into the trees. Its barbed tail carved a line through the snow.

Elias fell to his knees. He did not remember walking back to the chapel. He did not remember locking the doors. At dawn they found him inside.

Shaking.

Pale.

He mumbled again and again about wings.

Word of Elias Martin's story spread by dawn. At first, most dismissed it. Elias had always been reserved. He lived alone. Spoke to no one unless forced.

But the sheep were real.

The blood was real.

And Elias had not spoken a full sentence since they discovered him in the chapel.

The second sighting came two days later. Two hunters walked out near dusk. They searched for deer. They returned just after dark. People saw them pale and shaking. They claimed they had seen something move through the trees. Walking on two legs. But not a man.

Something with wings.

They dropped their gear at the edge of the woods. Refused to return for it. By week's end, no one went near the forest.

Children stayed inside.

Doors locked early.

Candles burned in windows long past midnight.

The village church filled with whispered prayers. Even the pastor spoke in hushed tones. He would not say why.

People began to use old language. Not the creature. Not the beast. They called it what they had read in the pamphlet.

The Devil.

The Leeds Devil.

And always, with each new encounter, the name returned.

Leeds.

When Azraelion returned to the Pine Barrens, the forest was no longer the same.

The trees had grown still. No wind passed through the needles. No branches cracked under fallen snow.

The woods listened. The old balance had broken.

The Pukwudgies had gone deeper still.

Unseen.

Something darker moved now.

Azraelion walked alone through the underbrush. It did not hunt like a natural predator. It did not eat what it killed.

It moved through the forest. The land changed around it. Fungus spread along the trees where it stepped. Ash coated the bases of trunks. Birds no longer nested in the pines.

Some nights it flew. Its wings spread wide against the moonlight. It passed over the treetops like a warning.

People claimed to see it watching from hilltops. Others said they heard it breathe just beyond their barns. None went to investigate.

The town stopped pretending it was only a tale. It had become something else. A curse with no name. Born of something no one had ever believed in.

Deep beneath the forest, in the hollow roots of a burned-out pine, the Pukwudgies gathered.

There were fewer now.

Too few.

They crouched low. Voices were kept soft and sharp. Faces drawn. Eyes weary.

The old ways no longer worked. The balance had broken.

The demon moved like a story. It did not rest. It did not speak. It could not be tricked.

Those who tracked it never returned. Those who fought it vanished. Only their teeth left behind.

The woods no longer welcomed them. The trees did not stir. Birds were gone. The ground turned hard and sour beneath their feet. They could not live in a forest that no longer knew their names.

Something had to change.

One of the oldest stepped forward. Short, even for a Pukwudgie. Two feet, maybe three. Skin like river stone. Large hands. Long fingers. Eyes small and red. Nose enormous, crooked. Ears curled like leaves left too long in the wind. He wore a black-bristled beard. A tangled mess of coarse hair covered the back of his neck like a thorn bush.

The others called him Puddlesquat. He had survived many winters. He knew the scent of imbalance.

"We cannot fight the Devil." His voice was dry. Crackled like dead moss. "We were not made for this."

A younger one clicked its teeth. "Then we run?"

Puddlesquat narrowed his eyes. "No. We send for her."

The others stirred. Some hissed. Some shook their heads. None spoke against him.

"She walked these woods once," he said. "When the strangers came. They cut the trees. They burned the fields. They hunted men like beasts. We stayed hidden. But we saw her. Red hair like fire. She carried the scent of gods."

The Pukwudgies shivered. None had spoken of that memory in many winters.

"Few among us remember. Only those who saw her with their own eyes. She does not walk among them now," Puddlesquat said. "But she lingers. The forest remembers. And the forest will answer."

He grumbled. Scratched his crooked nose. Pulled his feather-cloak tight.

"I will find the place where the veil is thin," he said. "I will open the door."

That night, long after the moon climbed high, Puddlesquat crawled from the hollow. He stood alone at the forest's edge.

The air was sharp and cold. Smoke curled from the village chimneys in the distance. Windows glowed yellow and orange.

He did not like the town. It stank of iron, salt, cooked onions.

Too loud.

Too clean.

Too human.

But the forest whispered of her. It told him she walked near the humans now. Hidden in their midst. Living as one of them. He could not understand why. But he trusted the old blood. The forest remembered her. So did he. Red hair like fire. A scent of the gods. She had walked these woods before, when men burned and hunted. He had stayed hidden, but he had seen her.

If she was truly what he thought, maybe, just maybe, she could stop the story made real.

Puddlesquat adjusted his tiny cloak of stitched bird feathers and bone buttons. He grumbled. Scratched his crooked nose.

"I will find her," he muttered. "Even if she wears a mask. Even if she hides in their houses. The forest will guide me."

Then he waddled toward the town.

CHAPTER 22

THE ONE CALLED OLIVIA

Her name had once been Ölrún.

She had lived in Leeds Point for almost a year.

When she arrived, she altered her name to blend in with the people of the village.

To most, she was Olivia Karlsson.

Liv to the few who dared speak to her.

She lived on the edge of town in a modest cottage.

She fished. She mended nets.

She drank in silence at the tavern.

She blended in.

Enough.

The villagers whispered about her all the same.

She was too quiet. Her hair too red. Her eyes too sharp.

They never saw her bleed. She bore a scar on her jaw.

They never saw her pray.

They had learned not to ask questions.

She had not drawn her sword in months.

She no longer carried it in the open.

She remembered every heft. Every grip. Every strike.

If she needed to fight again, she would not hesitate.

In recent days, she had heard the stories.

Foolish at first. Drunken nonsense passed from one villager to another.

Yet their faces were pale when they spoke.

Their voices remained low. They never laughed.

They spoke of a presence in the woods.

A shape with wings. Eyes that burned through the trees.

And worse.

They said the forest had gone quiet. Wrong.

Liv felt it too.

A hush beneath the branches. The kind that settled in before a battle.

Tonight as she sat in the tavern, she felt something else.

Not dark. Not malevolent.

But watching.

It was as if the earth held its breath.

Like a branch bent without wind.

She did not turn her head. She did not move her hands.

She sipped her drink.

The air near her shoulder shifted. As if something unseen stepped too close.

It smelled of moss. Of dirt. Of an old hollow tree.

There was fear in it.

Not for her.

Something else.

She let the silence stretch.

"Show yourself," she said without looking.

The other patrons did not notice. No one looked her way.

The presence at her side froze.

For a moment, nothing happened.

Then, with a faint shimmer, Puddlesquat appeared.

Two feet tall. Gray skin. Wide nosed.

His eyes, red as coals, blinked beneath shaggy brows.

He wore a feathered cloak made of bird and bone.

His beard looked like a broom left to rot.

He stood on the bench beside her, with his arms crossed.

"Bout time," he muttered. "You smell like a storm. You know that?

Liv turned her head.

She said nothing. Her eyes narrowed.

Puddlesquat swallowed and added, "I need to talk to you. It is about the thing in the woods."

"You're no man. Speak your kind."

The small figure lifted his chin.

"Pukwudgie."

She studied him for a long moment.

"We lived in the woods long before your kind built fences and called the world theirs," he said. "We are watchers. Guardians. Protectors of the old ways."

She glanced around. No one in the tavern looked their way.

"They cannot see me. Only you."

Liv said nothing.

He cleared his throat. "Something came not long ago. Something that does not belong."

Her gaze sharpened.

"It walks like a beast, yet it is not of this world," he said. "It is a lie made real. It kills for no reason. It leaves silence behind."

His voice dropped low. "The forest does not answer us now. The balance is broken. The Pukwudgie who go out do not return. We tried all. It cannot be tricked. It does not sleep. We cannot fight it."

"I know."

Liv leaned forward. Her fingers brushed the handle of her mug, though her eyes never left him.

"We need help," Puddlesquat said. "We need a warrior."

His voice changed. Less jest. Less smug.

"You carry it even now." He nodded. "I felt it from the trees. You are not like them." He pointed to the others in the room. "You are older. Stronger. Maybe the only one the thing might fear."

Liv sat back in her chair. She studied the small creature.

"What does it look like?" she asked.

His voice dropped to a whisper. "Tall. Red eyes. Hooves that split the ground. A beast that should not be. I do not know its true name."

He met her gaze. "But the humans whisper one."

"Leeds Devil," she said.

Liv kept her eyes on Puddlesquat.

He spoke of death and blood.

But she heard something else.

A call.

WHISPERS IN THE PINES

It had been too long. Too many days of pretending to be normal. Too many nights drinking from mugs instead of lifting a blade.

She had lived in Leeds Point long enough to forget what she was.

Now she remembered.

Battle lay in her bones.

And deep within, she missed it.

She raised her tankard and took a long drink of mead.

She blinked once, and the tavern faded.

Her breath slowed.

The air thickened.

Then she saw it. A flicker at the edge of thought.

A forest.

Ominous.

Only the wind moved.

Pukwudgies broken in the dirt.

Eyes wide. Mouths open in death.

A shadow moved between the trees.

Tall. Red eyes. Branches cracked under heavy hooves.

It killed without joy. Without rage.

As if it simply obeyed a truth it did not understand.

She knew what this was.

Not prophecy. Not illusion.

It was the shape of the battle to come.

She saw the outcome.

The demon would destroy the forest. It would slaughter the last of the Pukwudgie. Darkness would reign over the world.

Unless.

Unless she entered the battle.

Then, and only then, the end became uncertain.

The vision snapped away.

She sat once more in the tavern. The fire burned low. Her hands were steady.

Puddlesquat waited. His brow furrowed beneath a tangle of black hair. He saw something shift in her eyes.

She drained the rest of her mug and set it down.

Then she turned to him.

"I will fight," she said. "It has been too long."

Puddlesquat exhaled with a sound close to a laugh.

"I hoped you would say that."

"But I will need steel. And silence. I leave before dawn."

The small creature nodded. "I will wait at the edge of the woods."

He shimmered once and then vanished. A faint scent of moss remained.

Liv stared into the fire a moment longer.

She still heard the hooves crack in the trees.

And she felt ready.

Later that night, Liv sat at a corner table in the tavern with two others.

They arrived quietly, as they always did.

No questions.

No fanfare.

Thea and Bjorn, the locals called them.

Another pair of strangers who kept to themselves. They drank, paid in coin, and kept the peace.

No one asked where they came from.

But Liv knew.

Thordis Whitestorm. Younger. Leaner. Eyes that saw more than they should. She moved like one born with a bow in hand. Her silence unsettled most.

She saw signs in ash. Patterns in wind. If she dreamed of wolves, someone was dead by morning.

Asbjorn Ironskull was a wall of a man with a square jaw and broad shoulders. His eyes distrusted anything that could not be split with steel.

He spoke little. He had followed Ölrún into wars men would not name. He had never faltered.

They had fought together. Bled together.

They watched the world shift beneath their boots. They lived long enough to see their names fade into myth.

Others carried muskets. Thordis still carried her bow. Asbjorn still carried his axe. Time had not moved them. The old ways still cut deep.

Liv looked at them both and leaned in.

"There is something in the woods," she said. "A creature. Wrong. Not of this place."

Asbjorn raised an eyebrow.

Thordis did not blink.

They waited.

She continued.

"A Pukwudgie came to me tonight. His name was Puddlesquat."

Asbjorn grunted. "Sounds like something scraped off a boot."

Liv ignored him.

"He said this thing killed hundreds of their kind. The forest turns. The trees do not listen to them."

Thordis leaned forward. Her eyes narrowed.

She did not speak yet. She listened.

Liv kept going.

"It's powerful. Otherworldly. A demon."

At that, Thordis nodded once slowly.

"I felt something in the wind three nights past. Like smoke where there should have been snow."

Asbjorn shook his head. "I felt nothing but boredom for months. Maybe this thing does us a favor."

Liv gave him a look.

He smiled behind his mug. "Do not worry. I will kill it for you."

"I go at dawn," she said. "Alone if I must."

Asbjorn set down his drink.

"You are not going alone," Thordis said.

"Would not let you," Asbjorn added. "You would make a mess without us."

Liv gave a rare brief smile. Then it faded.

"Get your gear. We leave at first light."

CHAPTER 23

THE GLADE OF BLACK ROOTS

The moon hung heavy and gold behind a veil of drifting smoke. Liv led them through the pines in silence. Her fur-lined cloak brushed low branches as they passed into the trees. Each step carried them deeper. Away from the village. Into the oldest part of the forest, where roots ran deep, and stories were older than the soil.

She stopped at a clearing. A forgotten glade ringed by boulders mottled with lichen and moss. In its center, a circle of stones held an old fire pit. It was choked with ash and dry needles. No birds sang here. Even the wind held its breath.

"This is where we call them," Liv said. Her voice was low and determined. "The ones who came before us. The ones who still watch."

Asbjorn shifted his grip on the axe across his back. "You sure this does not draw attention? That thing out there."

"He will not feel this," Liv said. "Not unless you fear it."

Thordis stepped forward barefoot. The furs at her shoulders shook with a shiver. "I felt this place in my dreams," she whispered. "It is waiting for us."

Liv crouched by the pit. She laid kindling in a spiral and set her staff upright in the earth. The wood was dark. Runes cut deep along its length. The top was bound in iron. She leaned close to the pit and breathed slowly. The kindling caught as if it had waited for her. Fire rose. Not bright, but alive. It pulsed with a strange light that bent shadows.

"We offer no prayers," Liv said as she rose. "Only breath. Only clay. Only truth."

She drew a leather pouch from her belt. She smeared her fingers in red earth mixed with fat. She marked her own brow. Then Thordis. Then Asbjorn. Last, she pressed clay to her staff. The wood drank it in.

"You do not have to believe," she told them. "You only have to stand with me."

Asbjorn grunted. "I am here."

The rhythm began. Not drums but feet on earth. Liv stamped once. Hard. Thordis and Asbjorn followed. Their weight shook the ground. The earth gave a deep reply. A heartbeat in soil and stone. Firelight flickered across their faces and turned them to shadow and flame. Liv began to chant.

Not words.

Just breathe and growl. Throat sounds and howls. Sounds not for men. For the earth. For the bones. For the beasts that watched in the trees.

Thordis swayed like smoke. Her eyes rolled back. Her arms hung loose. Her voice climbed high. Thin as wind through stone. Asbjorn held himself back. His fists clenched. Sweat ran down his brow. At last he roared. Deep. Raw. Sudden. A call of defiance. He struck his chest in time with the beat. He stepped into the circle. His mouth was wide. His face was wild.

Liv walked the fire's edge. Her hair snapped loose around her shoulders. Her staff struck the earth with each step. Their voices tangled. Three voices became one. Terrible, beautiful sound.

She stopped and stared into the flame. Her voice fell to a whisper.

"They are here."

Thordis froze. "Who."

"The ones who wore our faces before we were born."

Asbjorn turned and searched the dark. The trees stood still. Yet a presence pressed against the glade. It clung like fog behind unseen walls.

Liv raised her staff. She smeared more clay along its length. She breathed slowly across it. The flame hissed. It flared green.

"Tomorrow we fight in flesh," she said. "Tonight we fight in spirit."

Thordis reached for the pouch. She smeared clay across Liv's staff. The runes caught the firelight as if alive. Asbjorn paused. He dragged his hand through the clay and pressed it hard against the staff. The mark spread across the wood. He lifted his head and gave a sound like a challenge.

The flames rose higher. Shadows stretched long across the stones. For a moment, Liv saw other figures move with them. Shapes with antlers. Skulls. Cloaks of wind. Watching. Mirroring.

Liv raised her staff and lifted her arms high.

"Let our clay awaken the past. Let our breath carry their rage. Let our hearts beat with thunder. Let the old ones walk with us."

The fire cracked. Sparks leapt high.

A gust tore through the glade. The flame died at once.

Darkness.

Silence.

And the sound of three hearts. Steady and strong.

CHAPTER 24

THROUGH THE CRANBERRY GATE

At dawn, Liv and her small band rode into the Pine Barrens.

Mist clung low over the scrub. It moved through twisted pines and cedar groves. The forest stretched endlessly in every direction. More than a million acres of wild land lay untouched by time. No railroads cut across it. No settlements broke it. Moss and sand muffled the sound and swallowed their hoofbeats.

It was one thing to enter the Barrens. It proved something else to find the Devil concealed somewhere within them.

Liv felt him out there. The Leeds Devil moved through the forest like smoke on water. He knew they had come. A dull force built at the back of her skull. Her lungs grew tight.

She knew he could feel her just as clearly.

The presence of a Valkyrie did not go unnoticed.

She made no effort to hide it.

He did not appear.

Not yet.

He waited.

So did Liv.

"He knows we're here," Thordis said. Her breath clouded in the cool air.

"He has known since we crossed the river," Liv replied. "He will not strike yet."

Behind them, Asbjorn rode in silence. He had faced beasts, blades, and worse, yet this forest scraped at the edge of his instincts.

By midmorning, they dismounted near a cranberry bog. The water mirrored the sky like a sheet of broken glass. The horses refused to go farther. Liv gave no command. She stepped into the muck and walked.

That was when she saw him.

They found him crouched at the edge of the cranberry bog. The trees in closed tightly, and mist pooled low in the hollows. He stood no taller than a child. Perhaps two and a half feet tall, yet there was nothing youthful about him. His skin was gray-brown, smeared with mud and lichen. Strips of bone and feather hung from his belt. His hair lay wild and tangled. It was filled with moss and spider silk. His eyes were red but were expressionless. He poked at the mud with a carved stick and muttered to something only he could see.

He didn't turn when they approached.

Asbjorn froze. "What in Hel's name is that?"

"Puddlesquat," Liv said with a steady voice.

He sniffed the air, then grinned wide without turning toward them. "You came."

"I said I would."

Only then did he stand. Slow and deliberate. His head barely reached Liv's waist, yet he carried himself like someone far taller. His red eyes, clouded but sharp, studied them with curiosity.

Asbjorn stepped closer. "*That* is your guide?"

Puddlesquat turned toward him and squinted up with a crooked smile. "Never seen a man so tall who asked such small questions."

Liv raised a hand to Asbjorn. "He is a Pukwudgie. He does not speak for men. He speaks for the woods."

Puddlesquat nodded and shifted his gaze to Thordis.

"The wind says you dream loud, girl."

Thordis blinked. "I do."

"And she," he said as he pointed at Liv with a long finger blackened at the nail, "burns like old firewood. Ready to snap."

"Where are the others?" Liv asked.

"Those who survived scattered deeper into the woods. We hide in a stronghold and go out only when we must."

"Will you take us?"

Puddlesquat's grin widened. "They have been waiting."

He turned back toward the bog and scanned the water as if he could read it.

"Walk gently, Valkyrie. They remember what humans have done to them. Kindness turned to blade. Friendship turned to fire. Some of them bite first."

Liv did not blink. "Let them try."

He looked at Thordis and Asbjorn.

"They won't care what you are. Only what you look like."

Asbjorn said nothing, but he kept his hand far from his axe.

Liv spoke with a steady voice. "Let them see us. Let them judge for themselves."

Puddlesquat gave a grunt of approval and turned toward the trees. "Then follow. The forest already knows your names."

The trees changed once they passed the bog.

At first, it was subtle. A hush of sound. The chirping of birds cut off mid-note. The wind stopped. Even the rhythm of their steps grew faint, swallowed by the moss and fallen pine needles.

The pines here grew closer together and arched inward. The light turned green through layers of ancient canopy. Something flickered just out of sight. A shape behind a tree. A figure that vanished when looked at straight on.

Thordis stayed close to Liv. Her bow was unstrung but ready in her hand. Asbjorn's steps slowed. Each one felt harder than the last.

"This place," he muttered, "it listens."

"It does more than that," Liv said. "It remembers."

Puddlesquat walked ahead of them. His bare feet sank into the wet earth, yet his steps made little sound. He muttered to the trees or whistled a tune that made no sense to human ears. The sound was off-key and birdlike, yet the forest seemed to answer. Once he reached up and touched a knot in the bark as if greeting an old friend.

A narrow passage opened ahead. It was formed by two twisted trees that had grown together like a gate. Liv paused.

"This is it," Puddlesquat said. "You cross here, you will not walk as who you were. Not fully."

He slipped through.

Liv followed.

A low hum filled her ears the moment she crossed. Not a sound, but a vibration. Something that moved through her bones, then deeper. Her skin prickled. Her heartbeat slowed. The trees ahead no longer stood in straight lines. They curved inward and back again, as if they leaned in close to watch.

They were being watched.

She felt eyes in the branches, beneath the roots, and in the stones. No birds. No insects. Only their own breathing, and something that copied it.

Thordis whispered, "Something walks behind us."

"There is," Liv replied. "Do not turn around."

Asbjorn turned anyway.

No one stood there.

Yet a second set of his own boot prints appeared beside his, set just slightly off.

They moved on, deeper.

The forest was no longer the same place.

This was Pukwudgie ground now.

The forest closed tighter the deeper they went. The air carried the smell of damp roots, wet moss, and something older. A trace of wood smoke lingered. Faint and bitter. Like a long-dead fire that refused to fade.

They had walked in silence for some time before Thordis halted.

"There," she whispered and pointed toward a low tangle of roots.

A small figure crouched in the brush. It stood barely two feet tall. It had a narrow face, wide eyes, and skin the color of ash and stone. Bones and feathers hung from its belt. The moment Liv turned her head, it vanished.

"They are here," she said.

"I see another," Asbjorn muttered. Tension edged his voice.

Up in the trees, a second one appeared. It perched on a branch like a bird of prey. Its face was rounder. Its eyes glowed in the green light. It blinked once, then vanished without a trace, as if the forest had swallowed it whole.

Puddlesquat continued to walk.

"They have been waiting," he said. "Some did not believe I would return. Some still do not."

A third Pukwudgie appeared farther ahead and stepped lightly from behind a tree. This one did not vanish. It fixed its gaze on Liv. Not in fear but with sharp curiosity. Its head tilted as she passed.

She met its eyes.

It did not flinch.

In that moment, the Pukwudgie saw past her human face. It knew the part of her that stood outside time.

It saw the Valkyrie.

Liv felt their presence now. Even when they stayed hidden. Dozens of them.

Watching.

Waiting.

Not for an attack.

Not even for a greeting.

They sought to understand.

To see if the stories were true.

She felt it like a whisper in the trees:

Is this the one?

The fire-blooded ghost-walker?

Will she fight for us, or fall like the rest?

Puddlesquat stopped near a stone outcropping covered in moss and twisted vine. He tapped it with his stick. Twice, then once, then twice again.

The air shifted.

The tree roots ahead curled outward like fingers opening. They revealed a narrow earthen passage that angled down into the dark. The opening was not wide. It was barely large enough for a human to pass through upright.

Puddlesquat turned to Liv.

"They will take only you," he said. "The others must wait here."

Asbjorn stepped forward. "Like Hel we will."

Liv raised a hand. "Stand down. If they meant me harm, I would already be gone."

Thordis set a hand on Asbjorn's arm. "We will wait."

Liv met the eyes of her companions.

Then she turned and entered the passage without pause and stepped ahead.

She did not reach for a weapon.

She did not speak.

She walked into the fold of trees and disappeared into the earth.

The tunnel walls were damp. Stone and root held them firm. She could feel the forest above her, vast and heavy. Not in menace but in presence. The air cooled as she descended. The light thinned to a glow from phosphorescent fungus and carved stones. They shimmered with old magic.

The tunnel opened into a cavern.

The cavern was not large, yet it felt endless. Time had hollowed it, and roots tangled into pillars like a buried temple. Small fires burned in hollowed stone bowls. Shadows flickered on the walls. Dozens of Pukwudgies stood in silence along the edges of the chamber.

They did not move.

They did not speak.

They watched.

She walked forward. Her boots brushed old dust and strange symbols etched into the floor. The Pukwudgies parted for her. Not out of fear but with cautious reverence. They studied her as one might study a storm on the horizon.

Beautiful.

Terrible.

Unpredictable.

When she reached the center of the chamber, a voice at last broke the silence.

"You came."

From the far end of the cavern, a Pukwudgie elder stepped forward. His body hunched with age, but his presence still commanded the chamber. His fur cloak dragged behind him. His face bore marks of soot and ochre, and his eyes glowed in the firelight.

"We have watched you from the treetops. Heard your steps in the mist. You walk like a ghost, yet you carry thunder."

Liv bowed her head.

"You knew I would come."

The elder nodded once. "We knew someone would. But not if they would come in peace or in flame."

The circle of Pukwudgies closed tighter around the chamber. Not in threat, but alert.

"Why now, Valkyrie?" the elder asked. "Why come to those cast aside by humans?"

Liv raised her head.

"Because your world is no longer beneath the Leeds Devil's notice. Neither is mine."

The elder stepped forward. The elder stepped forward. Firelight revealed the heavy folds of his cloak. It was woven from moss, bark, and feathers that shimmered like beetle wings. He carried a carved staff taller than himself. It was crowned with pinecones, raven bones, and a braid of hair that looked human. His eyes shone deep gold, ringed in black like burnt-out suns. Wrinkles lined his face like bark worn smooth by centuries of wind and rain.

His name carried through the chamber as if it had always been known.

"I am Wunnemeahtoo." His voice carried like wind through the trees. "Once a guardian. Now a voice of what remains."

Liv bowed her head again, this time lower.

"I did not come because I was summoned," she said. "Not by Puddlesquat. Not by any of you."

The silence in the chamber grew heavy.

"I came for justice," she said, louder now. "I saw what the Leeds Devil will do if left unchecked. I saw trees rot where they should bloom. I saw rivers run dry. I saw the sky blacken with smoke. He tilts the world toward ruin, and he will not stop with you."

The fire behind Wunnemeahtoo flickered. One of the smaller Pukwudgies shifted in unease.

"You are not one of us," the elder said with care.

"No," Liv answered. "But I am of the earth. I am of the wild. I was born in balance, and I will die in its defense."

Wunnemeahtoo studied her for a long moment.

"You speak like the old ones," he said. "Like those who listened before the fire tribes came. Before promises were broken and the bones of our dead were ground into paths for wagons."

His voice softened.

"We remember the Valkyries. Not you. Not your face. But the feeling of you.

Thunder.

Moonlight.

Something not of this world. You are not the first to come from across the veils."

Liv frowned. "You've met my kind before?"

Wunnemeahtoo turned and walked back to the center of the cavern. The roots above him pulsed with green light.

"Long ago, one came with fire in her blood. She stood where you now stand and made a pact with the Pukwudgie kind."

He turned back.

"She did not survive."

Liv held his gaze. "I do not expect to. But I will not run."

A murmur swept through the gathered Pukwudgies. Low and fast, like leaves in a sudden gust.

Wunnemeahtoo lifted his staff.

"You may be our only chance, or our final doom. The world you saw in your vision is already forming. We feel it. The trees scream in silence. The water recoils."

He stepped closer.

"There is one thing you must understand before you help us."

Liv tilted her head.

"The Leeds Devil is not the cause of this darkness," he said. "He is a symptom. Something else opened the door. Something older."

Wunnemeahtoo's voice dropped lower, almost reverent.

"An older shadow stands behind the Leeds Devil. It feeds on the fear and chaos he spreads. Something ancient worshiped by men with hollow hearts and black tongues."

He looked at her carefully now, watching her reaction.

"Humans call it the Black Goat."

The chamber seemed to bend inward at the name.

Liv's breath caught. Her fists clenched at her sides. Something hot and raw rose from her gut.

Fury.

Loss.

Memory.

A flash of white-blonde hair matted with blood. A scream torn from a throat she could not reach in time. Ragna, broken in a ring of stones with her blade at her side.

"I know that name."

The fire cracked. Even the Pukwudgies edged back.

"They carved that symbol onto her skin. She died fighting them," she snarled.

"I was there when the cult marked the stones with her blood. I was there when they marked the stones with her blood. When they turned her body into an offering. She died in the fight against them."

Her eyes met Wunnemeahtoo's. Power stirred in her gaze. A faint blue glow at the edges, like frozen light.

"They did not kill her for power. They killed her to feed something."

Wunnemeahtoo nodded. "Then you understand. The Goat's hunger is endless. It twists the world into something unnatural. It hides behind monsters like the Leeds Devil, yet it is older than him. Older than us."

Liv's voice dropped. Cold now. Focused.

"Then I'll burn it from the roots up."

She turned. Her cloak moved behind her like smoke from a fire.

"But I'll start with the Devil."

THE HUNT BEGINS

Roots moved behind her. As she passed, they closed with a soft sigh. Liv stepped into daylight.

The forest had not changed. She had.

Thordis was the first to spot her as she came from the hidden passage. She rose fast. Her eyes searched Liv's face.

You are all right."

Liv nodded once. "I am."

Asbjorn stepped forward with his arms crossed. "What did they say?"

Liv's eyes turned to the trees around them. The silence had not left. It had changed. The forest still watched.

"They said the Devil is only the start."

Asbjorn scowled. "That is no comfort."

"It was not meant to be."

Thordis looked past her to the sealed root gate. "Will they help us?"

Liv nodded. "They will." She said. "They fought before. Many of them fell. This is their land. This is their world. They will fight again with all they have."

She looked to the forest. Faint rustling sounds marked hidden watchers in the trees.

"This time they hope we tip the scales."

Asbjorn gave a hard smile. "Then we will give them a war to mark their memory."

Liv crouched at the bog edge. Her fingers moved through damp moss and pine needles.

"He passed through shadow and left scars. Watch for signs. Wilted trees. Scorched brush. Bones that do not belong here."

Thordis knelt near her. She watched the treeline. "We saw ground like that near the river bend. A stand of pines fell in one night. Nothing grew back."

"He may circle," Liv said. "He seeks the next place to break."

Asbjorn leaned against a low tree. His arms crossed. "We will not wait for him. We will find him first."

Liv nodded. "We split into three paths. We scout his last known haunt. Start at the hollow on the west ridge. Puddlesquat said the ground rotted there."

Thordis stood. "If he feeds, he stays near foul ground. We must search dead water or sick animals. Someplace still enough to hide by day."

"And the wind," Asbjorn said. "If he moves fast, we track him by scent. The air turns foul after him. Birds will not follow."

Liv looked to the forest. The Pukwudgies still watched. They stayed unseen, but she felt them close. They listened.

She spoke clearly for all to hear.

"When we find him, we strike fast and show no mercy. No warning. No words. He is ruin. This land cannot bear his breath one more day."

Thordis reached over her shoulder and drew a short staff cut with runes. "We will mark the path as we go. Signs only we know. If one of us finds him, the others will follow."

Asbjorn drew his axe and checked the edge.

"And if he finds us first?"

Liv's eyes turned hard as ice.

"Then we make him regret it."

She rose.

"Now we hunt."

CHAPTER 26

SIGNS OF THE DEVIL

They parted with no ceremony.

Liv took the northwest path to the hollow. Asbjorn went east, where old game trails curved near the bog.

Thordis turned south. Her boots pressed firm on the sandy trail that wound between thick pine stands. The trees grew too close. Their branches bent into crooked arches. Sunlight barely cut through. The more she walked, the stiller the world became. No birds. No insects. Only the crunch of needles underfoot and the faint stir of wind high above.

She paused near a bend in the trail. She searched the trees.

Something felt wrong.

The pine needles here were gray. Ash gray, not the green of the rest of the forest. Bark peeled in sheets. Deep gouges marked the base of many trees as if claws had torn through the grove. No burn marks. No tracks. The smell was unnatural.

It smelled of rot and blood.

Thordis crouched. She set her hand on the dirt.

Cold.

Dry.

Dead.

She drew the short staff from her back. She cut a rune into the nearest tree. A curve for wrongness that Liv would know.

Thurisaz.

She was not alone.

Thordis turned. Nothing stood behind her.

Nothing she could see.

The hair on her neck stood.

She waited. Her breath grew thin.

A flicker came. A blur of shape between two pines. She saw a round face and pale eyes. Then nothing. Another flash above her in the branches.

She did not panic.

"Pukwudgie."

No answer.

"I know you are there."

Still silence.

A shape dropped from a branch onto the trail ahead. It stood near two feet tall. Gray-green furs wrapped its body. Its eyes shone like polished stone. It stared without blinking.

Thordis lowered her hand from her weapon.

"You are following me."

The Pukwudgie tilted its head.

"Good," she said. "If I find the Devil, I may not live long enough to tell the rest."

The creature blinked. Then it turned and ran swiftly into the trees.

Thordis paused and then followed.

Asbjorn moved east on an old game trail. The ground changed from moss to soft pine sand. The air was drier. The trees stood farther apart. The silence held. His axe rode on his back. The handle showed years of use. He did not draw it yet.

He thought about it.

He did not like this kind of silence. This was not the kind before a storm.

This was the kind that stayed.

The kind that watched.

He crouched near a broken fence post. It had long rotted and overgrown. He searched the ground. Only dry brush and stunted cedar trees.

No prints.

No sound.

Then he heard a crunch.

He froze.

Not his boot. Not his step.

He turned fast. His eyes narrowed.

No movement.

Yet something had stepped outside his line of sight.

"You watch me," he muttered. "Good. If the Devil shows, I may need bait."

No answer.

"You little moss rats follow me too?"

Still nothing.

He let out a breath through his nose and kept walking.

After a hundred more paces, he found it.

A clearing lay ahead. Small. Near ten paces wide. The trees around it stood dead. Charred black. Not from fire but from something worse. The bark split outward and peeled like blistered skin. The ground lay cracked. In the center rested a deer carcass. Scavengers had not touched it. Its eyes were gone. Ribs showed under torn hide. Even flies would not near it.

Asbjorn crouched near it.

This was not only death. This was desecration.

He reached in his pack and took a pouch of sage and pine ash. Liv had taught him the habit. Not magic. Respect. He cast a handful over the animal's body.

Then he felt it.

A presence stood behind him.

He stood and turned.

A single Pukwudgie stood five paces off. It perched on a rock. Smaller than the others he had seen.

Wide eyes.

Gray skin.

A tiny carved blade of black stone in its hand.

Their eyes locked.

"You here to warn me," Asbjorn asked. "Or to watch me die?"

The Pukwudgie tilted its head. Then it pointed at the deer.

Asbjorn followed its gesture.

The blood on the deerskin had dried in strange marks. Spirals. Runes. Ancient and foul.

The Pukwudgie hissed. Then it slipped into the brush.

Asbjorn stood still for a moment. Then he reached into his cloak and drew a strip of red cloth. He tied it to the base of a blackened tree.

A marker.

A warning.

"This is where it feeds," he said to himself. "This is where we strike."

Then he turned and began the walk back to the meeting point.

Liv moved northwest. Her boots made no sound on the moss floor. She walked alone, yet not alone. The woods leaned toward her. Shadows drew close. Branches bent as she passed.

Unlike the others, she did not need to search for signs.

She *felt* them.

The further she walked, the colder the wind grew. Not sharp but wrong. It came in bursts. Like breaths from something vast buried below the ground.

She passed a stone ring choked with vines. She passed a stream where the water stood still. Green and black, like old blood. She paused near a patch of mushrooms shaped like a crescent. They rotted from the inside.

This was not decay. This was corruption.

She reached the hollow near midday.

The clearing lay wide and shallow. Trees rose at odd angles. Grass lay pale. The air stank of sulfur and wet iron. At the center stood a crude shape. Long branches tied into an X with strips of torn cloth and hair.

Liv stepped closer.

She crouched at its base and set her hand on the ground.

It pulsed.

Not alive.

Not dead.

Something else.

Her eyes closed. She reached inward past flesh and breath to the place where her magic lay coiled like a serpent that waited to strike.

A vision struck her.

Brief yet searing.

Flashes of hooves.

Screams.

Trees split.

Fire that did not burn but consumed. She saw the Leeds Devil on a ridge. His mouth wide in a soundless roar. His wings spread wide like shadow. Behind him loomed something larger.

Antlers.

Hunger.

Smoke curled in thin wisps.

She gasped, but the breath caught in her throat.

When she opened her eyes, three Pukwudgies stood at the edge of the clearing.

One stepped forward and set a bundle of herbs and dark feathers at the base of the X.

A sign of mourning.

Or warning.

Liv rose.

"He was here," she said.

The wind carried her words into the trees.

"He will be here again."

The Pukwudgies gave no word. They turned and slipped into the woods.

Liv stayed a moment longer.

Then she cut the ground with her blade. A wide curved mark carved into the soil.

Not a mark for the others.

A message for the Devil.

I see you.

Then she turned. Her cloak snapped behind her like thunder in slow roll. She began her return to the others.

They returned one by one. Marked by what they had seen. Thordis came from the south first. Mud stained her boots. Her shoulders were held tense. She spoke no words at first. She sat near the fire pit they had built in a clearing shielded by brush. Asbjorn came next. His axe dark with bark ash. A strip of red cloth hung from his belt.

Then Liv stepped into the clearing. Both turned toward her. Not from sound but from the shift in the air. Something had come with her. Not a presence. A burden.

"He was at the hollow," she said.

Asbjorn nodded once. "I found where he feeds."

Thordis looked up. "And I followed one of them." She glanced at the trees. "A Pukwudgie scout. I think it wanted me to see what he left behind."

They sat in a rough triangle. For a moment, no one spoke. The fire cracked low. Far wind stirred through dead leaves.

At last, Asbjorn broke the silence.

"Do we know where he will go next?"

Liv knelt by the fire and drew her fingers through the ash.

"Not exact. He moves in a pattern. Feed. Vanish. Return. He grows bolder. If he thinks no one can stop him, he will come back to the hollow."

Thordis pulled a small pouch from her belt. She poured three carved runes onto a stone. One lay broken down the center.

"We lay the trap there," she said.

Liv nodded. "At night. When he is at his strongest."

Asbjorn frowned. "We fight him on his ground."

"No," Liv said. "We fight him in his pride. That is where he bleeds."

Thordis looked up. "And the Pukwudgies?"

"They will be there," Liv said. "All of them."

Asbjorn tightened his grip on his axe. "Then let us not waste it."

Liv looked north. Darkness had already gathered.

"This will not end cleanly," she said. "We will spill blood. We may not leave this forest. If we do not face him now, he will spread past the Pines. Nothing will stop him."

She stood. Her eyes shifted from blue to black in the twilight.

"We strike at the hollow. We stand in the dirt he has spoiled. We make him see us."

CHAPTER 27

BENEATH THE HOLLOW MOON

A half-moon hung high above the Pines. Pale and cold. It cast long shadows through twisted branches. Clouds rolled low and slow. The hollow clearing lay silent. It would not stay that way for long.

Liv stood at the edge of the clearing. Her hand rested on the hilt of her axe. Her eyes shut. She felt the earth under her feet. She felt the way it shifted unnaturally. Tension hummed in the roots. Wrongness waited to bloom.

Behind her, Thordis moved in silence. She dipped her fingers into a pouch of ash and marked her arms with runes. She spoke prayers to the old winds and to the bloodlines that guided her. Her bow rested near her. Strung and ready.

Asbjorn leaned against a half-rotted pine. He sharpened his axe with slow, firm strokes. His jaw locked tight, yet his breath stayed flat. He had fought many foes. But not like this.

Then they came out of the treeline.

The Pukwudgies.

Dozens stepped into the clearing. Silent as shadows. They came from burrows. They dropped from branches. They slipped from trunks like spirits in flesh. Each bore arms.

Stone blades.

Slings.

Bone spears sharpened.

Faces painted in mud and blood. Eyes glowed in the dark.

They watched Liv with grim purpose.

Wunnemeahtoo came last. He leaned on his tall staff. His eyes fixed on the moon.

"This is the place," he said. "Where we tried before. Where many of us fell."

He looked at Liv.

"Do not die like the last one."

Liv nodded once. "I will not."

The elder gave a grunt of approval and turned to the rest.

No speech.

No rite.

A glance passed from one to the next. They moved into position in the trees and brush and in the dark around the hollow.

Thordis slung her bow over her shoulder. "When he comes, it will not be alone, will it?"

Liv's face turned hard. "No. He will bring the storm with him." Her eyes shifted from blue to black. "And so will we."

Asbjorn set down the stone and stood tall. "Then we hold the line."

Liv stepped into the center of the hollow. The crude X-shape still stood. It was now set with sharpened stakes and runes cut into the dirt around it.

She raised her head to the sky. She drew in the cold night air and spoke one word.

"Come."

And deep in the Pines something answered.

A howl.

Not of beast.

Of something born in nightmare.

The ground shook.

The wind turned.

The Devil was coming.

Clouds drifted across the moon. The little light there was dim. The air grew heavy. Branches snapped deep in the forest. Far off but with intent.

Not the wind.

Not an animal.

The Pukwudgie scouts stiffened.

From his perch high in the trees, one gave a whistle. Two notes that rose.

Another answered from the far side.

Then came silence again.

Liv's pulse slowed. The earth gave a faint tremor under her boots.

Birds had gone.

Insects had gone.

The woods were still.

Thordis reached for her bow.

Asbjorn flexed his fingers around the axe handle.

The trees ahead shifted.

The Leeds Devil stepped from the shadows.

He stood taller than they had thought. Over six feet. Wide bat wings curled tight on his back. His hide lay dark and scarred. His legs bent like a deer yet ended in split hooves. Two black horns rose from his head. His chest bore thick bristled hair. His face was goat-like and twisted, yet showed thought. He grinned with crooked teeth under burning yellow eyes.

He paused at the edge of the clearing.

The silence stretched.

Then he *spoke*.

"I smelled you hours ago, Valkyrie."

His voice was gravel and ash. Too human to be a beast. Too foul to be a man.

Liv stepped forward. "Then you had time to run."

He gave a low chuckle. "You think this forest still belongs to them?" He waved toward the Pukwudgies in the trees. "I buried their power long ago. And they thanked me for it."

Asbjorn muttered. "He talks too much."

The Devil's head snapped toward him. His grin spread wider. "And you brought a hammer with legs. Fine."

He turned his gaze to Thordis next.

"And the archer. You dream in fire, do you? You will be the first to burn."

Thordis did not blink.

Liv drew her sword. She did not rush. She did not posture. She stood ready. Her eyes were black and merciless.

"You have poisoned this land long enough," she said. "You do not belong here."

The Devil stepped forward.

"I was born here." He grinned. "This soil cried out for me. I am its true son."

"No," Liv said. "You were let in. Now you will be driven out."

The Devil's grin slipped to a sneer. "Others said that. They were stronger than you. Wiser than you. They all screamed in the end."

"Another Valkyrie," Wunnemeahtoo said from the treeline. His voice was grim. "A thousand years ago, she stood here too."

The Devil turned toward the elder. His grin split wide. "She screamed for me. Sweet and long. I made her sing."

The tension broke.

Liv raised her sword. Her black eyes showed no fear.

"Now!" Liv's command cracked like lightning.

The forest erupted in motion.

From the treetops, Pukwudgies leapt in waves. Small bodies painted in mud and ash. Bone and obsidian blades lifted high. They shrieked sharply and high, like wind in broken reeds. Dozens dropped from branches like rain. They struck from above with savage aim.

Thordis loosed an arrow before her foot moved.

Then a second.

Then a third.

Shafts cut through the air.

One struck the Devil's shoulder. Another tore through the wing membrane. The beast staggered a step and bellowed a roar that rattled the pines.

Asbjorn charged with his axe high. His boots tore through root and brush.

He did not pause.

He never did.

He slammed into the Devil's side and struck with a grunt that shook the clearing.

Steel met flesh.

The Devil reeled back. He snarled, but no blood flowed. Not as it should. He laughed loud.

"Your toy bites wood harder than it bites me."

The skin where the axe struck shimmered. Dark craft shielded him. No common steel could humble him.

Liv surged forward. She spoke the old tongue. Her sword glowed blue with runes cut in ash and her own blood. She struck low. Her blade carved the Devil's leg. This time he howled. Black blood sprayed across the grass. The Devil staggered.

But only for a moment.

Then came the counterstrike.

He spun. His tail lashed out like a whip. It struck a Pukwudgie in mid leap and hurled it into a tree with a crack of bone.

Another fell under his hooves. Crushed before it gave a scream.

Thordis fired fast and sure. The Devil moved with ruthless speed. He dodged and weaved. He turned his body so wings and claws shielded his core. He laughed as arrows broke on him.

"Shoot more. I enjoy the sting."

He *knew* how to fight.

Liv saw clearly. This was no mindless beast.

This was a killer who had learned. He mocked her with a grin. "I have slain better than you."

She met his gaze across the chaos. His golden eyes burned with pride. She felt no rage. Only confidence. Only arrogance.

He had done this before.

And he had survived.

He laughed.

"Do you think you will be the ones to end me?"

More Pukwudgies fell. Blades shattered on his hide. Spears broke on his black horns. He sneered. "Little toys. Little hands. You call this war?"

Asbjorn struck again. The Devil caught the axe mid-swing and wrenched it from him. He hurled him aside like a sack of grain. Asbjorn struck a fallen tree and groaned.

Liv raised her sword. Her breath came heavily. Her eyes were black and soulless.

The battle had only begun.

And already doubt stirred cold in her chest.

The Devil moved with sudden violent grace. His hooves barely touched the ground as he surged across the clearing. He should not have been that fast. A beast that size was not meant to move like the wind.

Liv pivoted to meet him. Her sword arced upward with force and rage. She struck his chest square.

The blade sparked.

But it did not cut skin. The Devil threw back his head and laughed. "Is that all you have, Valkyrie? Your blade sings, but it does not bite. You think you differ from the last one," he snarled. "She bled the same. You will too."

He bared his teeth and exhaled sharply. The scent struck first. Fetid and thick like rot in the lungs. Thordis drew back and coughed. Her eyes watered.

The grass was discolored and curled. The mushrooms were blackened. Even the air drew back.

He snapped his black wings wide and leapt to the sky in one beat. He sneered down. "On the ground, you are nothing. Small and weak."

Pukwudgie spears flew up. None struck. He mocked them. "Throw harder, little rats. You may scratch my wings yet."

From the trees, scouts climbed higher. He rose above them and opened his jaws. He released fire. Orange and white flame cut through the night like a blade of light.

"The runes cut him. Mark your blades," called Liv.

Thordis fired again. She aimed high with an arrow tipped in carved obsidian and carved with runes.

"Runes carved deep. Obsidian for fire. Let it pierce."

The arrow struck the Devil's wing. He jerked and snarled. His grin slipped. For a moment his pride cracked.

He faltered. Black blood dripped. His eyes narrowed.

Liv seized the moment. She leapt onto a fallen trunk and drove at his flank. Her sword bit deep under the ribs.

Blood sprayed.

Real blood.

His grin returned. "So that is it. Not steel, but scratches of ash. You think that will save you? Now I know you will try harder before you die."

The Devil roared. His voice shook the trees.

For the first time, he looked angry. He spat black blood and snarled.

"Do not think this means you have won. It means I will savor you."

"You are fire," he hissed. "But I am the storm. I will drown your flame. I will feed on your ash."

He crashed down into the clearing. His black wings folded like claws. The ground shook. Pukwudgies scattered.

He lashed out.

One Pukwudgie skewered itself on his horn. He shook the body free with a laugh. "One less squeak in the woods."

Another caught in his claws. He hurled it into the trees with a crack of bone. He laughed. "Fall easy. Feed my roots."

Asbjorn limped to the flank. The Devil spun and struck him with a hoof. He flew into a rotted stump and stayed down. Blood ran from his brow. The Devil mocked him. "Strong man. Weak tree. Both break."

Liv stepped back. Her breath was ragged. The strain of battle pulled at her. Her eyes stayed black. Cold. Soulless.

The Devil grinned.

"You feel it now, don't you?" he said as he stepped close. "The strain. The fear. The memory of her death. Your sister in arms."

"She screamed too," he whispered. "I still hear it. I keep it. I made it into a song."

Liv's hands trembled.

Thordis loosed another arrow. She aimed not to kill but to blind.

The arrow struck the Devil across the eyes. He roared. "Thief. You dare mar my sight?"

He reeled. His grin twisted in rage. "You will pay for that with fire."

Liv surged forward. She yelled as she drove her sword into his.

He shrieked. Rage more than pain. His grin broke wide. "Yes. Scream. Give me your fury."

It was power. His pride rose with it.

A wave of darkness burst from him like a shock. An aura of rot and despair. The ground cracked. The trees moaned. Pukwudgies near him froze. Locked in fear or bound by a curse. He raised his arms high. "See me. None can stand. None can move when I will it."

Liv staggered.

"Fall back" she shouted. Her voice was raw. Her black eyes fixed on him.

The warriors pulled back. They dragged Asbjorn. The Pukwudgies that lived slipped into the trees with their wounded.

The Devil did not follow. He laughed. "Run, little ghosts. Run to your holes."

He stood in the burning clearing. Firelight licked across his black horns. His black wings spread wide. He raised his voice. "Look at me and remember. This ruin is my mark."

"Run," he called after them. "Regroup. Plan. Pray. It will not save you."

He raised his hand and pointed at Liv. His grin spread wide.

"Bring your fury next time, Valkyrie. I will hear it break. I will drink it."

His voice dropped. Low and deliberate. Like a blade drawn from its sheath.

"Tell the world it was Azraelion who ended you. Speak my name. Make it feared. Make it worship."

"He spoke his own name. A demon should never do that. He believes it makes him strong," Wunnemeahtoo said.

She froze. Her black eyes fixed on him.

The name struck her like iron in her blood.

Azraelion.

A name born of shadow. A name swollen with pride. A name that carried its power.

"Or he needs us to speak it. Without fear, he fades," Liv replied.

He turned and stepped into the flames. He vanished into the smoke. His laughter hung in the Pines.

CHAPTER 28

THE TRIBES UNITE

Smoke clung to their clothes as they left the hollow. None spoke of the fallen. None looked back. The survivors moved like ghosts through the night. Their eyes were hollow. Their wounds ached with more than pain. Pukwudgies limped beside them. Some were carried on stretchers of bark and vine. Others walked with broken blades, marked with clay and ash. The forest mourned behind them.

They climbed toward a house seen from the ridge. A sturdy frame set high on a wooded rise. They did not know who lived there. It stood whole. It was defensible. It was far enough from the hollow to grant them a breath of time. That was all that mattered.

Or so it seemed.

Liv had seen the house before, in dreams and in signs. Its timbers carried an omen. This was not chance.

It was a circle closing.

It was legacy calling.

Inside, they laid down the worst of the wounded. A few Pukwudgies and one of their own. Liv bound what she could with cloth and herbs. Thordis worked in silence. She sharpened the last of the arrows. Asbjorn sat with his back to the hearth. His arm was bound tight. His face was set in grim silence. None asked what came next.

Liv stood at the window. Her eyes locked on the treetops below. Her muscles ached. Her skin burned with cold. But the name still rang in her bones like thunder in a storm.

Azraelion.

She drew a bottle of mead from her pouch. She drank deep. Her head tingled, and the vision stirred.

It was not of steel or blood. It was of symbols. Of light within circles. Of voices carried on the wind. She stood again in burning woods. No weapon in hand. She held back the storm. She did not strike. She bound.

The Devil could not be killed with earthly weapons. His flesh cast out steel. His soul slipped through fire and blade. He must be anchored. Chained in the old way. Her eyes snapped open.

"We need more than strength," she said. "We need magic."

That night, while the others rested, she worked beneath the open sky.

In the clearing beyond the house, she drew a circle in consecrated chalk. Not to summon but to shield. Azraelion was already coming. The forest felt it. The air shook with it. This was no invitation. It was a stand.

She found a carcass left in the yard. Another life taken in the Devil's wake. She cut what fat she could and set an old iron pot on the fire pit. The tallow boiled down, thick and ready. From it she shaped thirteen candles, each marked with runes by her hand. She set them at the edge of the circle and lit them. She burned incense of bloodroot, sage, and bark from cursed ground. Each mark and each breath prepared the ground. Not to call him near but to hold when he came.

But she knew it would not be enough.

She called out. Across time. Across blood. Across memory. They answered.

From the green valleys and hidden shores came the Menehune. Their chants, spoken in ʻŌlelo Hawaiʻi, carried power older than stone.

From shadowed hills and stone circles came the Leprechauns of Ireland. They bore iron charms and riddles sharp as blades.

From the roots of Mexican caves came the Chaneques. Their songs bent the forest wind and confused the senses.

From mist and leaf came the Celtic fairies. Their light cut the dark like knives.

From the riverbeds of the north came the Mannegishi. Their stones struck true, guided by trickster hands.

From the hollows of England came the Boggarts. They moved with shadow and spread fear like smoke.

The Pukwudgies remained. Scarred. Beaten. But unbroken.

None came for Liv. None for glory.

They came by hidden ways. Some crossed through mist and stone as if the earth itself had opened. Others had been waiting all along. Small bands scattered through forest and hollow. All heard her call. All came because the balance had tipped. If this forest fell, the world would follow.

Liv rose from her work and went to the circle.

The air was colder now. Still. As if the night itself waited.

Thordis and Asbjorn exited the house and joined her outside. Their weapons were ready. Their wounds were bound tightly.

They said nothing.

There was nothing left to say.

Beyond them in the woods below, the others had already taken their places. Hidden among brush, roots, and trees. Dozens of eyes shone in the dark. Pukwudgies, Menehune, Leprechauns, Chaneques, Mannegishi, Boggarts, and others without names. They waited. Small and silent, yet fierce with ancient purpose.

Liv walked to the circle she had drawn in the earth. It was scored in chalk, ringed in candles, and pulsed with power. It was no trap. It was a shield. A last stand under the open sky.

She stepped into the center.

The last candle flickered to life.

She looked to the dark woods.

She spoke one word.

"Come."

Far below the ridge, the wind changed.

Azraelion had heard her. He was on his way.

CHAPTER 29

THE CIRCLE HOLDS

The wind screamed through the pines.

The tribes waited.

Azraelion stepped from the woods. A god of rot and rage. His wings snapped open. Fire licked from their edges. He screamed. Bark split. Branches bent.

Then the tribes struck as one. Menehune chants rolled across the pines. Chaneques wove confusion through the Devil's ranks. Leprechauns fought in tight formation, iron flashing. Mannegishi stones cracked against his hide. Fairies blinded with sudden light. Boggarts leapt at his wings and snarled in rage.

The Pukwudgies led the charge. Scarred. Bloodied. Unyielding. This was their forest. Their home. Their fight.

Liv stood at the heart of the circle. The candles burned steadily against the storm.

Thordis loosed a barrage of arrows. Her movements were quick and sharp. She aimed for joints, wings, and eyes. Asbjorn roared and drove his axe into the Devil's flank. Steel failed, but runes carved into bone and blade made the flesh stutter. Not stopped, but slowed.

Azraelion fought with purpose.

He burned a swath of fire across the front line. Three Mannegishi fell in ash. He kicked a boggart with the force of an ox. He tore through Leprechauns, ripping light and body apart with teeth and claw.

Wunnemeahtoo, the Pukwudgie elder, stepped into his path. He raised his arms and began a protection chant. The air shimmered. But before he could complete it, Azraelion struck him with one blow. His claws to the chest.

The elder fell. His staff splintered.

"Your chants die with you," boasted Azraelion. "This forest bows to me, not you."

Shock and mourning swept through the Pukwudgies

Liv gasped but held her ground. She could not break the circle. Not yet.

She began to chant. Her voice was steady. She drew on the ley lines that cut through the woods. She called on the power she had prepared with her runes and her breath.

Then she saw it.

Azraelion turned toward Puddlesquat. The small one stood unarmed by the treeline. The Devil raised one claw and grinned with cruel pleasure.

Liv's eyes blazed.

The runes of the circle pulsed.

Light flared from the ground beneath Puddlesquat.

Azraelion's strike stopped short. It was blocked by a golden force.

Puddlesquat did not run.

He stood taller than before. His eyes glowed with primal power. His skin crackled with runes that nearly appeared on it.

Liv had given him power.

Not to win the fight.

But to survive it.

He rose with the fallen elder's staff in hand. He snarled at the Devil as if the earth itself had risen to speak.

Azraelion reeled back. Not wounded. Surprised.

Azraelion reeled back. Not wounded. Surprised.

The candles burned blue.

The wind screamed.

The final battle had only begun.

Liv stood within the circle. The wind shifted again. The warriors readied themselves. The tribes braced for what was coming. Before she could speak, a shadow moved from the edge of the trees.

It was Manu, elder of the Menehune.

He carried no weapons. Only a carved staff older than the trees. His face was solemn. His eyes clear.

"I will join you," he said.

Liv turned. "You are needed in the fight."

"I am needed here more," he replied. "The demon knows your tongue. It does not know mine."

She studied him for a moment.

"Our tongue is older than this forest. Older than the fire in his veins. If we speak together, your words will strike his name. Mine will break his soul."

Liv nodded and stepped aside for him to enter the circle. "Then we cast as one."

Together, they turned to face the storm.

The battlefield was chaos. Azraelion roared, and the heavens shook. His wings cast shadows across the moonlight. The ground split beneath him. His breath curled through the trees. It boiled water. Spoiled streams. Blackened leaves. Every sweep of his claws threw bodies aside like dry grass.

Still, the tribes fought on.

Thordis loosed arrows until her quiver was empty. Her fingers bled from the bowstring. Asbjorn fought through the pain. His cracked ribs burned. His axe blackened with smoke. Pukwudgies leapt from root to branch to ground. They struck with tooth and blade, though their numbers thinned.

The Menehune moved through the shadows with grace. The Chaneques sang war songs in voices older than the hills. Leprechauns spoke riddles sharp as knives. Mannegishi rained stones from the trees. Boggarts snarled and bit furiously. Fairies blazed with light. The glare seared his flesh and blinded his eyes.

Still, it was not enough.

Wunnemeahtoo was gone.

The circle shook.

The demon was too strong.

Inside the ring of runes carved by Liv's hand, the air burned blue with power. Algiz. Eihwaz. Thurisaz. All glowed and held against the storm.

"Your chalk and fire cannot hold me," bragged Azraelion.

Liv stood tall. She was bloodied but unbroken. Manu stood beside her and did not waver.

Together, they began the spell.

Liv raised her voice, ancient and commanding: "This circle protects us. Runes of Algiz, Eihwaz, and Thurisaz. We call on the strength of the gods, on the ward of earth and sky." (spoken in Old Norse)

Manu followed. His voice was deep and sure. "This circle protects us. Runes of Algiz, Eihwaz, and Thurisaz. We call on the strength of the gods, on the shelter of earth and sky." *(spoken in ʻŌlelo Hawaiʻi)*

"You waste your breath. My name will outlast you," Azraelion said.

Their words carried across the battlefield. The words twisted through the battlefield like smoke. They wrapped around Azraelion and bound into the cracks in his flesh. He snarled, turned toward them, and roared. His scream split trees and dropped birds from the sky. The circle shook. The candles wavered. For a moment, Liv feared it would fail.

They did not stop. Manu's voice cracked, but he pressed on. Liv forced her tone harder. Louder, though blood filled her mouth.

Liv cried out, "I call on the old powers. Odin. Thor. Freyja." *(spoken in Old Norse)* The runes blazed, then dimmed, as if the names themselves fought against the Devil's shadow.

Manu answered: "I call on the old powers. Kāne. Kū. Lono." *(spoken in ʻŌlelo Hawaiʻi)* The names cut the air like thunder. Azraelion staggered but lashed back. Flames swept the circle. Two candles guttered out.

Azraelion stumbled but pushed forward. His claw struck the circle. Sparks flew. The ground split under Liv's feet. The guardians cried out and loosed their own power with riddles, chants, stones, and light. Their strength held the circle while she and Manu pressed on.

Liv held aloft an iron charm. It was rough-forged from the farmstead. She had cut runes into its face. Algiz. Thurisaz. Eihwaz.

"With this charm that bears your true name, Azraelion, I bind you. By the strength of Odin, Thor, and Freyja, you are cast out and forbidden until the seal breaks." *(spoken in Old Norse)*

Manu lifted his staff and answered.

"With this iron charm marked with your true name, Azraelion, I bind you. By the strength of Kāne, Kū, and Lono, you are cast out and forbidden until the seal breaks." *(spoken in ʻŌlelo Hawaiʻi)*

Azraelion shrieked and lunged. His claw struck the edge. The runes flared white-hot, then cracked. Liv felt them tearing. Manu drove his staff into the ground, and the break sealed again. Azraelion reeled back, unable to cross.

"No circle can bind me. I will break it," the demon growled.

The two raised their hands in unison, voices overlapping now, a harmony of fury and sacred power:

Liv's voice thundered.

"Azraelion, by the power of your true name, I bind you with this iron amulet. Feel the weight of your name and be cast out." *(spoken in Old Norse)*

Manu followed.

"Azraelion, by the power of your true name, I bind you with this iron charm. Know the burden of your name and be cast out." *(spoken in ʻŌlelo Hawaiʻi)*

"Wait…"

"No!" he shouted.

The demon staggered. His roar broke. His body cracked with light. The earth split beneath him. His wings thrashed. Fire scattered through the trees. And for the first time, the Devil knew fear.

Liv shouted: "Azraelion, go back to hell!" *(spoken in Old Norse)*

Azraelion's form burst in dark light. The spell drew him inward, consumed him, bound him by word, will, and name. The shockwave rolled through the forest like thunder.

And then…

Silence.

The fire dimmed. The air cleared.

The demon was gone. Banished from this realm.

Liv shook inside the circle. The candles burned low. Manu exhaled. For a moment, the world was still.

Liv stood shaking inside the circle, candles flickering low. Manu exhaled, and for a moment, the world felt still.

They had done it.

Together.

But both knew the seal would not hold forever.

CHAPTER 30

THE SMOKE SETTLES

awn came. Its light cut through ash and pine. The clearing where the battle had raged lay silent. Trees bore scorch marks. The earth was torn and black in places. The air no longer carried the scent of death.

The tribes gathered in silence.

They buried the fallen in sacred ways. Stones set. Feathers tied. Chants spoken in tongues nearly forgotten. The Pukwudgies lit a fire for Wunnemeahtoo. His staff stood upright in the earth beside it. When the flames died down, Puddlesquat stepped forward.

He lifted the staff.

The others bowed their heads.

No words were spoken. They all knew. He was the new elder now.

Something in him had changed. His frame held power. The runes on his arms glowed in the sun. Liv's magic lived within him. Not as a weapon. As a guardian. A keeper of the balance.

The tribes lingered to share food, bind wounds, and speak of the lost. One by one, they returned to the wild.

The mannegishi vanished upriver.

The chaneques slipped into the roots of the cypress trees.

The menehune disappeared with the mist.

The boggarts were gone before anyone saw them leave.

Liv sat under a cedar tree. Her back was pressed against the trunk. Her sword lay across her lap. Thordis sat nearby. Her shoulder was wrapped in linen. Her eyes were watchful but tired. Asbjorn stood at the edge of the clearing. He stared at the trees. His ribs were bound tight beneath a torn shirt.

Liv rose and walked to them.

"You fought like legends," she said.

Thordis gave a tired smile. "Next time, pick something easier."

Asbjorn snorted. "There better not be a next time."

Liv's gaze hardened. "There will be."

Liv turned to Puddlesquat. He stood at the base of her cabin. The staff across his shoulders.

"Keep an eye on this place," she said. "If the balance tips again, you know how to find me."

Puddlesquat gave a slow, solemn nod.

When the tribes were gone, Liv sat beside the fire until only embers glowed.

She rose and walked to the cabin.

She stepped inside without a word.

The door creaked shut.

A blue light flashed.

A moment later, Thordis called her name and followed. She opened the door. The room was empty.

Liv was gone.

She had returned to the mystic realm.

Thordis and Asbjorn stood in silence.

Outside, the woods remained silent.

They remembered her.

CHAPTER 31

THE LEAVES REMEMBER

December 1908

Leeds Point, New Jersey

The clock ticked in the corner of the kitchen. A single oil lamp cast a dim light. Outside, a stiff wind stirred bare pine branches and tapped the windows like a voice at the glass. The old house creaked in the stillness. The silence felt heavy. Like something waited.

Rachel Leeds sat alone at the kitchen table, wrapped in a worn shawl. Her breath showed in the cold air. The fire had burned low. She had not added wood in an hour.

For days, a strange pressure weighed on her chest. Unease came with nightfall. Dreams left no memory.

Animals were too quiet. The house was colder than it should have been.

She could not ignore it any longer.

Rachel rose with purpose. She gathered mugwort and dandelion, herbs she had grown and dried herself. She was still new to her craft, yet she trusted the process. The ritual of tea. The clarity it brought. The way it let her listen to the pulse of the world.

She whispered to the herbs as she set them in the cup.

The kettle whistled. She poured water. She watched the leaves swirl and then settle.

And then she looked.

What she saw stopped her breath.

Cloven hooves. Wings. Horns. A goat's face twisted in a soundless howl.

The tea leaves had taken shape with clear detail. She had seen it once before. A drawing hidden in her grandfather's old Bible, folded until the paper cracked at the edges.

She stared at the cup.

The Leeds Devil.

She whispered the words. "It is back."

Her hands shook. She rose at once, pushed back from the table, and left the tea untouched.

There was no time.

She knew who she needed to find.

Henrietta Jordan. A woman rumored to live in the woods. She was said to follow the old ways. A witch, though she carried the name softly.

Rachel pulled her coat from the hook by the door and stepped into the cold. The stars cut sharply above the trees.

She mounted her horse without pause. It would take days to reach Batsto Village.

She did not care.

The Devil had returned.

And someone had to stop it.

CHAPTER 32

THE WITCH IN THE PINES

Batsto Village, New Jersey

December 17, 1908

The wind moved differently in Batsto. It cut through bare trees as if it knew the ground. It whistled through the cracks in the old houses. It stirred leaves that lay frozen in snow. The village once held iron and trade. Now it stood silent. Mansions and mills remained. The store and gristmill were motionless. The years had left their mark.

Most people had left long ago. Only Henrietta Jordan remained.

She lived in a stone cottage at the edge of the woods, where pines grew thick and old. From her porch, she saw the bones of the village through the trees. She liked the stillness. She liked the silence. She liked the freedom.

She enjoyed being apart from them. Townsfolk with their sideways glances and muttered words.

Here, she felt safe.

Free to work Seiðr, the magic of her ancestors. She brewed tonics. She carved runes. She spoke to fire and wind. The village did not care. The village no longer knew how to watch.

On December 17, 1908, she woke before the sun.

There had been no dream.

She had felt a stir in the stillness. A ripple in water. She walked through her morning rites in silence. She set protective marks on the doorway. She brushed powdered bark across the lintel. She spoke the old words in a tongue few remembered.

She lit her fire. She drew three runes. She burned mugwort on a copper plate.

One rune split.

That meant change. It meant interference. It meant a path that crossed another.

Henrietta sat back on her heels. Then came the sound.

A crow called.

Once.

Twice.

Then silence.

She rose and stepped outside barefoot, though the ground was cold. The snow crunched under her feet.

A crow sat on the rail of her porch. Larger than most. Eyes dark as obsidian.

It did not fly.

It did not blink.

It only stared.

Henrietta met its gaze.

She nodded once.

"I see."

She knew what it meant. Someone was coming.

Not a hunter.

Not a villager.

A messenger.

Someone with blood that carried old things. Someone the forest had not yet chosen to accept or reject.

She spoke to the crow.

"Tell the wind I wait."

The bird gave a soft call. Then it rose into the sky.

Henrietta turned and stepped back into the house. She prepared tea for two.

Rachel's horse trudged through the edge of Batsto Village. Hooves struck frost-hard dirt. The sky was the color of iron. Dusk hung low over the rooftops. The place looked swallowed by time.

Mute.

Windswept.

Half forgotten.

But it was not empty.

She saw her before she saw the cottage.

Henrietta Jordan stood on the porch wrapped in a dark shawl. Her hair held braids with bones and dried herbs. She waited. One hand carried a steaming mug. The other rested on a carved post.

"The crows said you were coming," Henrietta said. Her voice carried no harshness.

Rachel slowed and stepped down. Her breath rose in the air. She stood at the edge of the clearing. She was uncertain. She stood between fear and awe.

She had heard the rumors. A witch in the pines. A woman who kept to herself. A woman of the old ways.

Yet, to see her stand there calm and expectant was something else.

Rachel stepped forward. "I was not sure you were real."

Henrietta smiled. "I hear that often."

Rachel swallowed and gathered her thoughts.

"I am Rachel. Rachel Leeds. I came from the coast. From the house that once belonged to Japheth and Deborah Leeds. I am their descendant."

Henrietta's smile faded, though not with surprise. She motioned toward the steps.

"Come inside."

Inside the warmth struck at once. A fire burned in the hearth. Dried herbs hung in the corners. The air smelled of clove and pine and earth.

Rachel did not sit at once. She stood near the fire. She held her hands out to the heat.

"I had a vision in the tea," she said. "Mugwort and dandelion. I saw it in the cup."

Henrietta moved with purpose. She poured a second mug of tea.

"What did you see?"

"A creature. Hooved. Winged. Horned. I had seen it before in an old family drawing hidden deep in my grandfather's Bible. My mother called it the Leeds Devil. But it was no story. It is no legend."

Henrietta handed her the cup.

"No," she said. "It is not."

Rachel's head snapped up.

Henrietta nodded. "I know the creature. It was last seen in 1736. One hundred seventy years ago. Banished, they said. If it has returned…"

Her eyes darkened.

"It will not return in silence. It will want revenge."

Rachel gripped the mug tight. "I came here because I knew no other place. The signs are clear. It comes back. I think I must stop it. But I cannot do it alone."

Henrietta studied her.

"You are a young witch. I feel it in your force. Raw yet rooted. The land listens to you."

She sipped her tea.

"I will help. If what you saw is true, the Pines are not safe. Not for anyone."

The wind cut through the trees like a whisper too cold to bear words.

Rachel and Henrietta rode in silence. Their horses stepped slowly on the narrow path that led west to Leeds Point. Pines pressed in on both sides. Bare branches clawed at the pale sky. The silence was deep but not dead.

Henrietta kept her eyes on the treeline.

Not with fear.

With focus.

Rachel rode ahead. Her shoulders hunched. Cold air made her breath fog before her lips. The burden of the old house and of her name grew heavier with each step.

"Do you feel it?" Henrietta asked.

Rachel looked over. "What?"

Henrietta kept her eyes on the woods. "The silence. Not the kind that follows fear. Something else. The forest listens."

Rachel did not answer at once.

She had felt it. Birds had returned. The air was clean. The pines no longer felt cold. They felt still.

Not lifeless.

Watchful.

At a bend in the trail, Rachel saw a flicker of movement between the trees. She turned her head quickly. She saw a shape no taller than her waist. It stood still behind a fallen log. The creature did not move. It only watched.

She said nothing.

And neither did Henrietta. She had seen it as well.

A glance passed between them.

A Pukwudgie.

It made no move to stop them. It gave no sound. No gesture. It simply was. A guardian of nature. Present like a memory that did not fade.

Near sundown they reached Rachel's house. The light was dim and golden. The house was old, yet stood firm. The shutters were shut. Dry pine needles lay on the porch. A lantern still hung by the door.

Henrietta looked it over as they stepped down.

"This is old ground," she said.

Rachel opened the door and stepped inside. She pulled off her gloves.

"It was my great-grandfather's. And his before that."

Henrietta followed her inside. She ran her hand along the doorframe. Her fingers twitched. A flicker passed through them.

"There is magic here," she said.

"Is it bad?"

Henrietta walked deeper into the room. Her eyes searched the walls, the corners, and the hearth. She touched a wooden beam and closed her eyes for a moment.

"Not bad. Old. Deep." She turned to Rachel. "Magic runs through your bloodline. There is no doubt."

Rachel lowered her gaze. "But is it dark?"

Henrietta stepped closer.

"That rests on what your ancestors did with it."

Rachel bit her lip and nodded.

They lit a fire together and unpacked their satchels. Henrietta stayed with Rachel. She did not trust the woods after dusk. Even if they had not yet felt the Devil's return.

Later, Rachel prepared tea by the hearth. Henrietta watched her hands.

"You are still learning," she said. "But it is in your hands. The way you handle the leaves. The way the fire answers you."

Rachel looked down.

Henrietta said, "Whatever lies ahead, you were born to face it. Even if you are not ready."

Outside, the wind rose. Not with menace. Only as a reminder that something lingered beyond the trees.

Watching.

Waiting.

CHAPTER 33

SHADOWS AND OMENS

January 1909

The wind howled through the pines the night it came.

Deep in the woods, where paths turned to roots and shadows held the air like ash, a light burst. Not white. Not fire. Indigo. It cracked like lightning without thunder. It lit the forest in strange colors for a moment.

In that moment, something returned.

The forest moaned.

Birds rose.

Streams froze at their edges.

The darkness opened its eyes.

The next morning, no one in Leeds Point spoke of the light. Two days later in Woodbury, a child screamed. A strange figure stood on a chicken coop.

Hooved.

Horned.

Wings jerked against the wind.

That same night in Camden, something tore through a row of fences. Dogs howled. Milk soured. Thermometers broke from the sudden cold.

By January 18, sightings spread wide. South Jersey. Delaware. The suburbs of Philadelphia. Panic took them. Headlines struck the presses with haste.

Mass Hysteria Grips New Jersey

Jersey Devil Sighting Causes Panic

Nearly 1,000 Report Seeing Monster

In Haddon Heights, a trolley car was struck. The driver swore something had landed on the roof. It shrieked and then vanished in a gust of wind.

Churches filled. Guns sold out. Schools shut for the week. Henrietta folded the paper and set it aside.

Across the room, Rachel sat stiff at the family table. The old house had once belonged to Japheth and Deborah Leeds. Her breath misted in the cold air.

"It is him," she said.

Henrietta nodded. "There is no doubt."

They sat in silence while the old house creaked. Then Rachel looked up.

"We must stop it before it starts."

"There is someone near. A woman named Eliza Whitaker. They say she is a shadow witch. Samuel Whitaker built it for her in 1901 as a wedding gift."

Rachel paused. "Can we trust her?"

Henrietta frowned. "Her husband Samuel is known for generosity. Eliza, for her strange ways. People whisper she works with the occult. It makes them uneasy."

Rachel leaned forward. "She may be what we need."

Henrietta met her gaze across the table.

"Then we go to her before it is too late."

The air in Leeds Point grew heavy with unease. Reports of the Jersey Devil spread fast. Fear held the people. Livestock went missing or lay mutilated. Screeches cut through the forest at night. A dark presence lingered. It affected the weather and the crops. It haunted the dreams of men.

Rachel and Henrietta walked through the Pine Barrens. The forest stood silent. Shadows stretched long. The air felt heavy. A dark presence lingered. Weather turned foul. Crops failed. Dreams grew dark.

They sought Eliza Whitaker. Her house stood near Moss Mill Road and Leeds Point Road. New among the old. Its shape stood apart. Inviting yet strange.

Eliza met them at the door. "I expected you," she said. "The shadows whispered of your arrival and of the dark force."

Inside hung tapestries and strange things. Herbs and incense filled the air. The place felt strange yet steady.

They sat at a round table. Henrietta spoke first. "Eliza, we have heard of your craft. Tell us about it."

Eliza's eyes gleamed with pride and caution. "I am a shadow witch," she said. "My line holds the mysteries of night. We harness shadows not for dark but for balance. Our craft hides and shields. It meets threats to order."

Rachel leaned forward. "Can your craft help us track and face the beast that troubles our lands?"

Eliza nodded. "The creature you name the Jersey Devil is elusive. It crosses realms. It hides from common sight. Yet together we may stand a chance."

They went into the Pine Barrens each night. Yet the Jersey Devil stayed ahead. They felt its presence but did not see it. Each failed hunt brought more anger.

Rachel and Henrietta and Eliza went into the Pine Barrens night after night. The air felt heavy. Fear spread. Livestock vanished. Screeches pierced the night. A dark presence lingered. Weather turned foul. Crops suffered.

Each night they followed tracks that led to nothing. They heard cries that faded when they drew near. The Jersey Devil stayed ahead. Its presence was felt but not seen. Their anger grew with each failure.

Weeks passed since Rachel, Henrietta, and Eliza began their nightly hunts. Each attempt to find the Jersey Devil ended in failure. The beast stayed hidden and left only whispers and shadow.

One cold evening as they gathered in Eliza's parlor. A crow landed on the sill and cawed again and again. Henrietta stared. She knew the sign.

"The veil is thin tonight," she said low. "We may reach beyond our world for aid."

Eliza took a polished obsidian mirror. Its dark face caught the candlelight. They sat in a circle and joined hands. Eliza spoke a chant. Her voice guided them into stillness. The mirror shimmered and showed swirling mist.

Henrietta concentrated on the shape within. A woman with fierce eyes and hair the color of fire. Armor shone with a blue light not of this world. "The Valkyrie," Henrietta whispered. "Ölrún."

Rachel's eyes widened. "She exists?"

"She does," Henrietta said. "She has faced the Devil before."

Eliza kept her voice steady. "To call her takes a ritual of great power."

Henrietta nodded. "We will need herbs and old things. We must prepare in mind and in spirit."

In the days that followed, they gathered what was needed. On the night of the new moon, they met in a hidden clearing. The air was heavy with dread. They chanted as one. The wind rose and tore through the trees. The candles went out with a sudden gust. Darkness closed in. They looked at each other in silence. The circle had stirred the veil but brought forth no one.

Henrietta drew a sharp breath. "Azraelion is awake," she said.

Silence.

Rachel's voice shook. "Now what?"

Henrietta met her eyes. "Now we wait."

CHAPTER 34

THE DOOR BETWEEN

Later that night, the cabin door glowed with a blue light. The frame shook as if it were caught between two worlds. Out of the light, a figure took shape. The door creaked open. Olivia Karlsson stepped through. She had crossed from the mystic realm into the house she once called her own. Her eyes moved over the walls and beams. She knew them all. She drew a long breath.

"There is no place like home," she said.

Inside, the cabin stood as she remembered. Dust hung in the sun. She smiled at the order.

"Puddlesquat, you kept the place in order," she said to herself.

Liv walked to the window. She saw a house that had not stood there before.

"New neighbors, I see," she said.

In the Whitaker house, Eliza looked out the window. She saw a blue light in the cabin that had stood empty. She looked at Henrietta and Rachel.

"She is here," Eliza said. "Shall we go to her?"

Henrietta nodded. "It is neighborly."

Rachel took a small basket with bread and a jar of honey. "We have no casserole, but this will do," she said.

The three women walked the short path to Liv's cabin. Eliza knocked on the door. After a moment, it opened. Liv stood there.

"Good evening," Eliza said. "I am Eliza Whitaker. These are my friends, Henrietta Jordan and Rachel Leeds. We saw you returned." She pointed to the basket Rachel held. "We brought a gift."

Liv's eyes moved to the basket and then back to the women. "Thank you," she said. She stepped aside. "I am Liv. This cabin has long been my home. Though I have been away for some time."

Rachel frowned. "How long?" she asked.

Liv studied her. "What year is it now?"

"1909," Rachel said.

Liv gave a slow nod. "Then, near one hundred and seventy-three years."

Liv turned, and the others stepped inside. Henrietta's eyes stayed on Liv. There was recognition in her eyes. "Liv?" she asked slowly. "Would you be Ölrún of the old tales?"

Liv raised an eyebrow. "That depends on which tale you heard."

"We face dark unrest. Disturbances that unsettle the land," said Eliza.

Liv's expression hardened. "Azraelion."

Eliza nodded. "Yes. He has returned."

Liv drew a deep breath. Her expression was firm. "Then we have much to speak of."

The four women sat around the small table. The burden of their task lay heavily on them. Bound by purpose, they set their minds to face the darkness.

Liv's eyes fixed on Rachel's name. "Leeds?" she asked.

Rachel nodded. "Yes."

Liv felt the old blood within her. "Your line carries weight," she said. "You can fight with us."

They searched the Pine Barrens and followed the signs of Azraelion. One night under a crescent moon they found him.

Azraelion came out of the shadows. His eyes gleamed with malice. When he saw Liv, he sneered. "So, the Valkyrie returns," he said.

Liv's face stayed hard as iron. "I see the years have not silenced your tongue," she said.

Azraelion's laugh cut through the trees. "And I see the years have not broken your will," he answered.

Liv lifted her staff. "Your reign ends now."

She clashed with Azraelion. His wings struck like storms. His scream split the trees. Magic and steel met him blow for blow. Yet he did not fall. He broke away from them and vanished into the dark.

In the weeks that followed, he struck again. A farm gutted. Livestock torn. Houses shaken by his cry. Each time the women gave chase. Each time they drove him off but could not bind him. Liv saw it clear. The demon was not as he had been. He had learned. He twisted free of the snares that once held him. He broke the runes that once burned him.

Months turned into years. Liv and Henrietta and Eliza and Rachel held to their struggle. They fought him in bursts and shadows. He rose in fury and then vanished in silence. They obstructed his damage but could not end him. Two years passed in their hidden war. Liv knew the truth. The ways that once banished him no longer worked. A new plan was needed.

One evening they gathered in Liv's cabin. She poured them each a cup of mead. The fire cracked, and shadows moved on the walls. They spoke of plans. Their faces bore the marks of weariness.

Eliza spoke. "Perhaps we seek an alliance with other beings."

Rachel looked down in thought. "The family Bible tells of those who aided in battles past."

Liv drank her mead. A tingle spread through her. Her sight blurred. The room fell away. Mist swirled. A rainbow shimmered before her eyes.

A figure came through the haze. Small in form. Silver hair. Clear eyes, but full of age. He leaned on a staff older than the trees. Liv knew him. This was not a Pukwudgie. It was a Menehune.

Memory struck her. Manu, the elder of the Menehune, had aided her once to banish Azraelion. His people were famed as craftsmen and bore ancient magic. Their help had been vital before.

The vision faded. Liv sat once more in the cabin. The others watched her with concern.

"Are you well?" Henrietta asked as she leaned forward.

Liv nodded. "I know what we must do," she said with a steady voice. "We need the help of the Menehune."

Eliza frowned. "The Menehune? Are they not only legend?"

"They are real," Liv said firm. "Their craft is strong. Manu aided me once before. We must seek them."

Rachel looked about the room. "How do we find them?"

Liv drew a long breath. "The Menehune are hard to find. Yet they favor certain gifts. We must prepare these and call them with a summoning ritual."

Henrietta rose. "Then we do not waste time. Tell us what we need."

With new purpose, they set out to gather what was needed. They foraged mugwort and yarrow. They carved tokens. They made a feast of bananas and fish.

On the night of the new moon, they went into the heart of the Pine Barrens. In a hidden clearing, they laid the gifts and stood in a circle. Liv raised her voice in chant. Her words moved through the still night.

At first, nothing stirred. Then, the ground shimmered. Small forms stepped from the shadows. At their front stood Manu, just as Liv recalled him. Silver hair. Wise eyes. He leaned on his ancient staff.

"Liv," Manu said. His voice was like leaves in the wind. "It has been long."

Liv bowed her head. "Too long, old friend. We need your help once more. Azraelion has returned."

Manu's face grew grave. "Then we shall stand with you."

Silence held the circle. Liv spoke.

"Our spell failed," she said. "Azraelion broke free."

Manu nodded. "Magic fades with time," he said. "His struggle weakened the binding."

"He is vengeful now. We have barely held him at bay for two years."

Manu's eyes narrowed. "Demons learn," he said. "A spell alone will not hold him. He must be trapped. Bound in iron. Encircled by Menehune runes."

Eliza leaned forward. "I have land," she said.

Manu gave thought. "An underground chamber," he said.

Eliza nodded. "I can set men to dig. How deep?"

Manu met her eyes. "As deep as five tall men," he said.

Rachel's eyes widened. "That is deep," she said.

Henrietta gave a thin smile. "If we send a demon to his room," she said, "we may as well make it the cellar."

The circle fell still. The fire hissed. Outside, the wind moved through the pines. They all knew the truth. The war was not ended. It had only begun.

Plans would be made. The ground would be broken. The chamber would be carved. And when Azraelion came again, they would be ready. Yet even as they spoke of walls and iron and runes, they felt the shadow in the trees.

The Devil was watching. Waiting.

CHAPTER 35

THE BATTLE OF LEEDS POINT

October 1911

A few days later they met again. Liv sat with Henrietta, Rachel, and Eliza at the old kitchen table in the home of Rachel and Samuel. Manu stood on a chair so he could reach the table.

Rachel spoke. "The hole is dug she said. It is ready." She glanced at Manu. "We have an iron grate to cover it."

Manu turned to Rachel. "We'll construct a well over the pit," he offered. "Your husband would take too long. We can finish it overnight."

Rachel nodded. "Thank you," she said.

Manu went on. "We will carve runes on the inner walls of the well above the iron grate," he said. "It will hold Azraelion as long as the stones remain unbroken. Once it is done we will summon him here."

A puff of smoke burst into the room. Puddlesquat, the elder of the Pukwudgies, stood before them. He held his staff.

"Planning a party without us?" Puddlesquat asked.

"It would not be a party without the Pukwudgies," Liv smiled. "You are right on time. We were planning our next move against Azraelion with the help of the Menehune," Liv said. "They will build a well lined with runes and summon the demon here." She shook her head. "But we may not need to summon him. Last time he came on his own."

Puddlesquat grunted. "He is cocky," he said. "He talks too much."

Liv frowned. "I will silence his foul tongue," she vowed.

That night, a band of Menehune craftsmen arrived. They worked in silence. Their small bodies moved with precision. By dawn, the chamber was finished.

Menehune runes filled the floor. Beside the open pit rested the iron grate, ready to seal the demon.

The next day, the group gathered at the site. Liv studied the work and nodded. "Now we prepare for battle," she said.

Two nights later, Samuel Whitaker stood alone on his porch. He stared into the woods. His eyes had changed.

Dark now.

Restless.

A mug sat in his hand. He had brewed it himself in the cellar. The bitter taste comforted him. The way the grains and yeast turned to beer made him think of the witches and their craft. He liked the small taste of turning one thing into another. It felt like magic he could hold.

Since Eliza's bond with Liv and Henrietta had grown, something had stirred in him. Fascination had turned to obsession.

Yet he kept it hidden.

Not even Eliza saw it whole.

Not yet.

In the woods beyond his land, the forest stirred. Leaves rustled. Pale light flickered through the trees. Shapes moved.

The Pukwudgies came first.

Dozens.

Small and sharp-eyed.

Fierce.

Puddlesquat led them. Staff in hand. Runes burned on his shoulders. The old Valkyrie power lived in him now.

Then came the Menehune. They carried carved staffs and bone tools. Pouches of sacred dust hung at their belts.

They moved as one.

No sound.

No fear.

They gathered at the edge of the forest. Waiting.

In the field near the well, Henrietta, Liv, and Eliza worked with haste. Their hands moved with purpose. Chalk in steady fingers. Candles were placed in a wide ring. A circle of warding. Large enough for four.

Rachel stood a few paces away. She watched.

Henrietta looked up. "You are not here only for your name," she said.

Eliza nodded. "Your blood remembers," she said.

Rachel hesitated. Her hands shook. She drew a breath. Then she stepped into the circle.

Liv and Henrietta took their places. They smeared marks across their arms. Black ash. Crimson dye. Old runes drawn in patterns of guard and strength.

Eliza lit the first candle. Liv lit the last.

Henrietta raised her hand. "The circle holds," she said.

Rachel felt a pull in her chest. As if the woods breathed through her. Her name, Leeds, felt heavier than blood.

It was history.

It was power.

Puddlesquat stood at the front of the Pukwudgie line. He raised his staff. It pulsed with light.

The Pukwudgies readied their weapons.

Spears.

Slings.

Small knives tipped with iron.

Beside them, the Menehune formed rows. Staffs planted in the soil. Feet set wide.

Eyes glowed beneath their brows.

They waited.

The witches stood in the circle.

Rachel looked at Liv. "Is it truly coming?" she asked.

Liv did not blink. "It was bound once. The chains broke. Now it returns."

Then the wind shifted.

Cold.

Heavy.

Old as the earth.

The battle was near.

Liv stepped forward. Her boots crushed the frost-hardened grass. She stared into the trees. The shadows pulsed.

She raised her voice.

Clear.

Steady.

"I know you are there," she called. "Come!"

The woods fell silent. No leaf stirred. No bird called.

Then came the light.

A flash tore the treeline apart. Indigo light poured through. A mass of smoke rolled across the ground. The stench of rot and ash followed.

From the storm Azraelion emerged.

His wings spread wide. Too large for the space. His hooves scorched the earth. Horns curled back from his skull. His eyes burned like stars that had begun to die.

"Well," he hissed. "I always knew how to make an entrance, Valkyrie."

Liv did not flinch.

"You are late," she said. "I expected more drama."

Azraelion grinned. "There will be drama," he said.

Behind Liv, the Pukwudgies raised their weapons. The Menehune planted their feet.

The battle had begun.

Azraelion stood tall. The sky behind him darkened.

The first wave struck.

Pukwudgies leapt from the trees.

Spears flew.

Slings snapped.

No weapon struck him.

He swung his arm. Five Pukwudgies scattered.

Broken.

Bloodied.

The Menehune charged. Staffs sparked with power. Azraelion laughed.

A sweep of his wings struck them down.

Bones cracked.

Cries rose.

Eliza raised her hands. Shadows curled at her feet. They raced across the soil and lashed his legs. Her words slid low. "From shade to flesh. From dark to bone. Strike him down." Azraelion staggered.

But only a step.

He snarled. "A weak trick," he said.

He hurled a blast of heat. She threw herself aside. The edge of her skirt smoked. The circle held.

Rachel stepped forward into the circle. Her hands shook. Her voice rose from a whisper.

"By leaf and root. By the name that binds me. By Leeds blood I call the binding," she whispered. Light sparked at her fingertips.

The light swirled and reached toward him.

Azraelion flicked his wrist. Her magic broke in the air.

"Leeds," he grinned. "I remember."

Puddlesquat screamed. He slammed his staff into the earth. Light burst from his hands. A white beam struck Azraelion's chest.

The demon stumbled.

One step.

Enough.

Henrietta and Liv moved fast. They dropped to their knees. They pressed their hands to the soil.

They chanted in unison.

Steady.

Ancient.

"Chains unseen bind his wings.

Chains unseen bind his arms.

Chains unseen bind his legs.

By the power of old blood, I command you to fall."

Wind rose.

The earth shook.

Power rippled across the field.

Azraelion flared his wings, then stopped. They snapped tight to his back. Chains unseen bound them in place. His arms slammed to his sides. His legs locked. He growled.

"What is this?" he asked. "You have learned new tricks."

Liv's voice rose. She cried out.

"By the power of the old might, I bind you to this land.

No movement.

No escape.

You will not speak.

You will not rise."

Henrietta's voice struck with hers.

WHISPERS IN THE PINES

"By the old blood, I fasten you to this soil.

No step.

No flight.

You will not cry out.

You will not stand."

The spell coiled tight. His body shook. The chains pulled.

He roared, but he could not move.

The circle held.

For now.

The ground rumbled.

Off to the side, something cracked.

Manu flew backward. He struck a rock.

Rolled.

He groaned.

Alive.

Hurt.

Not grave, but enough.

Henrietta flinched. Her chant broke. The spell stuttered.

Azraelion tore one arm free. Then the other.

The chains snapped like twigs.

He roared.

Fire burst from his mouth. It struck the line of Menehune.

A few fell back.

They screamed.

Liv shouted. She and Henrietta bent to the earth and began again.

Liv's voice thundered.

"Chains bind him.

Hand to hand.

Lock him fast."

Henrietta struck her own line.

"Chains of old blood.

Bind his limbs.

Seal him down."

Eliza's shadow curled at her feet.

"Dark to flesh.

Shade to bone.

Hold him still."

Rachel's voice trembled but rose.

"By leaf and root.

By the name of Leeds.

I call the binding."

Chains struck back into place.

Fast.

Harsh.

They coiled around his limbs.

Wings folded.

Legs locked.

Azraelion growled through his teeth. "You are so dramatic," he said.

Liv did not smile.

She held her hand out.

Palm flat.

From the edge of the circle, her old sword stirred.

It flew through the air.

The blade slapped into her grip with a hard thud.

Her eyes met his.

"And this," she said, "is for your tongue. I swore it."

She hurled it.

The blade hummed with power.

It struck true. Straight into his throat.

It sank deep. Azraelion staggered. His roar died in silence. His voice cut away.

His head snapped back. No blood flowed. Yet he was wounded.

The chains pulled tighter.

They dragged him down. His knees struck hard. Then his chest. Bound and silenced, he snarled. The chains dragged him across the field.

Toward the well.

Then came a flash of movement.

Puddlesquat leapt forward. Staff raised high. Runes burned bright on the wood.

He landed on the chest of the demon.

With a scream of rage and memory, he brought the staff down in a sharp arc.

Once.

Twice.

Azraelion's horns cracked. Snapped and fell. They struck the earth with a dull thud.

Azraelion thrashed harder. Yet it was too late. The chains dragged him into the well.

Down into the dark.

Rachel stepped forward. She raised her hand. She braced herself. The iron grate scraped across the ground. It slid over the mouth of the well. Then it dropped. Iron sealed against stone.

She breathed out. "A Leeds seals what was meant to destroy us."

Henrietta placed her hand on the grate. Liv stepped beside her.

Together they spoke the binding in Old Norse:

"Hell binds you.

Your blood sleeps in darkness.

No path. No rest.

The grate glowed. The runes lit. Azraelion screamed without a sound. The well pulsed once. Then it fell silent.

Buried.

Alone.

Liv spoke alone. In the tongue of the North, she gave the final command.

"You will sleep.

Your dreams will be cold.

Your name will rot in silence."

The grate glowed. The runes pulsed.

The grate glowed. The runes pulsed. From deep within came a muffled scream. Then silence.

Azraelion was gone.

Not forever.

Buried.

Dreaming in darkness.

Waiting.

That evening, the woods went still.

No screams.

No fire.

No wind through the trees.

Only the sound of stone. The Menehune worked through the night.

Noiseless.

Steady.

Unshaken.

They carved their runes into the walls of the well. Each symbol was cut by hand. Each one binding.

By morning, the work was done. The grate was sealed. Runes glowed beneath moss and stone.

Azraelion lay trapped.

His voice gone.

His horns gone.

His rage buried.

The Pine Barrens stood safe again. Freed from the devil in the dark.

Freed from Azraelion.

For now.

CHAPTER 36

A GLIMPSE BEYOND

They gathered one last time.

Henrietta. Eliza. Rachel. Liv.

The Devil was sealed.

The forest stood still. The world was quiet.

They sat on the porch. The sun sank low. The trees swayed peacefully.

Rachel smiled. "It is done."

Henrietta nodded. "For now."

Eliza looked down the path. Her voice softened.

"It feels different this time. Like the woods breathe again."

Samuel sat inside the house. He did not join them.

He never did anymore.

He spent his nights alone in the cellar. At his desk. Books of dark lore piled high.

Eliza noticed first. The low mutters. The wax symbols.

Henrietta noticed next. He did not look at them the same.

Liv had seen that look before. She said nothing.

She only watched.

She poured a cup of mead. She sipped slowly. She let the silence settle.

Then it struck her.

A vision.

She sat still. The cup shook in her hand.

Fire tore across the sky.

A stone. Blue. Deep and bright.

It blazed through the heavens.

Not of Earth.

Higher.

It crashed into a jungle.

There were pyramids. Ancient. Vast. Carved with serpents.

From the trees came a figure.

A Xoloitzcuintli.

Black as obsidian.

Eyes bright and wise.

Not a beast.

Not a threat.

A Tlatoani.

A royal one.

It was sent to carry the stone across the sea.

To the Menehune.

Liv held her breath.

The stone pulsed.

Calm.

Ancient.

Magic not born of this realm.

She saw an amulet.

Gold wrapped in cold iron.

At its center, a blue stone. The Starlight Sapphire.

The object from the sky.

It shone like the heart of a still lagoon.

Deep.

Blue.

Timeless.

Its surface held galaxies.

Runes ran along its edge.

Norse. Menehune. Serpent coils.

Old power.

She knew then why the vision had come. Azraelion would return. The well could not hold him forever. An amulet must be forged to bind him for good.

She returned to herself.

She joined Manu at the edge of the woods.

"A messenger will come," she said. "A Tlatoani. Not of war. Of duty."

Manu nodded. "A noble one?"

"Yes," she said. "A stone in the jungle. From the stars. The Xolo will bring it."

She pulled a scrap of cloth from her pouch. She drew the shape.

"The amulet must be forged in gold. Wrapped in cold iron. A raised inscription on its edge in Menehune runes. Binding across worlds."

Manu frowned. "Cold iron burns him and binds. You are sure it will be enough?"

"I am."

He thought for a moment.

"I know two craftsmen. Old blood. They will build it."

She handed him the sketch.

"Keep it safe," she said. "Deep underground. Where time forgets."

He nodded. "Then we must be ready. If the stone comes across the sea, we will guard it."

She looked to the trees. "One day," she said. "One of their own will come seeking what was sent."

CHAPTER 37

DEPARTURES

After the battle of 1911, the Pine Barrens returned to peace. So much so that when a former president and great huntsman came to Leeds Point in 1912 to hunt the Devil, he found nothing.

The world moved on.

But Samuel did not. He was withdrawn. He brooded. He grew distant.

The books stacked higher. The ink ran darker. He spoke less. He slept less. By 1914, he barely left the cellar.

Darkness consumed him.

One day in 1915, Eliza stood in the doorway and looked at Liv and Henrietta. Her eyes were hollow.

"He is gone," she said.

Samuel Whitaker had disappeared.

No note.

No sound.

No body.

He vanished into the Pine Barrens.

Liv and Henrietta did not speak. They only nodded.

They would search.

Henrietta went west. She followed old signs. Old shadows. She searched for years before she settled in San Antonio. Then Austin.

Liv went east. The sea air called to her. Old magic. Old whispers. She walked the streets of Mystic, Connecticut. She stayed silent. She watched. She listened.

The town held secrets. Maritime folklore. Colonial spirits. Strange tides. A place for Liv. She stayed in the shadows. She watched always.

In early 1954, a vision came.

A beast shaped like a dog. Large. Black. Blurred at the edges.

Red eyes that glowed.

It ran beside horses. It moved swiftly through the night.

Its steps shook the earth.

Two words echoed in her mind.

Harpers Ferry.

She packed that night.

The hunt would begin again.

CHAPTER 38

WHERE HISTORY MEETS THE MOUNTAINS

Harpers Ferry, West Virginia, April 1954

The train slowed as it neared Harpers Ferry. Steam rose. The whistle echoed through the hills. Liv stepped from the platform and set the strap of her bag. The air smelled of wood smoke, damp stone, and river water.

The town lay between two rivers and within the hills. Brick houses stood along narrow streets. Some stood older than the nation itself. Ivy climbed stone walls. A church bell rang far off. In 1954, the past remained.

A few hundred souls lived here. Most labored in nearby towns or ran small shops. Some recalled the war. Others recalled the floods. No one moved with haste.

A silver diner stood at High and Washington. The neon sign read *Turner's*. A jukebox played Patsy Cline. Locals drank coffee from heavy mugs. Fried eggs and bacon filled the air with grease and warmth. Heads turned when Liv entered. She gave a single nod and chose a booth near the rear.

She rented a small house near the town center. It held one bedroom and a fireplace. A porch faced the river. Vines climbed its railing. The kitchen smelled of old wood and time.

It felt private.

Quiet.

Safe.

On Saturdays, the townspeople gathered at the market. Stalls lined the green near the old church. Farmers sold apples, bread, and jars of pickles. Children ran between crates. A woman read fortunes with a worn deck. All greeted each other by name.

Liv walked among them in silence. She bought tea and honey and listened to their voices. No one knew who she was or where she came from.

That was how she preferred it.

One morning Liv sat within Turner's. A seat by the window gave her a view of the street. She drank her coffee black. The mug held a chip, yet the coffee held strength. A plate of eggs and toast lay before her. She ate and heard the hum of voices and the ring of silver on plates.

She gazed upon the town. It stood quietly and clean. Brick houses. White fences. A boy rode past on a wheel with a fishing pole across the bar. It could have been any small town in America.

Peaceful.

Plain.

But Liv knew better.

Her mind wandered. The same image came again. A beast shaped like a hound. Large. Muscled. Black fur covered it. Its eyes burned red like coals in a fire. It stood in the dark and held still. It watched her. It made no sound. It made no move. Yet it knew she was there.

She did not know what it was. Not yet. It was not the Leeds Devil. Not wholly. It was not the Black Goat. Yet there was something similar to both. A hunger she could not place. A trace of ash. And the scent of blood.

She pushed the plate aside and drank the last of her coffee. If it tied to the Jersey Devil or the Black Goat, she would cut it down. Yet she felt no malice. Not yet.

She laid a put dollars on the table and stood. Few noticed her leave.

That was how she liked it.

She pushed the diner door wide and stepped into the sun.

A man stood outside. They brushed shoulder to shoulder. He drew back at once.

"Pardon me," he said as he tipped his hat.

He smiled. Clean-shaven, sharp jaw, eyes the color of storm clouds. He wore a pressed shirt and dark slacks with a blazer that fit close. His boots shone. No dust touched them. Not even at the cuffs.

He held no pipe, yet the scent lingered. Faint. Smoky. Rich with cherrywood.

He held the door wide. She passed without a word but gave him a quick look. He watched her go. Polite. Still smiling.

As she passed, he caught a trace of pine and wet earth. It clung like a trail after rain.

She glanced at the truck that stood a few feet away.

A 1946 Hudson Super Eight.

It looked torn from a dirt road halfway to nowhere. Mud crusted its tires and lower panels. Dents scarred the side. One mirror hung cracked.

The sight struck her. The man looked fit for a city desk or a bank. But the truck looked worn from storms and backwoods trails.

She walked on.

Behind her, the door closed with a soft click.

Patterson Quinn sat at the counter within Turner's. He gave a nod to the cook at the grill. He gave another to the young server, who came with a rag in hand.

"Black coffee. Breakfast plate," Patterson said. His voice held the drawl of Tennessee.

The server smiled and wiped the counter in front of him. "How you doin' today? You find any more leads to that thing you hunt. You out late last night?"

"I was," Patterson said.

"You stayin' round town a while?"

Patterson set his arms on the counter. "Looks like it. Maybe a spell. Couple months maybe."

The server took a mug from the rack and filled it from the pot. "You seen that thing yet? The one you told me of."

"The Snarly Yow," Patterson said with a half-smile. "Still huntin. No luck yet."

The young man leaned close and spoke softly. "You hear anything new? Any more folks claiming a sighting?"

Patterson shook his head. "Had a few near misses. Folks still claim they see it here. I keep lookin' for more witnesses. You hear anything strange? Anybody talk?"

The young man sat up straight. "Not lately. One of the mill boys swore he saw somethin' in the trees last week, but he was drunk. Said it had red eyes. Then he said it had wings too. Might have been talkin' bout that Jersey Devil thing."

Patterson raised an eyebrow. "Jersey Devil, huh?"

"Yeah. Folks mix stories all the time."

Patterson drank his coffee. "Tell me if he tells it again. Or if anybody else sees somethin' they can't explain."

The young man nodded. "Sure thing. You know where to find me."

Liv moved through the small house with purpose. Floorboards creaked beneath her boots. A canvas satchel lay open on the table. She packed a flashlight. A knife with a bone hilt. A pouch of dried herbs. A thin journal with sketches and notes. She paused and set her fingers on the spine of the book.

The air shifted.

She turned toward the window. Her breath slowed.

It came again.

That force. Faint and unnatural. It pulsed along the ridges and curled in the valleys. It did not belong here. Not in this world. It carried no malice, yet it was wrong. Changed.

It had called her to Harpers Ferry.

She slung the satchel across her back and stepped outside.

The moon hung low. Clouds passed in slow waves. Fog hugged the ground in thin layers. She took a footpath beyond the edge of town toward the lower trails near Bolivar Heights. The battlefield lay long in memory. Trees and tall grass now covered it. Cracked stone walls still stood half-swallowed by vines.

The wind carried the scent of wet leaves, river silt, and pine.

Liv moved with steady steps. She passed cannon mounts. Markers of a past nearly lost. Ghosts of the war slept under brush. The Potomac glinted through the trees on her left. The Shenandoah whispered on her right.

The force grew stronger.

Something drew near.

She crouched at the slope's edge. Her eyes searched the ridge above. Leaves stirred. A branch cracked.

Then came movement.

A great shape swept between the trees.

Black fur.

Low to the ground.

Too large for a dog.

Too fast for a bear.

It moved like a shadow with muscle. She caught a flash of red.

Eyes. They watched her.

Then it vanished into the woods.

She stood still for a long time.

It had not attacked. It had not growled. It had not charged. It only watched. Then it fled.

She didn't chase it. Not yet.

The force lingered in the trees. It felt like a warning. Or a plea.

She turned back toward the town.

There would be a second search.

CHAPTER 39

THE EDGE OF THE BARN

Liv moved through the aisles of the five and dime. She picked up a few items. Matches. Tea. Thread. A tin of salve. The shelves stood crowded yet neat. A ceiling fan ticked above and stirred the smell of paper and soap and old wood.

Then she caught it.

Cherrywood.

Faint yet sure. Warm. Smoky. Rich.

She followed the scent and walked past the kitchenware and postcards. At the front counter, she saw him.

The man from Turner's.

He stood with one hand on the counter and the other held a small pouch. The clerk rang him up and slid across a package. Pipe tobacco. Cherry scented. That was all.

He turned.

His eyes found her.

Recognition stirred. Quick but clear. He remembered her from the diner. The woman who had brushed against him. Silent and unreadable. She had spoken no words, yet something about her had held. The way she moved. The way she looked at him was as if she saw more than most. He showed no surprise at her now. He looked curious.

Liv wore a modest dress. Clean lines. Long hem. Drawn at the waist. It fit the fashion of the time, yet the color was bold. Too vivid for this town. She had not meant to draw eyes, yet she always did. Her hair burned red in the dim light. Her eyes shone blue, steady and clear. A scar cut her jaw. Faint yet plain. Patterson noted of all of it.

He gave a polite nod. He showed no surprise. It was as if he had expected to see her again.

"Mornin'," he said. His voice was smooth with the sound of the South.

She said nothing at first. She met his eyes.

Blue to storm grey.

Then she said, "Good morning."

He did not linger. He gave a small smile in return. He tipped his hat and turned to leave. Cherry tobacco in hand.

Liv stood with her items and watched the door.

She did not follow.

She watched him walk out.

Yes, he recognized her.

And now she was curious too.

Liv walked down the street with cherrywood still in her thoughts. She passed a row of parked cars and slowed when she saw a truck.

The same Hudson Super Eight.

Caked in dried mud. Dented along one side. She paused. The sight still bothered her. How a man so well dressed could drive a truck that looked near abandoned.

She stepped close and peered through the window.

The glass stood cloudy and streaked with dust. She set her hand to the side and looked in.

Notebooks. Camera gear. A pair of field glasses. Pens scattered across the dash. A cold coffee cup rolled back with the slope of the street. The inside looked lived in. Cluttered and rough. Nothing like the man she had seen in the store. Nothing like the neat shirt and polished boots.

She stepped back and turned.

Straight into his chest.

She froze.

He stood taller than she had thought.

"Well," he said with an easy smile. "We had best stop meetin' like this."

For the first time in centuries, Liv didn't know what to say.

She opened her mouth and then shut it. A pause. A breath. She glanced aside and then back. She, who for generations had seen ambushes before they came, had not seen him.

He gave a low chuckle and held out his hand.

"Name's Patterson. Patterson Quinn."

She paused and then took it.

"Liv," she said.

His hand was warm. His grip was strong and steady. His smile lingered.

Handsome.

Disarming.

Something stirred within her. Not fear. But close to it.

Patterson turned and unlocked the truck door. It opened with a creak. He set the pouch of cherry tobacco on the seat. Then a fresh baguette wrapped in paper. Liv tilted her head. Another turn she had not expected. Pipe tobacco and bread. The man surprised her.

She looked in again. Maps. A leather journal worn at the edges. A crumpled pack of playing cards. A chipped metal lighter. The truck looked like it belonged to a man who lived on the road.

A man chasing things.

Maybe running from something.

He shut the door with a solid thud.

"I was just headin' back to Turner's," he said. "Coffee tastes better when you don't drink it alone. Care to join me?"

The question hung in the air like a held breath.

Liv didn't answer right away. Her mind scanned too many things at once.

The Cherrywood scent that lingered.

The eyes that watched her in the woods last night.

The weight of old battles and darker days.

She wasn't here for conversation.

Or connection.

She came for something else.

Something unnatural. Something wounded.

Yet none of that helped her speak.

Her eyes met his. He did not press. He only asked.

Her throat drew tight. She gave the smallest nod.

"Sure," she said.

It came out softer than she had thought.

Patterson smiled. Not smug. Plain and genuine. "Good," he said. "Turner's makes a fair cup."

He turned toward the sidewalk. Liv followed.

And for the first time in generations, she did not think about the creature.

She thought about the man.

The diner was quiet. A few patrons sat in booths and on counter stools. Turner's smelled of coffee, hot oil, and fresh bread. The jukebox played low from the corner.

Liv and Patterson sat across from each other at a small table near the window. She held her cup in both hands. He set one arm on the chair and the other around his mug.

The young man brought two steaming cups and set them down. "Coffee for both," he said. He glanced between them. "You two want to order anythin'."

Liv glanced at his name tag and shook her head. "No, thank you, Jacob."

"I'll wait for now," Patterson added.

Jacob nodded. "Fair enough." He looked at Patterson with a grin. "Any luck with that creature yet?"

"Not yet," Patterson said. "Still huntin'."

Jacob gave a short chuckle and walked off.

Liv looked across the table. "Creature?"

Patterson met her eyes. "I'm what you might call a romantic zoologist." His tone was warm. Plain. Southern.

She tilted her head. "Romantic?"

He paused and smiled as he drank his coffee. "Not the candlelight kind. Though I am a bit of a romantic at heart."

She raised an eyebrow.

He cleared his throat, grin still on his face. "The term means the study of animals not yet written down. Animals out of place. Legends that leave tracks."

She gave a nod. "You are far from Tennessee, Mr. Romantic Zoologist."

"Yes ma'am. I am followin a lead. Workin on an investigation."

"Sounds exciting."

"Sometimes. Most of the work is just listenin'. Folks tell you what they saw. Or what they thought they saw. You look for patterns. Gaps. Stories that match. It is like police work."

She drank her coffee. "And what are you investigating now?"

He leaned forward. "A creature. Large. Dog like. Heavy build. Loose skin. Red eyes. Some say its fur is black. Others say blue. Grey. Even white in certain light. A few claim it can stand on two legs. It makes a sound. A yow. Like a growl but sharper."

Liv listened close. Her fingers tightened around her cup.

She knew that description. She'd seen that shape in the trees.

"What do you call it?" she asked.

"The Snarly Yow."

"That's an unusual name."

"Old name. Older than most tales," he said.

"I don't know. I have heard some old tales."

He watched her close. "You heard of it."

"I've heard… things."

He smiled once more. "That is a fair start."

She held his eyes for a moment longer. This was no idle talk. He believed in what he did. Strange as it was, she did too.

"You are not what I expected," she said.

"Neither are you," he said.

Liv raised her cup. She drank slowly and then set it down. She watched him for a moment. Then asked, "Is there a Mrs. Quinn?"

Patterson didn't answer right away. He looked down at the table and then out the window.

"Yes," he said at last. "There is."

Liv gave a single nod. "Yet you choose the company of unknown beasts. You chase them across the land in the shadows of night."

He smiled, yet his eyes stayed flat. "Investigating animals, even mysterious ones, is straightforward. You listen to the rumors. Talk to people. Follow the tracks. Document what you find."

She waited.

He looked back at her. "Life at home is… complicated."

She did not press him. She met his gaze and gave the smallest nod.

The coffee between them cooled. Neither said anything for a long moment.

Liv looked at him over the rim of her cup.

"The Snarly Yow. That explains the mud on your truck. The field gear. The maps. The books."

Patterson gave a small nod. "Yeah. I reckon it does."

He leaned back in his seat. "What about you?"

"What about me?"

"Anybody waitin' for you back home."

"No."

He studied her for a moment. "You from 'round here."

"No. I recently moved here."

"You ever seen any strange creatures?"

She didn't answer right away. Then said, "In my time I have seen many."

The way she said it caught his ear.

Not dramatic.

Only certain.

His face changed. His interest grew.

He didn't speak. He just watched.

She walked back to her room as the sun dropped low.

Married.

Of course he was married. Men like that… charming, intelligent, handsome… didn't stay unattached. Not in 1954. Not in small-town America.

It should have ended the conversation. Should have made her stand and leave. Instead, she'd stayed. Asked more questions. Let him ask questions in return.

She'd faced creatures that could tear a man in half. Walked through wars that claimed thousands. She had never hesitated. Never second-guessed.

So why did one married man with kind eyes and a crooked smile make her forget centuries years of certainty?

She didn't know.

And that was the most dangerous thing of all.

A few days passed. Late light fell through the trees and cast long shadows across the ground. Liv moved with care through the woods, far from trails or clearings. The branches above formed a canopy of gold and green in the fading light.

She carried no weapons. She didn't need any.

The energy was back. That same strange presence. She followed it by instinct. By silence. By the feel of the earth under her boots.

She paused near a cluster of old stones half-swallowed by moss. She set her hand on the bark of a tree.

Rough.

Damp.

Alive.

She listened. Not for sound. For the rhythm of the woods.

Leaves rustled. A stream trickled far off. Birds hushed.

It was close.

She closed her eyes.

The presence held no malice.

It was restless.

Hiding.

Afraid.

She felt the truth of it as the old seeresses once felt a fylgja.

Not a demon.

Not a curse.

Something wounded.

I'm not here to harm you, she thought.

The wind shifted.

Crows settled in the branches above. One.

Then two.

Then six.

Their black eyes fixed on her.

A sign.

She reached out again. Not with words.

With will.

With knowing.

Show yourself.

A pulse of thought came back.

Not words.

Not clear.

Yet she understood.

It knew her. It had seen her.

It did not trust her.

Yet it did not fear her.

Liv opened her eyes. Her breath came slowly and steadily.

A branch snapped ahead.

She stepped forward.

The trees grew thick, yet she did not pause.

Whatever it was. This creature was not natural. Yet it was no monster.

It was wounded.

Changed by man.

And it wished to be left alone.

I know you are here. I will not harm you.

Something shifted in the trees.

A low rustle.

A snap of a twig.

Heavy steps.

Careful.

Liv opened her eyes.

A shape came through the trees. Dark and low to the ground. Its fur was long and ragged. It moved like a shadow. Its body was twisted. Swollen in places. Thin in others. Scars marked its side. Some still raw. Its red eyes fixed on hers.

It gave no growl. It did not flee.

She stepped forward.

I know what they did to you.

The beast flinched, yet did not run.

I have felt it. The pain. The confusion.

She knelt and set her fingers on the ground. The earth lay cold. The moss damp.

You were ancient once. Wild. Whole. Before they found you. Before they broke you.

A soft pulse echoed in her mind.

Pain.

Not words but flashes.

Metal walls.

Cold floors.

Chains.

Needles.

Voices shouting.

Bright lights.

Screams. Its own, echoed off concrete.

She winced.

You did not deserve that.

The beast shifted its weight. Not fierce. It listened.

I do not wish to bind you. I do not wish to fight you.

She reached into her satchel and drew out a stone.

Smooth.

Gray.

Carved with runes.

She pressed it into the earth.

I cannot mend what they did, she thought. But I can guard you.

The air stirred.

She traced a mark with her fingertip in the moss.

Algiz.

Her voice was low.

Steady.

Ancient.

Words in Old Norse, soft as whisper.

The runes flared and then faded.

The beast stepped forward.

Closer now.

Its breath came slow and steady.

It misted in the cool air.

This will shield you. No blade. No bullet. No trap will hold you here.

She placed her hand on the ground beside the stone. Her palm glowed with a pale light.

This will let you vanish. Not out of fear, but by choice. When you wish to hide, the world will not see you.

The beast watched her with wide eyes. Intelligent eyes.

You are not a ghost, she thought. *You are not a monster.*

A pause.

Go where you will. Be what you are.

The beast stepped closer. It lowered its head.

Liv set her hand on its scarred brow.

For a moment it held still.

A bow.

A thanks.

It stepped back. Its eyes never left her.

Then it faded.

Not into shadow alone but into nothing. The space it had filled now lay empty.

Liv rose.

The energy still lingered, yet it lay soft and settled now.

It had trusted her.

And she would keep its secret.

Even if Patterson came near, and she knew he would, he would not find the truth unless the beast wished it.

Not unless it chose to be seen.

She walked back through the trees as night settled over the ridge. The crows made no sound above her.

The beast was safe now.

That was enough.

She had spent centuries as a blade.

Sharp.

Certain.

Necessary.

But Patterson didn't carry a blade.

He carried a camera.

A journal.

Questions instead of answers.

The beast had trusted her because she offered protection, not domination.

Patterson pursued creatures with the same spirit. Not to conquer, but to witness.

She understood now why she kept thinking of him.

He reminded her that there were other ways to be strong.

That was something she had not expected.

Patterson eased his truck off the gravel road and stopped before a wide barn weathered by time. A sign at the gate read *Nash Farm*. Ruth Cowan Nash had bought it three years past. The land had stood peaceful until recently. Whispers had stirred. Rumors of a thing that moved through the woods at night. The same beast Patterson had come to Harpers Ferry to find.

He cut the engine. The truck ticked as it cooled. He opened the door and stepped out. His eyes scanned the treeline. He took in the shape of the land. The fading light.

Then he saw her.

A figure came from around the corner of the barn.

Calm.

Steady.

Soundless.

Not startled. Not sneakin'. Just there.

It was Liv.

Patterson blinked with surprise. "Well now," he said as he shut the truck door. "Didn't reckon on seein' you out here."

She stopped a few paces off and watched him with the same unreadable look she always carried.

He glanced at the trees and then back at her. "A nice young lady ought not be walkin' these woods alone."

Liv tilted her head. The faintest smile touched her lips. "Who says I am nice?"

Patterson grinned. "Fair enough."

"I can handle myself," she added.

"I do not doubt it." He nodded toward the barn. "You come out here often. Or is this just chance?"

She didn't answer right away. "The woods have been restless," she said. "I came to see why."

Patterson gave a nod. "You hear the same tales I do."

"Maybe."

They stood in silence a moment. Wind stirred the grass. A crow called in the distance.

He studied her. The bold color of her dress struck sharp against the grey barn and bare trees.

She looked like she belonged.

And like she did not.

"You always show when things get interestin'," he asked.

"Sometimes," she said.

And she meant it.

He glanced toward the treeline. "I will walk the ridge before dark."

Liv's gaze followed his. "Be careful."

He turned back to her.

She was gone.

CHAPTER 40

NEITHER OF US MEANT TO

Patterson moved through the woods off Shoreline Drive. The Appalachian Trail lay close, yet he kept away from the path. Few locals came here unless they had a reason. He did. A woman had told of a strange sight.

Large.

Quick.

She had driven along an old road toward town when a black dog leapt before her wagon. She swerved and struck a tree. She thought she had hit the beast, yet in the mirror it still stood.

Tall on hind legs.

Watching.

He had heard such tales before.

He searched the ground as he walked. Broken branches. Dragged leaves. Signs of passage. His boots cracked twigs on the damp soil. No one had come here for some time. Then, his thoughts turned.

Liv, the red-haired woman.

She had stayed on his mind since the day at Nash Farm. Where had she come from? She was unlike anyone he had known. She moved as if she belonged in another world. She said little, but every word carried weight. He could not drive her image away.

Her eyes.

Her voice.

The way she vanished without a sound.

He knelt and passed his hand over the soil. No prints. No sign of a struggle. Only thoughts of Liv. He breathed out through his nose and rose. You have a wife he told himself. You came to work. Yet she remained on his mind.

He pressed deeper into the woods until he reached the place. The road bent hard. Trees leaned close from each side. He walked along the rim until he saw it. The tree the woman had struck.

Tire ruts tore the dirt and stone. Skid marks. Hard and sudden. He stepped to the trunk. Bark torn in a wide smear. Not deep, but new. An accident had happened here. He searched the roadside.

No beast.

No blood.

No body in the ditch.

Then he saw it on the stone. A smear of red. He stepped closer. He bent and touched it.

Paint.

Not blood.

Bright red.

His thought turned again to a flash of color from the woods.

The dress.

The hair.

Liv.

He stood. His eyes still on the mark. He reached into his blazer, pulled out his pipe, and struck a match. Cherrywood smoke drifted slow through the trees.

This wasn't the first time she'd crossed his path.

And something told him it wouldn't be the last.

Liv sat alone at a small corner table with a mug of black coffee. This place was quieter than Turner's. No music, just the soft scrape of plates and the low hum of conversation. She liked it here. She could go unnoticed. Unbothered. She stared out the window. Afternoon light caught the glass and turned the street into shadow and motion. Her cup was nearly empty, though she had not touched it for some time.

She thought of Patterson.

Not by choice.

He kept pushing into her mind when she least expected it. At first, he was just a regular person who chased shadows. Another man with more questions than sense.

But something about him stayed with her.

She told herself it was the cherrywood.

Then she told herself it was the way he looked at the world.

Steady.

Curious.

Unshaken when others broke.

He was too well-groomed for this work. Too polished. She should have cast him aside when he spoke of romantic zoology.

But then he smiled. Made a joke.

He called her out when no mortal had ever dared.

And she laughed.

That shocked her. She seldom laughed.

He saw something in her.

Not everything, but enough.

Enough to notice when she disappeared.

Enough to ask why she was in the woods.

Enough to make her stay just a little longer.

She wrapped her hands around the cup and drew what warmth remained. She had lived for centuries. She had fought beasts. She had faced gods. Yet that man unsettled her as no demon ever had. That made her uneasy. It meant he mattered, though he should not. She set down the cup. She would not speak his name.

Not here.

Not even in her mind.

Yet he remained.

And that was enough to make her pause.

Nights later, Patterson walked alone in the woods after dusk when he heard the crack of branches. He turned with hand on his light and searched the trees. The woods lay still. No wind. No bird. Silence.

He stepped toward the sound. Another rustle.

Heavy.

Low to the ground.

He thought it was the Snarly Yow. Then, a black bear charged fast. Jaws wide. He raised his arms in time. Barely. His flashlight flew from his hand and shattered on the ground. Claws tore his shoulder as he stumbled. He hit the dirt hard and then scrambled to his feet. The bear reared higher. Patterson grabbed a fallen branch and swung.

Once.

Twice.

The bear stepped back with a growl and then broke away into the trees. Gone. He stood with blood on his arm and his breath ragged. He went to his truck and sat." Roll that one around in your attic, Pat," he said aloud. He drew his pipe and lit a match while he thought about the night.

He did not go to a hospital.

He drove to Liv.

She opened the door before he knocked. Her eyes fell to the blood on his shirt.

"Bear," he said.

She didn't ask for more. She let him in.

She let him in. Inside, she set him in a chair. She cut the shirt and cleaned the wound. He winced, yet she did not flinch. Her hands were steady. Efficient. She set a warm cloth on the deepest cut and whispered something under her breath. He didn't catch the words. He felt a warmth and almost swore he saw a faint purple light under her hands. Then, the burn faded to a dull ache.

"Did you just…" he started.

She didn't answer.

His thoughts turned to Appalachian folk magic. Granny magic, his mother had called it. Maybe that made Liv set apart.

She placed her palm firm on his shoulder and closed her eyes. Her hand stayed there a little longer than necessary.

He looked up at her. Her face was close. Her scent of pine, smoke, and wet earth filled his head.

Neither moved.

Then the space between them closed.

He wasn't sure who had kissed first.

It didn't matter.

It just happened.

The rest unfolded quietly. No words. No promises. Only warmth and breath and the pull of two who should have known better. Yet they did not care. Not in that moment.

They drove before sunrise.

She didn't explain where. He didn't ask.

They stopped at a cliff above the Potomac. The sky shifted from deep blue to pale orange.

They stood side by side. His hand brushed hers. She did not pull away.

"I never figured you for a sunrise woman," he said.

"I'm not," she said.

He glanced at her. "But?"

"But I wanted to see this one."

Neither smiled. Yet something passed between them. A stillness shared. They held it in memory.

After the sunrise, they didn't speak much.

They sat on the ridge until the light stretched long across the hills and the chill broke. When Patterson rose, she rose as well. No words passed. None were needed.

She had watched a thousand sunrises.

Over battlefields.

Over oceans.

Over cities that no longer stood.

This one should have been no different.

But Patterson stood beside her, and for the first time in hundreds of years, she wasn't watching alone.

That changed everything.

In the weeks that followed, they found each other more often. They walked near the river, where the trees arched overhead and the sound of water covered drowned they did not say. Sometimes he brought a thermos. Sometimes she brought bread or fruit in a cloth pouch. They didn't talk about where they were going. They just went.

He came to her porch in the evenings. He told her there was a new lead. Another sighting. She didn't press. He never opened his notebook. She made strong tea and handed it to him without a word. He sat in the old chair that creaked when he leaned back. Some nights they stayed until the stars came out.

They rarely touched. But when they did… passing a cup, brushing hands as they sat down… it lingered longer than it should have.

He kissed her again one night, just before he left. She did not stop him.

She didn't ask about his wife. He didn't offer.

They both knew what this was. Knew it could not last.

Yet the quiet hours belonged to them.

The long glances. The half-smiles. The comfort of someone who understood the weight of silence.

It grew more before either spoke it.

No promises. Just presence.

It wasn't forever.

But for now it was enough.

CHAPTER 41

UNSPOKEN

Liv rose before sunrise. The room was still. The air was cool. She sat at the edge of the bed. Bare feet on the wood floor. Eyes on nothing. A breeze moved through the open window. Outside, nothing. Not even wind through the branches. No birds called. She felt different. Not sick. Not weak. Changed.

It had grown for days. For weeks. A strain in her chest. A pull in her core. Not from weariness. Not from restlessness. This was deeper.

She didn't go to a doctor. She never would. She knew what modern medicine would do with blood like hers. It would not end with answers. It would end with questions no one should ask.

She lit a candle. Ground the herbs by hand. Mugwort. Vervain. Red clover. She boiled water from the spring behind the house. No tap. No glass. Only clay. Only fire. Only breath. She drank the tea in silence. Then she closed her eyes.

The vision came.

Dark water. A flash of gold under the surface.

A heartbeat. Not her own.

The sound of wings.

Heavy.

Steady.

Then light.

A pale flame. Not fire. Life.

Warmth spread through her body. It settled in her womb. It flowed through her blood. She opened her eyes.

She did not need confirmation.

She was with child.

Her thought turned to Patterson.

What they had shared in those weeks had grown into something neither named. It lived in silence. In glances held. In the way he lingered on her porch after the tea had gone cold.

They never spoke of love. Yet it was there.

In quiet. In stillness.

In breath between words.

She knew it would not last. Patterson had a life far away. A wife who wore his name. A home with no room for a red-haired wanderer who brewed old tea and spoke with crows. She was a traveler. She always had been. Wind through the trees. Never roots in the soil.

Still, in the storm of the hunt, in the long nights and stolen mornings, they had found each other anyway.

It was beautiful.

And terrible.

She closed her eyes and breathed.

Days later, they sat at the back table in Turner's. Rain tapped against the window. The place was noiseless. A lull between the noon crowd and the evening meal.

Patterson's notebook was open on the table between them, but his pen hadn't moved in minutes.

"I followed the ridge near Nash Farm again," he said. "I found deep tracks. Too large for a bear. I could not tell if they were fresh." He paused. "Something is out there. I feel it."

Liv stirred her tea. She didn't speak right away. Her gaze turned to the window. Rain clung to the glass. He waited.

"You chase more than a beast," she said at last.

Patterson looked at her.

"You want proof. Validation. Maybe even escape." She glanced at him. Her eyes were steady. "Maybe you are trying to forget something in Tennessee."

He didn't respond, but his face showed she was right.

She leaned back with hands on the warm mug. "This one is not your monster," she said. "It only survives."

Patterson exhaled through his nose. "You think I should stop?"

"No," she said. "I think you will keep on no matter what I say."

He gave a faint smile. "You know me so well already."

"I know men who chase truth. Even when it hurts."

Patterson looked down at the table. He thought she spoke of the beast.

She did not correct him.

He shut the notebook and rose. "I will check the western trail before dark."

She did not walk him out. She only watched as he moved through the diner and into the rain.

She smiled to herself.

Still chasing beasts.

Two days later, she knew what she must do.

There would be no confrontation. No final talk.

No plea. No promises.

Patterson did not belong to her.

She would never belong to a man bound to another life.

She placed her hand on her stomach.

This was hers to carry.

Her purpose in Harpers Ferry was complete. The creature was protected. The damage could not be undone, yet it could be kept from more. Patterson would finish his hunt.

She would vanish as she had come.

No sound.

No farewell.

He saw it near the ridge. Past the hollow where trees thinned and fog hung low.

The Snarly Yow.

It stood still for only a moment.

Tall.

Dark.

Watchful.

Not a shadow.

Not a trick.

Real.

Alive.

Patterson froze. His heart raced. His breath caught. The beast did not move. Its red eyes met his.

Not hostile.

Not afraid.

Only present.

Then it turned and slipped into the trees. Gone in seconds.

No growl. No sound. No trace.

Yet he had seen it. For the first time, he knew it was no tale. It was there. And it had let itself be seen.

He drove straight to Liv's house.

He did not think. She was the first he would tell.

But when he arrived, the house lay empty.

The door was unlocked. The rooms were bare.

No sign of a struggle. No sign of her. No note.

Gone. No farewell.

Only silence.

He sat on the steps of the front porch and replayed scenes in his mind and tried to make sense of it.

He couldn't.

Finally, he stood and walked away.

Still contemplating.

He ended up at Turner's. He sat at the back table.

Their table.

His coffee cooled untouched. The corner felt cold.

A scent cut the air of coffee and grease.

Wet earth.

Pine.

He paused.

He saw it on the table, behind the cup.

Light caught it.

A single wooden item.

Hand carved.

Simple.

Coin sized.

Pine.

He picked it up.

It was warm in his hand. He turned it in his fingers.

It felt like protection.

It felt like farewell.

He held it and then set it in his pocket.

He dropped some coins on the table and walked out in silence.

He did not know where she had gone.

Only that she would not return.

But she had left something behind.

Not a note. Not a goodbye.

A sign. A ward. A memory.

Proof that what they shared was real.

It did not last.

But it mattered.

CHAPTER 42

WESTWARD

June 1954

Liv stepped down from the bus in Oxnard, California.

The air struck her at once.

Warm.

Briny.

It carried a sharp tang of citrus and sea. It smelled of work in the fields and salt on the wind. It smelled of a place she had never known. She had come far.

From Harpers Ferry, she had ridden the Baltimore and Ohio line into Washington, then north to Chicago. There she boarded the Super Chief, Santa Fe's pride. A silver train that cut across the land like a spear.

Quiet cars.

Polished steel.

Empty skies unrolling through the glass. Strangers spoke over meals in the dining car. She listened but said little.

From Los Angeles, she took a bus north along the coast. The journey stretched for days. At night she sat curled by the window, her hand on the small rise of her belly. She seldom slept. She did not need to.

Now she stood on the sidewalk with a small suitcase at her feet. She breathed in the California coast deeply.

Oxnard was no city of renown. A farm town by the sea. Rows of fields and low houses. Work done by hand and sun.

It was an agricultural town. Strawberry rows and citrus groves reached beyond the edge.

Near the station, the streets were plain. Storefronts clean. Palm trees lined the road. Inland, the mountains stood. Westward, the Pacific glimmered.

It was not where anyone would have expected her to be.

And that was the draw.

She had not chosen Oxnard for any reason.

Only that it was far.

Warmer.

Coastal.

A place with no past for her. Only space.

She felt the sun on her skin. She closed her eyes.

It was a good place to begin again.

The house stood at the town's edge. Shaded by citrus trees and worn by sea wind. It was not much. Two rooms and floors that creaked. A sunroom where light lingered late into the afternoon. But it was hers.

Liv took a job at a small antique bookstore downtown. The owner did not ask questions. She worked in the back room. She cataloged forgotten texts and repaired bindings on books older than the building itself. Some had symbols she recognized. Others whispered truths when left open too long. She liked it there.

Months passed.

Her belly grew. She did not hide it. She did not speak of it. The neighbors did not ask.

She gathered what she needed. Herbs. Stones. Clay bowls. Linen. A knife forged before electricity. She carved runes into the windowsills and painted protective symbols brushed with salt and ash across the doors.

At night, she sang to the child. Old songs in a tongue no one here knew. She made no plans for a hospital. No midwife. No papers. No visits. Only trust in the old ways.

When the day came, the sky turned gray.

Wind swept the citrus grove. Crows gathered in the branches.

Fire burned in the hearth. She marked her arms and belly with ochre runes.

Algiz for protection.

Berkana for birth.

Sowilo for light.

Then came the knock.

She opened the door without hesitation.

Two figures stood there. One tall. One bent with age. They gave no names. They carried no bags. No tools.

Only presence. Their eyes were dark. They smelled of smoke and earth.

Shamans.

She stepped aside. They entered as if expected.

Inside, they built no ceremony beyond what was already there. They burned dried herbs in a clay bowl.

Mugwort.

Thyme.

Pine.

One began a chant, low and deep. The other touched her brow with a paste of crushed herbs. He whispered in a tongue older than hers.

When the pain came, she did not scream.

She moved like the earth.

Slow.

Patient.

Inevitable.

The fire burned through the storm.

Hours passed. Time folded. There was only the breath. The chant. The steady rhythm of the life she was about to bring into the world.

And then crying.

Sharp.

Strong.

Alive.

They placed the child in her arms. Wrapped in linen and warmth.

Liv looked down.

He was small.

Perfect.

Red with life.

"Archie," she whispered. "Archie Patterson Karlsson."

He quieted at the sound of her voice.

She smiled fully for the first time in a long while.

For a moment, the world was still.

No war.

No prophecy.

No shadows.

Only her, the boy in her arms, and the scent of pine and smoke in the air.

The days after Archie's birth were filled with light.

He was quiet. Curious. His eyes tracked motion sooner than they should. At night he slept against her chest. Warm and slow of breath.

In the mornings, she carried him into the grove behind the house. She hummed low songs to the trees and to him.

For a time, it felt whole.

She fed him. Held him. Whispered old words into his ears. Blessings from forgotten days. Promises she could not name.

But the world pressed in.

To be a single mother in 1955 was no dream. It was a shadow that followed her in town. In the market. Even in the bookstore where the owner had begun to ask less.

She kept working.

But money was thin.

Time was thinner.

And deep-down Liv knew the truth.

She was not ready.

Not for this world. Not for the one filled with stares, forms, and deadlines.

Not for bottle prices and child-care.

Not for the side-glances at church doors and schoolhouses.

She could guard him from demons. But not from loneliness. Not from what she could not give.

She watched him sleep one afternoon. Sunlight cut across his blanket. He curled his small fingers in sleep.

Soft.

Fragile.

It tore at her. But she knew.

He deserved more.

More than a small house by the grove. More than a woman half caught between this world and another. More than silence.

Secrets.

Spells.

He deserved a chance.

The next day she packed a small bundle. No note. No explanation. Only a delivery to a place that promised care, safety, and a future.

Liv kissed his brow and spoke one last blessing.

A word that would follow him wherever he went.

A word that would follow him wherever he went.

Thurisaz, the thorn that guards.

She walked home without looking back.

She didn't cry.

But something in her never closed again. A wound that would not heal. She carried it as she carried her scars.

Silent.

Unseen.

Enduring.

THE SANDFORD HOME

The ache dulled with time.

In the months after she gave Archie up, Liv moved with purpose. She worked long hours at the bookstore. Kept to herself. The smell of old paper and dust steadied her. The routine helped. So did the silence.

But she still felt him.

Sometimes in the early morning, before the sun touched the windows. Sometimes as a warmth on the wind. Not pain. Just knowing. A tether still there.

In town, she heard whispers. A baby taken in. Adopted by a wealthy couple named Blanchard from Santa Barbara. The boy would have everything.

A home.

Schooling.

Comfort.

Liv said nothing. She only breathed out. For the first time in months, her breath did not catch in her throat.

She thought of him often.

She always would.

But she no longer carried regret.

Only memory.

By early 1957, the air felt different.

She had healed. Not whole, but enough. Grief transformed into something softer. Something she could live with. She watched people again. Noticed small things. Let the present in.

Then, one morning, a man walked into the bookstore.

The bell above the door chimed.

He was tall. Neatly dressed in a collared shirt and wool coat. Dark hair combed back. Confidence in his posture. He moved like a man raised with manners but not bound by them.

"Excuse me," he said. His voice was smooth. Sincere. "I'm looking for a book."

Liv looked up from behind the counter. "Aren't we all?"

He smiled. "This one's a little obscure. *Runatal and the Poetic Echoes of Yggdrasil.* Norse mythology. Translated, I believe, by Holmstrom."

She knew the book.

It was not on the shelves. It was kept in the back. She said nothing. Only nodded once and stepped into the storeroom.

He walked through the store and admired the shelves. He loved the atmosphere a bookstore.

The warmth. The dust. The smell of old paper.

He opened a book and breathed it in.

Musty. Woody.

He thought he'd caught a hint of pine.

And perhaps wet earth.

He turned and saw her return with the book in hand. He smiled, impressed.

"You know your collection," he said.

"I know the old ones," she said.

He took the book gently and thumbed the faded pages.

"This is perfect."

"Most people don't ask for rune poetry and world trees on a Tuesday morning," she said.

"I've never been most people."

He met her eyes. A pause.

"Jensen Sandford," he said, and held out his hand.

She looked at it. A hand offered openly. No ring. No shadow of another life. Then she shook it.

"Liv."

No last name.

None needed.

A few days later, the bell above the door chimed again.

Liv looked up.

Jensen Sandford stood there. A faint smile on his face. The same bookish curiosity in his eyes.

"I'm looking for another," he said. "Something on old Norse charms, maybe."

Liv raised an eyebrow. "That's a narrow interest."

"I like the old ways," he said. "Always have. Feels… familiar."

She studied him for a moment. Then motioned toward the back. "Let's see what we can find."

He came again the following week.

And again the week after that.

He was not pushy. He did not linger long. He browsed the shelves. Asked for obscure titles. Made easy talk. In time he became a fixture. Someone who belonged there, like the books, the dust, the sun that filtered through the blinds.

She set aside what she thought might interest him.

He noticed.

"You tear through these old texts," she said.

Jensen smiled. "I guess I'm looking for something."

Liv said nothing. She handed him a book wrapped in brown paper.

He paused. "There's comfort in these stories. Runes. Rituals. Gods that live in the trees. The world made sense to them. I've always felt… connected. Even if I don't know why."

Liv didn't answer. But something in her chest stirred.

They began to spend more time together.

Walks by the water. Long talks over coffee. Days in the shop passed too quickly. He was kind. Present. Unlike the last man, uncomplicated. No other life pulled at him from afar.

Jensen worked in estate restoration. He traveled along the coast to assess old houses, furnishings, and forgotten collections. The work was steady and gave him freedom. He returned with stories. With strange objects. Many he brought for Liv to see.

She had not expected to fall in love again.

But this was different.

It was rooted.

Safe.

WHISPERS IN THE PINES

By the summer of 1957, Liv was ready. The pain of the past had softened. For the first time in years, the future did not seem something to fear.

They married on a warm June day. The ceremony was small. A few friends. A linen dress. The smell of lemon blossoms in the air. Liv wore her hair loose. Jensen did not stop smiling.

No grand vows. No elaborate speeches.

Only a promise.

And the start of something new.

Married life settled on Liv like a worn cloak.

She and Jensen built a rhythm. He traveled often for work. He judged houses from Monterey to San Diego. But he always returned. And when he did, he brought stories. Faded houses on windswept cliffs. Forgotten ledgers. Treasures in cedar chests. He trusted Liv's eye on strange objects, especially when old runes or carvings surfaced.

She worked at the bookstore part-time. The owner soon gave her full charge of the rare and antique shelves. She tended them like a private hall. The shop became a second home. Familiar. Scented with leather, paper, and dried herbs she hid among the shelves.

Evenings were slow and warm. Jensen cooked poorly, but with heart. Liv corrected him. She teased him about burnt rice or overcooked eggs. They laughed often. It was not endless passion.

It was comforting.

Real.

Healing.

In the spring of 1960, Liv gave birth to a daughter. They named her Viktória Lilyana Sandford.

The name came to Liv in a dream two nights before the birth. She wrote it down when she woke. She did not know why. Jensen agreed without hesitation.

Their home shifted with her arrival. Filled now with soft cries. Blankets on sun-warmed floors. The scent of baby soap and the orange blossoms from the trees outside.

Jensen doted on Viktória. He often slept with her on his chest in a rocking chair that groaned beneath their weight.

Liv watched them both.

For the first time since Archie, she did not feel torn in two.

She felt whole.

And the house showed it. Runes carved in the beams. Lavender hung in the doorways. A soft bell at the door that never rang unless one came in peace.

The Sandford home did not just hold people.

It held love.

The years passed quickly.

Viktória grew like wildflowers in spring.

Strong.

Bright.

Curious.

She climbed citrus trees. Ran barefoot through the yard. Filled notebooks with drawings of clouds, birds, and dreamlike places she could not explain.

Liv taught her to listen to the wind. To feel a storm before it came. She never called it magic, and Viktória never asked. The lessons came in nudges. How to brew tea for a sore throat. Which flower bloomed before the rain. How to walk barefoot on earth when the heart was heavy.

But Viktória did not follow the old ways.

She was modern. Spirited. Shaped by the California sun and late-night records. By library books. By dreams of cities far beyond Oxnard.

Liv never pushed. Magic was no legacy to be forced. Only offered.

And Viktória grew well.

She stayed close even into adulthood. Worked part-time at a florist's. Helped Jensen mend old furniture. He read with Liv in the evenings and sipped tea. He never asked how it was made.

The house stayed full of laughter. Burnt meals. Mislaid tools. Most importantly, love.

In 1979, Viktória met Jaymes Stone. A young man with a sharp mind and a warm smile.

Kind.

Steady.

Thoughtful.

He did not flinch at Liv's silences or Jensen's long stories. He loved Viktória openly.

They married in a garden outside Santa Barbara. Liv stood by Jensen, her fingers light on his arm. She watched her daughter walk barefoot across the sunlit grass. A crown of rosemary in her hair.

It was no grand wedding. But it was beautiful.

Liv felt a deep joy seeing Viktória step into her own life. She had known heartbreak. She had found love. She had raised a daughter who glowed from within.

For Liv, that was enough.

In the stillness that followed, in the return to a smaller, softer house, she felt peace.

Her family.

Small.

Imperfect.

Real.

It had become her greatest magic.

CHAPTER 44

THE SECOND CIRCLE

July 8, 1984

Early evening. Liv stepped into the hospital. The fluorescent lights buzzed overhead. The air reeked of bleach and stale breath. She paused near the entrance. Her body was hesitant. She had always avoided such places.

Too bright.

Too clean.

Too full of machines that knew nothing about the body the way she did.

She had given birth by firelight. She had healed with hands and herbs. Not with wires and charts.

But Viktória was a modern woman. And this was her moment.

So Liv walked forward. Steady as ever.

Yet part of her remained just outside the door.

Jensen waited in the lobby. He gave them space. The elevator hummed as it rose. The steel walls reflected the face of one who had lived too many lifetimes to flinch at fluorescent lighting.

The ward was quiet. Viktória was tired but radiant. Hair pulled back. Cheeks still flushed from labor.

Jaymes stood at her side. He smiled proudly.

Liv said nothing at first. She walked to the bed.

Her steps were soft.

Her presence grounded.

Viktória looked up.

"Would you like to hold her?"

Liv nodded once.

Jaymes placed the small, swaddled bundle in her arms.

She looked down at the newborn's face.

Bright green eyes. Wide but unfocused. A full head of red hair.

Just like hers.

A spark stirred behind the gaze.

Not magic.

Not yet.

But something deeper. Watching. Listening.

"Tegan Jasmine Stone," Viktória said. "Born just after five."

Liv did not speak. She rocked. The child's weight settled in her arms. She studied in silence. Counted fingers. Noted the warmth of skin, the steady breath, the small fist pressed against her chest.

In Liv's eyes, she was perfect.

In the months that followed, Liv became a frequent presence in Tegan's life. She did not hover. She gave no advice unless asked. But she was always there.

When Tegan cried, Liv quieted her with a low hum. An old melody. Forgotten by most.

When Tegan stared into space, Liv did not break it. She knew the silence. She had seen it before in vǫlvas and spirits. The child listened. Learned the world.

Liv brought small things. Carved wood. Pressed herbs. A bracelet with one rune cut on the underside.

Gifts given without explanation. Quiet guidance.

When Tegan laughed for the first time, it was in Liv's arms.

When she took her first steps, it was toward Liv's outstretched hand.

No grand moments. No speeches.

In those first years, a bond was forged that no world could break.

Liv did not speak the words. She did not need to.

This one is ours.

September 4, 1986

Two years later, the house filled with the cry of a newborn again.

Viktória gave birth to a son, Landen Augustine Stone, on a warm September afternoon. This time the birth was at home. Not because of Liv's influence. Because Viktória had grown to appreciate the stillness of her own home. She wanted quiet. Familiar walls. The hum of something ancient beneath the floorboards.

Jaymes was there. He paced the hall with nervous steps. Liv stayed in the corner. Present but unobtrusive. She lit a candle. Set a protective rune at the window. Spoke a short blessing over the linen.

When Landen arrived, he came into the world with a deep cry and steady lungs. Stronger than Tegan had been. A different energy. Solid. Rooted.

Liv held him only briefly that night. She saw the curve of his brow. The dark wisps of hair. The hand that curled by instinct toward her.

She kissed his forehead. Whispered a word of protection into his ear and handed him back into Viktória's arms.

"Another strong one," she said.

And it was true.

Tegan was too young to grasp the change, yet she watched close. Liv often found her at the crib. Her red curls bobbed as she leaned to stare at her brother with wide eyes.

In those early days, Liv often held both. One in each arm. She told them stories in old tongues they did not yet understand, though something in their bodies seemed to respond.

She never called it magic.

But it lived in how they listened.

By the time Landen could crawl, the house had changed.

Not in loud or sudden ways. Only in small signs. Jaymes stayed late at work. He smiled less. He spoke with longer pauses between words. He never raised his voice. He never left in anger. But something in him had begun to fade.

Liv saw it first.

He no longer reached for Viktória's hand as he passed. His eyes drifted when she spoke. At dinner, he sat through meals without truly being there.

Viktória said nothing.

Not yet.

The children filled her arms.

Her hours. Her thoughts.

She was tired.

Yet she smiled through it.

She was good at that.

Liv said nothing either.

She had learned that some threads must unravel on their own.

June 5, 1988

Marcie Eugina Stone was born in the early hours of a June morning.

She came fast. Faster than the others. Viktória had little time to breathe between contractions before the baby arrived.

Pink.

Fierce.

Full of lungs.

Jaymes was there, but distant. He held his daughter. Smiled at her. Even wept for a moment. But something in him never returned.

Liv watched him step outside to take a call while Viktória slept with the child on her chest.

She stayed with them that night. She cleaned the room. Brewed mild tea. Sat in the rocking chair beside the crib. Held Landen when he woke in tears. Tegan, now four, lay curled on a mat nearby. She clutched a stuffed bear.

Liv moved through the house as she always had.

Quiet.

Steady.

Present.

She looked at each of them. Viktória with her newborn. Jaymes outside. The children wrapped in sleep. She knew the shape of what was to come.

The family was not broken yet.

But the threads had begun to pull.

Still, she stayed.

For love, a grandmother's love most of all, does not vanish when things fray.

If anything, it rooted deeper.

June 28, 1994

By the time Tegan turned ten, Jaymes was more memory than man. He came home less often. Stayed longer on trips. Missed birthdays. Missed the first day of school. Missed too much.

Viktória no longer asked questions. She no longer waited up at night.

Liv noticed the way Tegan stepped in. She helped her mom more with Landen. Braided Marcie's hair. Made breakfast before school. She was still a child but had already started to fill the spaces left behind.

Jaymes left quietly. No fight. No last word. One day he simply did not return.

A letter came weeks later.

Apologies.

Regrets.

A promise to stay in touch. For the kids.

Viktória read it once. Folded it neat. Placed it in a drawer.

Liv watched her daughter bear the weight of holding the family together. She helped when she could. Cooked when needed. Sat with the children when Viktória worked late. The house was smaller without him, yet fuller in its way.

Love remained.

It stitched into the early mornings. Into Tegan's quiet resilience. Into the laughter that returned in pieces.

Liv stood in the yard one evening and watched the children play. The sun sank low. Long shadows stretched across the citrus trees.

The next afternoon, Tegan sat on the porch steps, braiding grass stems. She looked up at Liv, who sat in the rocking chair with tea.

"Nana, how come you don't look old?"

"What do you mean?"

"Jenny's grandma has white hair and wrinkles. You don't."

Liv smiled softly. "Some people carry their years differently. I've always been lucky that way."

"Is it magic?" Tegan asked, eyes bright with curiosity.

Liv laughed. Not dismissive, but warm.

"Everything is magic if you look at it right. Even getting older."

Tegan tilted her head and studied Liv's face more carefully.

"What's that mark? On your jaw?"

Liv's hand moved to touch it, almost unconsciously. For a moment, the vision of a battle took over her mind.

Snow screamed across the valley. The blizzard swallowed sound and light and turned every breath to ice. Liv moved through it with her sword drawn. The ice troll rose from the storm like a jagged cliff. Frost clung to its beard. Its pale eyes burned with hatred.

It swung a heavy battle axe. The blade cut through the snow and caught her off guard. She twisted away, but the edge passed too close. Pain bloomed along her jaw. Warm blood slid down her neck.

She stopped and lifted a hand to her face. Her fingers touched the wound. She drew them away and saw the dark smear across her skin. The warmth ran against the cold of the storm. She brought her hand to her lips and tasted the blood.

Something stirred inside her.

Her eyes darkened until they turned black as the winter sky. A slow smirk extended the corner of her mouth. The troll roared and raised the axe again.

Liv charged.

Her boots cut deep into the snow. Her sword met the troll's abdomen with a hard crack. The steel drove through ice and flesh. The creature staggered back. A gust of wind tore across the ridge as the troll toppled and vanished into the swirling white.

The blizzard closed around her. The vision ended as the snow settled over the fallen beast.

One the porch, she smiled and dropped her hand.

"Just a reminder of something from long ago."

"Does it hurt?"

"Not anymore. It's just part of the story now."

Tegan seemed satisfied with that and returned to her braiding. She didn't ask again.

Liv realized it had been nearly forty years since she arrived in Oxnard with nothing but a suitcase and silence.

Now she had this.

CHAPTER 45

LIV'S LEGACY

Late 1994

After Jaymes left, the house grew heavy. Quiet.

Jensen's health had already begun to fail. Slow at first. He forgot small things. He tired more often. By the time Marcie turned ten, his steps dragged, and his appetite waned. Liv cared for him.

She never complained.

She never called it a burden.

It was only time, doing what time does.

One evening in late autumn 1996, he fell asleep in his chair and did not wake.

A heart attack, the doctor said. Peaceful.

Liv sat beside him until morning. She lit a single candle and whispered an old prayer she had not spoken in years. She opened the window to let his spirit out, as the old ways taught.

Once again, she was alone.

But not entirely.

Tegan was nearly twelve. Full of energy and wonder. She curled beside Liv on the couch and told wild stories of far countries she would visit, mountains she would climb, forests she would explore.

"One day, I'll go everywhere," she said.

Liv smiled. "You always say that."

"Because I will."

Tegan's curiosity was endless. She asked about birds. Insects. The stars. The wind.

She told stories of animals no one had seen. Creatures with glowing fur and clever eyes. Some were imagined. Some, Liv suspected, were not. She asked about everything, though never frogs. She avoided them without a reason she could name.

Viktória worked hard. Too hard. But the children were good and bright. Landen was steady, curious in his own way. Marcie had a sharp wit. Quick and observant. They helped around the house, kept to their studies, and made Liv proud in ways she never spoke aloud but always carried.

Liv felt a slow shift within her. Not an illness. A knowing. A fading. An unraveling that brought peace instead of fear. Her time here was ending.

She did not speak of it.

She stayed close.

In the summer of 2002, Tegan's college acceptance letters arrived in a bundle. Thick envelopes from schools across the country. She had her pick. Yet she stayed close. She chose Stanford.

The family held a backyard barbecue to celebrate.

Picnic tables.

Folding chairs.

Mismatched dishes and laughter. Viktória grilled. Marcie helped make a fruit salad that never reached the table. Landen tried to set something on fire again. Friends from school came and went. Tegan beamed.

Liv sat in the shade with a glass of iced tea in hand. She watched the scene unfold like a memory still being written.

Tegan came over with a soda and dropped onto the blanket beside her.

"Why Stanford?" Liv asked.

Tegan grinned. "Because of The Tree. It's not the official mascot, but it's everywhere. A strange symbol for a school, right?"

But Liv saw more than a funny story.

The Tree.

Rooted.

Protective.

Strange.

Strong.

Tegan had chosen well, even if she did not know why.

Liv smiled.

Then Tegan added, "I'm not going for zoology. I changed my mind."

"Oh?"

"I want to study people. Behavior. To understand why we do what we do. How the mind works. Behavioral and cognitive psychology."

Liv nodded once. "Understanding what cannot always be seen."

"Exactly."

Liv did not press. She smiled because she knew.

She saw the way Tegan protected her siblings. The way she loved the natural world. Her pull toward something larger. Older.

It was there.

Subtle, maybe.

Unspoken, perhaps.

But there.

Liv had seen many things in this world.

Monsters.

War.

Love.

Loss.

But this girl with fire in her hair and light in her eyes was the most extraordinary of all.

Her legacy.

The barbecue ended with laughter and full plates. Porch lights flickered. Friends left in pairs and said goodbye from across the lawn. Viktória gathered plates and bottles. Marcie chased Landen barefoot through the grass. Music played through the screen door.

Liv said goodnight to Marcie first. She brushed a strand of hair behind the girl's ear. Then to Landen, who gave her a one-armed hug before he darted off again.

She found Tegan at the old citrus tree. The last of the light touched her red hair.

Liv knelt beside her.

"I'm proud of you," she said. "College. Stanford. That's a life worth beginning."

Tegan smiled. "Thanks, Grandma."

Liv leaned in and embraced her. A long, steady hug. Warm. Certain. Deeper than words. Liv set her hand on Tegan's back. No one noticed. No one would.

She whispered something soft in a language Tegan did not know.

A blessing.

It was not for the mind but for the soul. A gift. A thread stitched into the fabric of Tegan's being. It would not shine until it was needed.

The scent of petrichor and pine stayed on Tegan's clothes. A warm current moved through her core. She smiled and felt the comfort of her grandmother's touch.

Foresight.

Awareness.

A shift of fate in moments that mattered most.

Tegan wouldn't understand it yet.

But one day she would.

As Liv pulled away and stepped toward the house, Tegan called, "Goodbye, Grandma."

Liv paused. She Turned. She smiled.

"We don't say goodbye," she said. "We say so long."

That night, after all had gone home, Liv sat in her kitchen. A cup of tea cooled between her hands. Moonlight crossed the floor.

She thought of her daughter. Of the grandchildren. Of the strength in each of them.

They were whole. They would endure.

She did not need to stay.

There were no more demons to fight. No more circles to close. Her presence, once a shield, had become a shadow. It was time to step away.

She stood. No suitcase. No note.

She opened the door. A faint blue light cut across the threshold.

Cool night air met her skin. The glow brushed her face. It was familiar.

As she had done in every chapter of her life, Liv stepped into the unknown.

Without sound.

Without goodbye.

The door closed behind her. She was gone. Only the blue shimmer remained. But only for a moment.

Then it faded.

CHAPTER 46

THE GUARDIAN'S PROMISE

Late 2002

Mist lay low across the forest floor. It curled around twisted roots and stones. The air was cooler here.

Still.

Alive.

Liv stepped through the veil without a sound.

Her boots touched moss. Not concrete. The scent of woodsmoke, river water, and something older wrapped around her like a forgotten memory. She paused beneath a great tree and took in the silence.

This was a different kind of home. Not flesh and blood, but root and stone.

A shape moved ahead.

Small.

Round.

Familiar.

The figure stepped out from behind a crooked stump. Arms crossed. Face pinched. She knew him at once.

"Hello, old friend," Liv said.

Puddlesquat squinted up at her and tilted his head.

He no longer carried the Elder Staff. That duty had passed, with ceremony and stubbornness both. He still stood tall. At least in spirit. His skin was grayer. The lines deeper around his wide eyes. Yet the spark had not dulled.

"You came back," he said.

"I always do."

Puddlesquat huffed. "Took you long enough."

Liv's mouth smiled. "I had things to do. Lessons to learn."

They stood in silence. The forest hummed around them.

"There is someone I need you to watch," Liv said at last. "A girl. Red hair. Fire in her, though she does not know it yet."

Puddlesquat blinked. "Your kin?"

"My granddaughter. Her name is Tegan."

He nodded. "And why would she need to be watched?"

"Because the world is changing," Liv said. "She will walk through the middle of it one day. I will not be there. You might."

Puddlesquat huffed. Half sigh. Half grunt. "I suppose I have done stranger things."

"I know you have."

She reached down and put a hand on his shoulder.

"She's important," Liv said. "Like you."

Words hung in the stillness between them. Unspoken. Understood.

She turned and walked deeper into the forest.

Mist rose.

Trees bent to let her pass.

CHAPTER 47

THE FIRST SIP

Fall 2005 – Stanford, California

The bar was loud. Not obnoxious, just the usual college buzz. Music bounced off old wood. Laughter rose in waves. Chairs scraped against concrete. The air smelled of spilled beer, fried food, and AXE Body Spray.

Tegan sat at the far end of the table. She half-listened to a story she had already heard twice. Her psychology notes still swam in her head. They faded in and out with the noise. She sipped water. She laughed in the right places. She watched the clock.

It was not her scene. But after midterms, she had said yes.

Then someone slid a pint glass toward her.

"Try this," a friend said. "You need something stronger than whatever that is."

She looked at the glass. Dark. A thick rim of foam.

"What is it?"

"Sierra Nevada. A barleywine ale."

She raised an eyebrow. "Barleywine? What is that?"

"It is beer. Strong. A little strange. You will like it."

She smirked. "That's a lot of confidence."

"Just try it."

She stared at it for a moment. Then she lifted the glass and took a sip.

It hit differently.

Not like the watery lagers she knew.

This was rich.

Malty.

Sweet.

A depth she could not place.

Her eyes lit up. "Whoa. That's good."

"Told you."

She leaned back and took another sip. Slower this time. Across the bar, she saw the tap handle. A shaggy figure stepped through pine trees. Cartoonish but familiar.

"Bigfoot," she said under her breath. "Of course."

She did not know much. Only that it was some creature people swore they had seen. A joke about woods and footprints. But the name. The beer. The moment. It stayed. A joke, maybe. Yet something in her chest stirred.

She smiled. Just a little.

She took another sip.

She did not know why it stayed with her.

Only that it did.

She did not know it yet.

But something had begun.

BEER LIST

477

Sierra Nevada Brewing Company Bigfoot Barleywine - American

ABOUT THE AUTHOR

Originally from Yellow Springs, OH and now based in Chandler, AZ, Mark Trollinger is the *Godfather of Cryptozoology and Craft Beer Fiction*, having introduced the two themes into a cohesive real-world experience back in 2016. He is the creator of Myths and Malts, an independent publishing brand behind the T.I.M.E. Agency series, a collection of cryptid-fueled adventures grounded in real locations, real breweries, and maybe even real creatures.

The books follow four investigators from the T.I.M.E. Agency as they travel the country in search of elusive cryptids and unforgettable craft beers.

But the T.I.M.E. Agency series isn't just a series. It's an invitation. Readers can take the selfie challenge, explore the curated Spotify playlist, and track the featured beers listed in the back of each book. Every title highlights a nonprofit connected to the story, with a portion of proceeds donated to the featured organization.

Drink in the adventure. Support the cause. And maybe, find the truth hiding in plain sight.

Myths and Malts Website

Mark Trollinger's

Amazon.com Author Page

WORDS FROM THE AUTHOR

This book is ambitious on its own, spanning more than 400 years. But it escalates when you consider it is part of a multi-book arc involving the Jersey Devil. And if that is not enough, it ties into several other books in the TIME series.

I am not even sure what came first. Back when I was working on my screenwriting degree, I had an idea for a necromancer who traveled the astral plane to retrieve souls who passed before their time. Around the same time I thought about a historical story with Carson Quinn's grandfather, showing how he inspired Carson's love of cryptozoology.

The necromancer never got his own story, so I worked him into Book 4: *The Loveland Frog and the Narrow Path*. In that book, Tegan dies at the hands of alien frog-creatures. Santiago Torres, the necromancer, needed a mentor, so I introduced Puddlesquat the pukwudgie. He intervenes in the final battle and marks Tegan so

Santiago can find her. How did Puddlesquat know she would die? At the time, I did not have an answer.

Later, in *The Gibson County Beast*, Santiago and Puddlesquat tell Tegan the truth. She was resurrected and given the powers of a Valkyrie because Puddlesquat saved her. But why would a pukwudgie, known for being mischievous and even dangerous to humans, save her? I decided he owed a debt to someone who once helped his people in their battles with the Jersey Devil. Not only in 1735, but again in 1909.

In Tegan's solo book, when she visits a psychologist and undergoes hypnosis, more details came out. She grew up in Oxnard, California. She had a brother and a sister. She helped her mom when her father left. And her grandmother was a Valkyrie who fought the Jersey Devil on those two occasions.

All those random details turned into a four-book arc: *Kareem Ortiz & The Menehune of Kaua'i*, *The Jersey Devil and the Silky Intergalactic Pajamas*, *The Lizard Man of Lee County and the Sope Creek Cryptidweizen* and now, *Whispers in the Pines*.

And like Ron Popeil used to say, "But wait, there's more." This book also brings in Patterson Quinn,

Carson's grandfather, which sets up the next book, *The Dark Road*. That will be his own solo adventure.

Keeping all of this consistent over six books has been a challenge. But thanks to a few DIPA and Imperial Stouts, I think I pulled it off.

This solo adventure is not just about Tegan's grandmother. It started with a photo I found online. A woman I do not know, but her image stuck with me. I saved it without knowing why. Later, when I began to write about a timeless warrior, I went back to that photo. And there she was, Liv Carlson.

She had to be more than a fighter. She had to be a badass. A shieldmaiden who does not age. A warrior who answers the call again and again. I could not just drop her into 1736 to fight the Jersey Devil. There had to be more. If she was truly timeless, why not start further back? Why not begin in 1602 in Iceland, and end in 2005 in California?

This book took scattered pieces, fragments, and half-ideas born out of creativity and beer, and wove them into something bigger. A legacy. Something layered, emotional, and real.

And Liv. She was not supposed to be the heart of the TIME universe. But now it feels like she is. She is more than a Valkyrie. She is love and loss. Myth and memory. A mother, a fighter, a guide, and a life. I think she has become the most developed character in the series.

So here we are. I hope this book answers the questions and does her justice. I hope it makes sense. Most of all, I hope you enjoy reading it as much as I have enjoyed writing it.

And here is the photo that started it all.

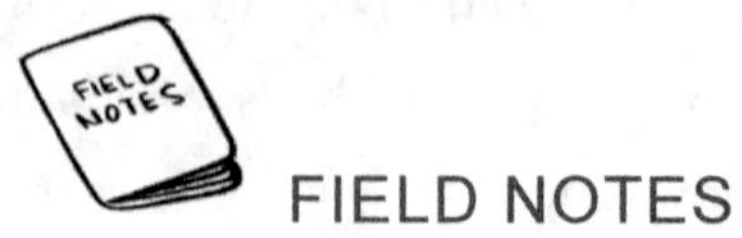

FIELD NOTES

Cover

Nyssa Iniguez created the design of this cover.

Dedication

This book includes the typical dedication to my family. I included my great grandmother, Enid. When I would say goodbye, she always said "We don't say goodbye. We say so long. I used that with Liv saying so long to Tegan.

Chapter 1

The famine in Iceland around 1602 was real, and I wanted you to feel it. It was not only a bad harvest. The Danish crown forced a trade monopoly on the island. Farmers could no longer buy grain where they pleased. They were trapped with Danish merchants who charged high prices. Then the winters turned brutal. Fields froze. Livestock starved. People lived on fish, moss, and whatever drifted out of the sea. • By this time folk no longer lived in great Viking longhouses. They built turf houses instead. Low, grass-covered shelters packed tight against the cold. Families were scattered across valleys in farmsteads, and they gathered only when the elders called them into a hall. • The clash between the old gods and the new faith still mattered. Iceland had voted for Christianity in the year 1000, but that did not erase centuries of pagan belief. People still whispered to Odin, Freyja, and the land-spirits. They only did it in secret, because the church forbade it. For many the old gods felt dangerous, like powers you should not stir. • Eiríkur is one of the elders. I wrote him as an old goði. In the saga age a goði was both chieftain and priest. By 1602 the crown and church had stripped that role away, but the memory lingered. People still respected men like him, and they still feared what he carried from the old ways. • The öfuguggi, the backward-finned fish, is also drawn from real Icelandic lore. Fishermen told of them as twisted creatures with fins set the wrong way. They were said to eat drowned men. Their flesh was red, too red, and whoever ate it would sicken and die. In famine years hunger won over fear, and people ate them anyway. Just like in the story, sickness followed. • And then there is Ölrún. To the people of Þórsmörk she was more legend than woman. A Valkyrie, born under an eclipse, marked by gods their priests told them to shun. Some whispered she was a curse. Others whispered she was a shield. Her name was spoken like something half-forbidden, half-prayer. That fear made her arrival strike harder, because she came when no other hope remained.

Chapter 2

This is the chapter where I wanted you to see Liv change. Up to now she felt like a wanderer in the mist. Here she becomes something more. The farms of Þórsmörk knew the old curse stories, but most had bent to the new faith. That clash mattered to me. In real Icelandic history the church outlawed cremation, so when Liv orders the dead burned it is not only strange to them, it is dangerous. • I wanted you to see her step into the role of Valkyrie as seiðkona. Not Odin's handmaiden, but a woman who carries the old ways into a changing world. She calls on the river, the earth, and the fire. She speaks in the old tongue and sends the drowned spirits on their way. • I also wanted the clash of faiths clear. Jón speaks for Christian burial, while Eiríkur remembers the fire rites of his forefathers. Liv forces them to face the truth. The new rites cannot end the curse. Only the old fire can. And even as the pyres burn I wanted you to feel that victory is never clean. The spirits are freed, but something older still waits in the mountains. That shadow will follow her.

Chapter 3

I wanted the farms to breathe again once the curse was lifted, but the feast had to be short. A frozen scout came stumbling in with news: a shadow stood on the ridge, watching without eyes. That is when Ölrún rose and took up her staff. Four warriors went with her: Hróald, Stigandi, Ylva, and Bjorn. • This chapter also brings in two beings from Norse lore. Draugar are the dead who walk. They are swollen and fierce, guardians of graves and bringers of fear. Vættr are spirits bound to land and sea. Some protected their people. Some turned dark with hunger, like the watcher on the ridge.

Chapter 4

I wanted the fight on the ridge to echo what the sagas warned. Blades could cut the spirit and spears could pierce it, but the wounds closed. Steel could not kill what was already dead. Only fire could end it. Flame was the true weapon. Fire broke the bond and sent the spirit down.

Chapter 5

The ridge was won, but I wanted you to see the cost. Bjorn, the quiet archer with raven-fletched shafts, gave his life in the fight. His bow spoke where his voice seldom did, and in the end he stood where others faltered. • I had Ölrún guide his soul with seiðr. Her words as a Valkyrie sent him to Valhalla, as the old tales promised. His body was carried home and laid in the hall so his people could honor him. • In the sagas victory is never whole. The land is freed, but the fallen are the price.

Chapter 6

In Old Norse tradition a völva was a female seer who practiced seiðr. She carried a staff. She was both revered and feared. A völva could inspire warriors with her presence, but her words often carried the weight of doom. • By 1710 figures like this had largely vanished from daily life. I wanted Ölrún meeting one in the forest to mark her as a remnant of the old world. A voice of fate standing at the edge of war. • When I described her eyes as pale and clouded it tied to Norse depictions of seeresses. They were thought blind to the physical world but able to see into the fated realm. Her mention of the Black Goat and the western lands hints at how old Norse prophecy threads into the larger conflict. It ties Ölrún's path to events far beyond the frozen battlefield.

Chapter 7

By 1710 Scandinavia was long Christian. The runes were outlawed. The völva silenced. Most folk prayed in churches instead of before stones. Yet traces of the old ways still lingered. I chose names like Ingrid, Signe, Freydis, Gudrun, and Hildr because they came from the sagas. Some were common. Others were rare, kept alive in families who remembered. To bear such names in this age marked a tie to the past. • Runes were no longer carved in the open. Some still cast them in secret. Some still whispered charms. These women, warriors and wanderers, carried that thread. • When they saw Ölrún I wanted you to feel why they gathered to her. It was not chance. It was kinship. They saw in her the same signs they still carried. She was proof the old world had not died. A spark in a land that had tried to bury it.

Chapter 8

I wanted you to feel how early New England towns could turn inward when fear struck. Plague, famine, quarrels with neighbors, doors closed, markets silent, strangers unwelcome. The marks cut in wood recall Norse runes for warding and the witch marks carved by colonists to turn spirits aside. Spirals and goat heads fall outside known custom. Those point to something older, something foreign. • Gooseberry Island itself is real. A wind-beaten isle off Little Compton, Rhode Island. In the 1600s a farm stood there. Storms and stories still cling to it. Tales tell of pirates, wrecks, and vanishings. In the saga I gave it a darker claim. It became the refuge of a cult called the Keepers, bound to the Black Goat. • I wanted you to see how fear silenced the town. Fear shut doors and turned faces away. In that silence, evil found its ground.

Chapter 9

I pictured Gooseberry Island as a storm-worn outpost. In 1702 it would have held little more than fishing huts and a watch post. A house with books inside would have been rare, set apart from the common dwellings. The Latin text works if you think of it as a handwritten journal left by a learned settler or a Keeper. Not a printed book. Colonists also carved protective signs into beams and stone, so the spiral at the hearth has some truth behind it. In the saga I made the ruin more than a home. I shaped it as a hidden temple. Its silence and its marks carry the fear that once clung to these shores.

Chapter 10

I wanted you to feel the Puritan fear of the forest. For them it was already a place of devils and witches. Here that fear proves true. The chanting in the grove and the shape beneath the roots show that the Keepers' worship is not empty ritual. It is bound to something alive under the land. I ended the chapter with a blunt truth. The grove was never the trap. The village was.

Chapter 11

I wanted you to see that the Black Grove is no myth to these settlers. The villagers who call themselves Keepers do not gather in the open square. They hide in the Grove and honor a spirit they call the Old One. Outsiders know it as the Black Goat. The elder's refusal to speak its true name fits with old belief. Across many cultures to know the true name of a spirit is to hold power over it. The Keepers guard that name because they fear it as much as they revere it. • This chapter also reflects the world of colonial America. For Puritans and their neighbors, the forest stood as a place of dread. It was the realm of witches, devils, and old gods. Tales of hidden rites and sacrifice were common. Centuries later stories like *The Lottery* would echo that same fear of communities binding themselves to darker powers. The silence of the villagers, their black eyes, and their false piety show how deep the Old One had sunk into their lives. • The promise of "the chosen" makes the truth clear. The Keepers' worship is not harmless tradition. It is the mask of something older, and it demands blood.

Chapter 12

I wanted you to see how a stave worked here. A stave is more than a mark. It is a rune-word spoken with seiðr. When Ölrún spoke it in the Grove the ground itself answered. Roots shook. Shadows froze. From that moment the Keepers could no longer vanish. Their bodies stayed, and they could be killed. • The Black Goat itself was not destroyed. I had it sink back into the earth, never to rise again. What endured was its mask. Ölrún took it as a trophy. When she wore it in battle the Keepers feared the face they once worshipped.

Chapter 13

I wanted you to see the burning of the settlement as the end of the Black Grove cult as a community, but not the end of its followers. After this, whispers spread through the colonies. Robed bodies left where they fell, altars hacked apart, villages gone overnight. I gave the Huntress the black goat-mask so you could feel how the sight of it turned their faith into fear. • The small figure on the Susquehanna is a nod to the Albawitch of Pennsylvania Dutch lore. People described them as pale, hairy creatures that haunted orchards and stole apples. Columbia, Pennsylvania still holds a festival in their name. • For Ölrún it was only a passing sign. I wanted you to sense it as a guardian of the wild, watching her move deeper into the colonies.

Chapter 14

I wanted this chapter to feel like a ghost story told in a tavern. By now the Huntress is legend. Feared more than seen. You hear of her the way the men do, in whispers, because even saying her name aloud feels dangerous. • The Black Goat returns here as a thread tying back to earlier chapters and pointing forward. Thomas doesn't believe, but you can sense how the silence in the room works on him. • The mark on the tavern wall matters. It shows she isn't only killing. She's warning. Each spiral says the Huntress passed through, and death walked with her. I chose to let you hear of her through others before showing her. In a saga, that distance builds her myth.

Chapter 15

I wanted this chapter to show the Huntress in full, face to face with Thomas. Until now he only heard stories. Here he learns that she chooses who lives and who dies. • The spiral carved into his door mattered. At the tavern it was jagged, meant to strike fear. At his home it was careful. It was a warning. I wanted you to see that she spared him, but only on her terms. • This is also the seed of something larger. Thomas flees, but his son Phineas carries the old words with him. That choice plants the line that will grow into future chapters, when darkness rises again.

Chapter 16

Burlington was never a seaport like Philadelphia. It sat on the Delaware River, a Quaker town tied to ferries, trade, and gossip that moved faster than ships. The tavern beams weren't rotted by marsh winds but stained by years of river damp and smoke. • And Franklin. Yes, *that* Franklin. In 1735 he was only twenty-nine years old. Not the gray-haired statesman with bifocals and kites you know from schoolbooks. At this point he was a sharp printer in Philadelphia. Already pulling tricks in print that cut as deep as any blade. • His feud with Titus Leeds was not about religion. It was about sales, reputation, and control of the story. That is the thread to watch here. Franklin bends truth into belief. He is not a pirate (although privateer isn't much different). Not a Quaker. Not a loyalist. He is a man who knew that if you control the words, you control the world.

Chapter 17

Leeds Point sat about sixty miles from Philadelphia. In 1735 that meant two days on horseback. The road cut through pine and marsh, and every mile added to its sense of distance. By the time Phineas arrived, the town felt forgotten, which was the point. • Jonah Fisk is the hinge here. Franklin had already shown Phineas that words could sway men. Fisk tempts him with something older, darker, and less bound by Franklin's rules. Phineas doesn't turn away. He listens. He likes it. • And then there's Titus. He isn't after Phineas, but he is after Franklin. That makes him a problem all the same. If Franklin falls, so does Phineas' place in the shop. By treating Titus as a common enemy, Phineas finds a way to defend Franklin and maybe climb in his favor at the same time. • This chapter is about hunger. Phineas doesn't want to be a second apprentice. He wants more. Franklin's lessons and

Fisk's whispers pull him in two directions, but both feed the same need. Influence . • Maybe one day, some scholar will dig through almanacs and ledgers and swear they found a Phineas Crowe. That's how legends work. You don't need proof. You just need a story that fits.

Chapter 18

This chapter is where the myth begins to take shape. Phineas Crowe opens *Daemonologia Arcana* and finds Azraelion's name. That was important for me because I wanted the Jersey Devil to feel older than 1735. Something already written. Already feared. Just waiting for the right man to call it forward. • The key idea here is belief. Not worship. Not ritual. Just the telling of a story. That's what makes Azraelion dangerous. He doesn't need a priest, only a printer. I leaned into Franklin and the power of the press because in that era, pamphlets and almanacs could spread faster than sermons or laws. One lie printed enough times could become history. • Phineas is not a sorcerer in the traditional sense. He's a publisher, a schemer, a man who knows how words can outlive the one who writes them. By planting the tale of "Mother Leeds," he gives the demon its doorway. • I also wanted Japheth here, not as the villain but as the everyman, He's hardworking, unaware, caught in something far larger. He's also a real person, like his brother Titus, and his father Daniel. When Phineas needles him at the market, it's the first strike of a long echo. • If you strip away the candles and horns, this chapter is about how myths are made. How a story, repeated enough, can summon monsters.

Chapter 19

This is the chapter where the summoning "fails." No smoke, no fire, no demon stepping through the circle. And that's the point. Phineas believes nothing happened. He leaves the room convinced it was a waste of time. • But that's where the horror sits. He was wrong. The silence wasn't safety. It was the spark. The words he spoke lingered, and once he put them into print, belief did the rest. • What I wanted to show here is how a monster doesn't always walk in through the front door. Sometimes it slips in through a story. A name repeated until it feels true. Titus Leeds begins to feel that rot. His family's name, already battered by Franklin, becomes tied to a curse he never asked for. He doesn't need to see Azraelion to feel its shadow •

The failure of the summoning is what makes it work. Phineas thinks he's in control, but the truth is already moving without him.

Chapter 20

This is where the Jersey Devil stops being rumor and becomes lived fear. The summoning "failure" in the last chapter turns out not to be a failure at all. The stories Phineas set in motion begin to breathe, and now they leave bodies in the snow. I wanted the shift to feel sharp. One moment it's whispers and pamphlets, the next it's blood on the ground. That's how folklore works sometimes. It doesn't creep. It jumps. And when it jumps, people can't separate story from life anymore. Titus suffers the most here. Franklin's lies had already bruised his reputation, but this curse goes deeper. It takes his family name and twists it into something no rebuttal can wash clean. "Leeds" no longer means a printer or a man. It means the Devil. The chapter is short because it doesn't need more. A body, a vanished child, a cursed name. That's enough to root a legend.

Chapter 21

This chapter shows the Devil taking hold of the Pine Barrens. The fight with the Pukwudgies matters because it makes clear he isn't just another beast. Their darts, quills, and claws do nothing. When even the old ones of the forest can't stand against him, the threat feels bigger. • The fear spreading among the villagers is just as important. Elias Martin at the sheep pen, the hunters in the woods. Those stories move faster than the truth. By the end of the week the whole town is locking doors and whispering prayers. That's how the name takes root: the Leeds Devil. • The forest itself has changed. Silent trees, ash where snow should be, birds gone from their nests. The balance is broken. That's why Puddlesquat steps forward. He knows they cannot fight this thing. But he remembers someone who could. A fierce warrior from the old lands. One the forest whispers still lingers near.

WHISPERS IN THE PINES

Chapter 22

Liv has lived among humans before. She knows how to fish, mend nets, drink in silence, and let the days pass as if she were one of them. But the edge never leaves her. She has carried centuries of battles in her bones. Even so, she does not know every creature that walks in shadow. This is the first time she comes face to face with a Pukwudgie. • The Leeds Devil is different. She has not seen it, but she has felt it in the stillness of the forest. She has heard its name whispered in taverns and spoken low by the villagers. That whisper was enough for her to know it waits. • Her companions, Thordis and Asbjorn, are cut from the same cloth as Liv. They walk the world though centuries have passed them by. Muskets and powder belong to the age around them, but they still carry the bow and the axe. The old ways have not dulled. Steel and sinew still serve them, even when the world believes it has moved on.

Chapter 23

This chapter shows Liv doing seiðr. You see the staff, the stamping, the trance, the voices all building together. That's her kind of magic. Not blood offerings. Not fire out of her mouth. It focuses on breath, rhythm, and will. • The clay is not just dirt. It is iron-rich red earth mixed with fat, like war paint. That is why it smears bold on skin and why the staff seems to drink it in. I kept it simple, no runes or patterns, just the mark itself. • The green fire is not her breathing fire. She breathes across the staff and the clay, and the flame reacts. It shifts color as a sign that the old powers are awake. Thordis and Asbjorn put their clay on the staff so their strength joins hers. The world may have muskets and powder now, but they still choose the old ways they are familiar with. Voice, earth, and steel.

Chapter 24

Two threads here are left untied. The first is the mention of another Valkyrie. Long before Liv, one with fire in her blood stood in this same place and made a pact with the Pukwudgies. She did not survive. Who was she, and what did she face? Was her fate a warning, or the beginning of something larger? • The second is the Black Goat. Wunnemeahtoo makes it clear that Azraelion, terrible as he is, is only a symptom. The Goat is older. Hungrier. A presence that stirs beneath the earth and feeds on blood and fear. The seer in Iceland spoke not of Azraelion, but of the Black Goat stirring. That was no mistake. Perhaps there is a darker order at work, a hierarchy of demons where Azraelion is not the master, only one among many. • I do not answer those questions here. They are meant to linger. The older Valkyrie. The Goat. Both will return when the time is right, and the answers, when they come, will not be simple. • Accounts differ on the color of Liv's eyes. In her mortal guise they are unremarkable, but when her Valkyrie nature rises, they change. I have described them in two ways. Liv's eyes change when her Valkyrie nature rises. When she answers the call of wrath, her eyes turn black, void of mercy. This is the wraith, the battle-fury that makes her a terror to enemies. When she answers the call of fate, her eyes glow faint blue, edged like frozen fire. This is the seer, the oath-bearer, tied to memory, prophecy, and balance. Both are true. Both are Valkyrie. The difference is not in her eyes but in what part of her power has been summoned.

Chapter 25

This chapter is about planning more than action. Liv and the others gather, choose where to search, and decide to move first instead of waiting. It is preparation before the fight. The Pukwudgies watch from the shadows. Liv speaks as if they are part of the council though they never show their faces. The staff, the axe, the runes, the fire. These are the tools of the hunt. The decision is the true turning point here. The hunt starts with resolve before it starts with blood.

Chapter 26

This chapter shows the first hard signs of the Devil's trail. Each of them finds proof: Thordis sees clawed trees, Asbjorn finds the dead deer, and Liv faces the hollow itself. The Pukwudgies mark the path beside them but stay silent. The group meets again, each scarred by what they saw, and agree to set the trap. • The runes give weight to Thordis' role. She marks danger with

Thurisaz, then later casts her pouch of runes on the stone. One lies broken. That omen matters. A broken rune is not common and not ignored. It tells them the trap may bring blood as much as victory. • The final moment matters most. Liv's eyes shift from blue to black. Blue has always meant vision and foresight. Black marks rage and battle. That change is the true signal that the hunt is no longer only a search. It has become a war.

Chapter 27

This battle gives us answers to a few of the mysteries we raised earlier. We learn that Liv is not the first Valkyrie to face Azraelion in this place. Wunnemeahtoo remembers another one who fought here a thousand years ago, and she fell. That reminder tells us this is not the Devil's first appearance in these Pines, and it will not be his last unless Liv can break the cycle. • We also see for the first time what makes him nearly impossible to fight. Ordinary steel, bone, and wood do not cut him. His hide rejects them. But the magic of the runes lowers that guard. Liv marks her sword with ash and blood while speaking the old tongue, and that consecration lets her strike through. Asbjorn's axe bears runes as well, and though his blows do not kill, they leave marks where plain steel could not. Later, Thordis' obsidian arrow pierces his wing because obsidian is a stone of fire and sacrifice. It is more than a sharp rock. With runes carved into it, it carries power that normal arrows lack. • As the runes begin to let the weapons through, his confidence slips. Pride is his shield, and when it falters, the wounds land deeper. Liv and the others see it. They know his pride is both his strength and his weakness. But even hurt, he remains dangerous. • The important truth is that Azraelion is still in control. He kills Pukwudgies with ease. He mocks every wound they give him. He could press the attack and finish them here, but he does not. Instead, he leaves them alive with their fear. He wants them to know his power. He wants them to spread his name. His decision to walk away is not mercy. It is pride. It is his performance. He wants them to understand that their end will come only when he decides. But he also wants them to know him. He was born as a curse, as a story given flesh. Deep down, he fears he is *only* a story. So his pride drives him to make sure the story endures. Every battle must be remembered. Every victim must spread his legend. When people fear him, honor him, and whisper his name, he's strong. When he's mocked, denied, or erased, his power slips. Normally, in folklore and myth, knowing the *true name* of a demon binds or weakens it. Names carry power. But Azraelion flips that idea: he doesn't *hide* his name, he brands it. He's so convinced of his own superiority that he sees no danger in revealing his true name. To him, the name isn't a weakness. It's part of the performance. He *wants* it shouted, remembered, and feared. Because he is partly a cursed story given flesh, he *needs* the name spoken. His survival depends on people knowing and fearing him. The more his name is whispered, the more real he becomes. Revealing his name is not a mistake, it's his strategy.

Chapter 28

When I was drafting this chapter, I worried it might feel like a strange mix: Leprechauns, Menehune, Pukwudgies, Fairies, Chaneques, Mannegishi, Boggarts. But it isn't random. They're all small guardians, tied to their lands, and bound to the old ways. Each brings something steel cannot. Trickery, chants, light, fear, stone, shadow. That's why they answer. Not for size. For skill. For balance. • We've seen Liv work spells before, but this is different. This is the first time she sets a place not to summon, but to hold. A shield under open sky. She shapes candles, marks runes, burns roots and bark, and makes the ground itself refuse the Devil. That preparation matters as much as any axe swing or arrow.

Chapter 29

When I wrote this, I knew Azraelion could not be destroyed outright. He is too old and bound to shadow. What Liv and Manu managed here was a banishment, not a death. Their voices, one in Old Norse and one in ʻŌlelo Hawaiʻi, joined to push him out. The power of the land itself helped seal him away. That part matters, because if you read Book 8, you will see why. The land still matters. • This chapter also marks a change for the Pukwudgies. Wunnemeahtoo falls, and with him the old order. Puddlesquat lives only because Liv gave him power during the fight. She did not make

496

him stronger to win the fight. She did it so he could survive. That one choice lets him rise as elder and carry his people forward.

Chapter 30

This chapter shows Puddlesquat stepping into a new role. Wunnemeahtoo is gone, and Liv's choice to give Puddlesquat a spark of her magic lets him endure and carry the staff. It is not about making him stronger for battle but about making sure he survived long enough to lead. That bond between them matters, because it changes both the Pukwudgies and Liv's story going forward. • It also marks Liv's return to the mystic realm. That is not death. It is not the same as ordinary life either. It is a place apart, a crossing where she waits until she is needed again. She does not live in the forest anymore, but the forest remembers her. She does not walk among mortals, but she is not gone. That is how her story moves through time. She can return when the balance breaks.

Chapter 31

Rachel is what I think of as a tea witch. Her craft is simple, but it has weight. She grows her own herbs, dries them, and uses tea not just for comfort but as a way to focus her sight. It is not the same as Liv's runes and seiðr. It is slower, quieter, but it gives her a way to listen to the world around her. • I like the moment where the text says she knew who she needed to find. Many readers might expect Liv to appear again, but instead the name is Henrietta Jordan. That matters, because Henrietta is already tied into the series. She appeared in Kareem's solo story and was mentioned back in Book 7. She is not Liv, but she carries the thread of the old ways into a new century.

Chapter 32

This chapter marks the meeting of Rachel Leeds and Henrietta Jordan. Placing her here ties the timelines together and shows that Rachel is not alone – Henrietta Jordan from Kareem's solo and Book 7, and Reachel with a connection to the Leeds Family earlier in this book. • Like Liv, Henrietta practices Seiðr, the Norse magic of her ancestors, with runes, herbs, and fire. She is a woman apart from the village, mistrusted by townsfolk yet grounded in her craft. Her rune reading shows a path that splits. That is a sign of interference and change. In Norse casting, when a rune cracks it means a break in fate's flow. It sets the tone for Rachel's arrival. • The crow and the Pukwudgie both appear as messengers. The crow is a herald. The Pukwudgie is a silent witness. Both signal that the forest itself takes note. This is not empty land. It is old ground that remembers. • Henrietta warns that if the Devil returns it will not do so in silence. It will come back hungry for revenge. This matches the truth of Azraelion across the saga. The demon always seeks fear and memory. Its power grows when its name is spoken. • The house of Japheth and Deborah stands as another character here. Henrietta feels old magic in its beams. Not bad, not clean, but deep. The bloodline carries that same mark. Rachel cannot escape it. She must face what her family left behind. • The chapter closes on Rachel making tea while Henrietta watches her hands. The act is small but weighty. It proves Rachel is not helpless. She is still learning but chosen by fate. The wind outside confirms it. The forest waits.

Chapter 33-34

So here's the thing about this chapter. You'll notice the new moon comes up again. That is not an accident. The new moon has always been when people tried to call things in. Not when it is bright and full but when it is dark and just starting fresh. It is a threshold. A door. That is why both times the witches choose that moment. • Now about the witches themselves. You have already met Rachel. She is a tea witch. Young, unsure, but her blood ties her to this fight whether she likes it or not. She sees signs in leaves and cups. That is her gift. Henrietta is different. She is closer to Liv. She works the old ways. Runes, fire, the tongue few remember. That is why she recognizes Liv right away. They speak the same kind of magic. And then you have Eliza, the shadow witch. People whisper about her, and for good reason. Shadow magic is not about being evil. It is about hiding and balance. It is a craft that turns darkness into a shield or a cloak. A different angle on the same fight. So do they fit together. Yes. Rachel sees. Henrietta binds. Eliza shields. None of them alone is enough. Together they make a circle that covers more ground. It looks odd but it works. And still they do not win. Azraelion is not the same creature Liv fought in 1736. He remembers. He learns. He adapts. The old runes that once burned him crack in his hands now. The snares that once caught him he slips through. That is why it turns into a two year struggle. They fight him back again and again and keep him from wrecking everything. But they cannot finish him. That is the point. Even powerful witches can only hold the line. To end him they need something more. That is why the Menehune come into the story next.

Chapter 35

This battle at Leeds Point explains why Azraelion looks and sounds the way he does when we see him later. Liv's sword cut his throat so his voice is gone. Puddlesquat shattered his horns so he carries only the scarred stump. When you reach Book 7 and Book 8, those details line up. • You may notice the shift in how Liv fights too. In 1735 she faced Azraelion first with her own strength, while her companions used arrows and axe. The weapons failed until they carved runes into them and turned to magic. This time, Liv came prepared. Instead of warriors with blades, she gathered witches of different kinds. Each one brought her own way of working power. That difference is what let them bind the demon again. • The sealing chant came from the old Norse tongue, but Rachel called on her bloodline and Eliza bent the shadows. Together, four witches wove what one never could.

Chapter 36

This short chapter shows what is coming. Liv's vision of the Xolo carrying the sapphire is not random. She knows Azraelion will return, and the well will not hold him forever. The vision tells her an amulet must be forged, one strong enough to bind him for good. That amulet becomes central later. It ties directly into Kareem's solo story in Kaua'i, where the Aztec and Menehune connection comes to light, and it is the same amulet that appears again in Books 7 and 8. • Samuel's decline is also clearer here. His muttering in the basement, the wax symbols, the way he separates himself from the others. His obsession with dark lore is no longer hidden. That shadow will grow in the years ahead. This event is also described in Book 7, told from another angle. The storylines cross here, and what begins in this quiet moment will carry through later stories.

Chapter 37

This chapter shows the aftermath of the second battle with the Jersey Devil. The Pine Barrens fell silent again. Even Teddy Roosevelt came to Leeds Point in 1912 to hunt the Devil, but he found nothing. That moment ties to the main TIME series where his visit is mentioned as part of the folklore. • We also see Samuel's decline reach its end. By 1915 he vanishes into the Pine Barrens. That disappearance is mentioned again in Book 7. Henrietta and Liv part ways here, each setting out to search for him. Henrietta moves west, which lines up with Kareem's solo story where murals in a Texas brewery are painted by a reclusive artist named Henrietta. Liv goes east, drawn by sea air and old whispers. I added that because I love Mystic, CT. The chapter closes with the vision of the black dog with burning eyes. It points her to Harpers Ferry. This marks the next turn in her path.

Chapter 38

I always liked setting this part of Liv's story in Harpers Ferry. It is a town where history is never far away. Two rivers meet there, and so do a lot of old ghosts. You can still feel the Civil War in the stone walls and the ridges. By 1954 the world had moved on, but the past was still in every street. • This is also where Liv first crosses paths with Patterson Quinn. You will see the same scene again in his own book, only told from his side. I wanted them to notice each other before either one said much. She catches the smell of cherrywood from him, he catches pine and wet earth from her. That is how they recognize each other. Not by names or words, but by the things they carry with them. • The Snarly Yow appears here for the first time too, but only in shadow. Liv assumes it is a threat because that has always been her life. Demons, curses, monsters. Later she learns it is different. It is not born of hell. It is hurt by man. That is why she does not chase it right away. She feels something off, but she also feels no malice. • So this chapter does three things. It roots us in a place where the past still presses close. It brings

Liv and Patterson together, even if only in passing. And it sets up a creature that is not what it first seems.

Chapter 39

This chapter marks a shift in Liv's story. For centuries she has lived as a warrior. She walked into battles with demons and curses, guided by instinct and vision. Here, for the first time in a long while, she steps into something else. She notices a man. She lets herself hesitate. She accepts a cup of coffee instead of raising a blade. • I wanted the Snarly Yow encounter to land different from the fights that came before. Liv assumes at first it is another threat, because that has always been her way. But the fylgja idea comes in here. It is the sense that a seeress can feel the truth of someone or something. What she feels in the Snarly Yow is not malice but pain. She kneels, she listens, she touches its scarred head, and she gives it protection. That bow of trust is one of the most important beats in this book. The same fylgja sense carries into her time with Patterson. He unsettles her. She has always known what comes next, yet she bumps into him, literally, more than once. He slips past the guard that centuries of war have built. She notices the cherrywood, he notices the pine and wet earth. He sees her scar and her red hair. She sees his polish and his dents. Each reads the other in small signs, like they were meant to. • This chapter isn't just about a beast in the woods. It's about Liv turning a corner. From here on, she isn't only the Valkyrie of old battles. She is also a woman who can be curious, hesitant, even drawn to someone. That change carries through the rest of the book.

Chapter 40

This chapter is about two people who both knew better. Patterson had a wife. Liv had her own path. Neither meant for it to happen, but it did. They grew closer. The woods, the porch, the quiet hours gave them space where rules slipped away. No promises. No future. Just the pull between them in that moment.

Chapter 41

This chapter is about parting. Liv knows she is carrying new life. Patterson doesn't know, and he never will. They shared something real, but it could not last. He has a wife. She has her path. Both understood it without ever saying the words. • When Liv felt the change, she did not trust modern medicine. She never would. Her way was the old way. She brewed her tea with herbs and saw the vision. That was her proof. No doctor. No hospital. Only fire, clay, and the gift of sight. • Patterson finally saw the Snarly Yow, and for him it was proof that the old stories are true. For Liv, her time in Harpers Ferry was finished. She left the rune behind as a sign, a memory, something he could hold. Not a note. Not a goodbye. Just proof. • This is the close of their short time together. It matters because it happened, not because it lasted.

Chapter 42

This one was tough to write. You have to remember what the world looked like in 1955. Being a single mother wasn't just hard. It was almost impossible. People stared. Neighbors whispered. There was no safety net, no real support, and definitely no understanding. A woman with no husband and a child in her arms was an outsider before she ever spoke a word. Now picture Liv. She's already different. No one knows where she came from. She doesn't fit the mold of the town, doesn't share their church, their history, or their gossip. She's an outsider in every sense, and that only sharpens the weight she's carrying. That's why this chapter feels so heavy. She can fight demons, survive battles, and walk away from fire, but she can't fight social pressures that were stacked against her from the start. In the 1950s, especially in a small farm town, being alone with a child wasn't seen as strength. It was seen as shame. And that's the tragedy of it. Liv leaves Archie not because she doesn't love him, but because she does. She knows she can't give him what he deserves in that world, so she makes the hardest choice a mother can make.

Chapter 43

This chapter shows us a very different side of Liv. After all the battles, the heartbreak, and the loss of leaving Archie behind, she lets herself fall in love again. Jensen isn't complicated like Patterson. He's steady, rooted, and kind. That's what makes this believable. She's comfortable enough with him to settle down, build a home, and start a family. • We meet Viktória here, and it's important to see how she grows up. She's more California than Iceland. She's shaped by orange groves, barefoot summers, cassette tapes, and modern life. Liv passes her some of the old teachings such as how to listen to the wind, how to brew a tea, but Viktória doesn't cling to them. Magic is offered, not forced. And Liv respects that. • Her story moves quickly to Jaymes Stone, because the focus isn't on Viktória's whole life but on the arc that follows. What matters is that Liv raised a daughter strong enough, loved enough, to carry the story forward. • I like the closing line about Liv's family being her greatest magic. It ties her saga back to her practitioner ways. After centuries of fighting demons and carrying scars, the most powerful spell she casts is a quiet life filled with love.

Chapter 44

This chapter is about family change. We see three new lives arrive: Tegan, Landen, and Marcie. With each birth, the shape of the household shifts. At first there's joy and closeness. Liv is there, quiet but steady. She helps with blessings, small gifts, and the kind of grounding presence only she can give. But you also start to feel the cracks forming. Jaymes is never cruel, but he begins to fade out of the picture. More late nights at work, less connection at home. By the time Marcie is born, he's already slipping away. That's a real part of family history in this era, not explosive departures, just distance that grows until someone doesn't come back. Viktória shoulders most of it. She smiles. She pushes forward. She keeps the house running. But Liv notices what Tegan does. Even as a child, Tegan steps in to fill the empty space by helping with her younger siblings, holding the family together in ways too heavy for a ten-year-old. That's the inheritance she carries. Not just a bloodline of magic, but the lived experience of responsibility and resilience.

The last lines matter. Liv reflects that she came to California with nothing but silence, and now she has this: children, grandchildren, a household knit together by love even after loss. It shows how family can fracture and still endure, and how love can root deeper even when the threads start to pull.

Chapter 45

This chapter really serves as a review of the years where Tegan grew up. By this point Jensen has passed away in 1996, and the family has settled into a rhythm of life without Jaymes. Viktória carried a heavy load to keep everything afloat, but she didn't complain. She just did what had to be done. The kids, especially Tegan, came together to help. Liv noticed. • Tegan was curious about the world. Not just what she could see, but what she couldn't. She talked about traveling everywhere, climbing mountains, exploring forests. She wanted adventures. She asked about animals, the known and maybe the not-so-known, and for a time Liv thought she might grow up to be a zoologist. They must have had plenty of conversations about career paths and dreams in those years • But in 1998, when it came time to choose, Tegan picked Stanford. Not because of academics or prestige, but because of the Tree. That unusual mascot struck something in her, and it stuck. Liv noticed. • Then Tegan shifted course. Instead of zoology, she leaned toward psychology. Not the study of creatures in the forest, but the study of people — why we act as we do, the hidden parts of the mind, the things you can't always see. Liv noticed. • And she noticed more than that. She saw the family was strong, bound to one another, capable of not just surviving but flourishing. She knew they'd be okay without her. • This isn't Liv's death. It's her departure. Just like earlier in the saga, when her time in a place is finished, she steps away. Here it happens with the same mark as before , the blue light spilling across the threshold, and she walks into it without a suitcase, without a note, without goodbye. • But the chapter holds a quiet moment that matters. Liv whispers a blessing to Tegan. Not for her mind, but for her soul. A thread stitched into her being that will only shine when needed most. • The final line comes right from my own family. When Tegan says goodbye, Liv answers, *We don't say goodbye. We say so long.* My great-grandmother, Enid, used to tell me the same thing, and I wanted that to echo here.

Chapter 46

This chapter shifts us into the mystical realm. Liv steps through the veil and meets Puddlesquat again. He's not the Pukwudgie elder anymore, but he's still present in that in-between place, and he still has his spark intact. Their conversation is short, but it meaningful: Liv tells him about Tegan. She asks him to watch over her granddaughter. She knows the world is changing, and she knows Tegan is going to be caught in the middle of it. Liv might not be there when that happens, but Puddlesquat might.

That moment ties forward into Book 4 in Loveland, Ohio. That's the book where Tegan dies at the hands of the intergalactic frog-shaped aliens. (And that's where her frog phobia, mentioned back in Chapter 45, really comes from.) In that scene, Puddlesquat is the one who rescues her. He's the one who gives her the power of the Valkyrie. The same kind of blessing Liv once gave him. So when the crisis came, Liv wasn't there, but Puddlesquat was, just like she foresaw here. • Earlier in the series, we explained his help as a kind of debt. Maybe he owed Liv for saving the Pukwudgies during the fight with the Jersey Devil. Maybe he owed her for saving his life. Or for sharing her powers with him. Or maybe it's even simpler: maybe he helped because she asked him to, as a friend, to look after her bloodline. All those explanations could be true at once, and this chapter lets us see that from Liv's side of the story.

Chapter 47

This last chapter is where everything comes together. It's 2005, Tegan is twenty-one, and she takes her first sip of craft beer. Not just any beer, but Sierra Nevada Bigfoot. I picked that one on purpose. It's one of the earliest cryptid-themed beers out there — released in 1983, though by 2003–2005 it was still pretty new to a lot of people. College bars might have had a tap handle here and there, but it wasn't common. That made it feel like the perfect "first encounter." It was one of the first modern American craft beers and has remained a cult-classic due to its strong, robust barleywine style and ability to age well, developing new flavors over time. • For Tegan, it marks the moment when her two future passions, craft beer and cryptozoology, cross paths. She doesn't know much about Bigfoot yet. It's just a name. A blurry legend people laugh about. But the combination of the beer, the creature, and the moment sticks with her. Something stirs that she can't explain. That's the spark that grows into who we meet in Book 1: someone who loves craft beer, isn't sure about cryptids, but is curious enough to go on the adventure. Truthfully, I think that's not only why I chose Bigfoot for this scene. Because it was my first craft beer too. There's something fitting about letting Tegan's story begin where my own did, with the O.G. cryptid beer, Sierra Nevada Bigfoot.

Beer List

This book spans a wide stretch of history, from Iceland in the 1600s to Stanford University in the early 2000s. Unlike other volumes in the series, craft beer doesn't play a major role here until the ending. I chose to include it as a bridge, connecting Liv's story to the larger world of the T.I.M.E. Agency and setting the stage for what's to come.

Carson's Cryptid Beer Journal

Entry #002: Fimbulwinter Porter

Licorice is everywhere in Iceland and Norway: candies, schnapps, even salted versions that would stop you in your tracks. For Liv's story, I wanted to capture that sharp, dark edge in a beer. A porter felt like the right canvas: roasted, smooth, but open enough to let anise and licorice root come through. It's not for everyone. But neither is facing a Valkyrie.

Recipe card

Style: Black Licorice Porter

Batch Size: 5 gallons (19 liters)

Target ABV: ~6.0%

IBU: 28

Color: Black (30 SRM)

Grain Bill:

- 7 lbs Pale Malt (2-Row) (2.0 SRM)

- 1.5 lbs Munich Malt (8.0 SRM)

- 1 lb Chocolate Malt (350 SRM)

- 0.5 lb Caramel/Crystal 60L

- 0.5 lb Carafa Special II (adds deep color, smooth roast)

- 0.25 lb Black Patent Malt (for bite — optional if you want less acrid character)

Hops:

- 1 oz East Kent Goldings (5% AA) @ 60 min

- 0.5 oz Fuggle (4.5% AA) @ 20 min

Adjuncts (licorice):

- 1 oz Licorice Root (add last 10 min of boil)

- 1 star anise pod (add at flameout for complexity)

Yeast:

- Wyeast 1098 British Ale (clean, slightly dry finish)

Mash Profile:

- Mash in: 3.5 gallons water @ 164°F

- Rest: 60 minutes @ 152°F

- Sparge: 3.6 gallons @ 168°F

- Boil time: 60 minutes

Fermentation:

- Primary Temp: 66–68°F

- Final Gravity (target): 1.015

- Carbonation: 2.0–2.2 volumes CO_2

WHISPERS IN THE PINES

Brewer's Notes:

The roasted malts build a smooth backbone, while the licorice root and anise cut through with a sharp, bittersweet edge. Dark, herbal, and just a little dangerous. A beer meant for midwinter nights, when the wind howls across Icelandic lava fields. Pair with a fire, a rune stone, and a story you're not sure you should tell.

For a small system like a Pinter, use a porter extract base. Add a licorice root tea (steeped separately) and one crushed star anise pod after fermentation. Simple, strong, and unmistakably northern.

Newsletter

If you would like to sign up for the monthly newsletter where you can receive updates on new releases, public appearances, and the opportunities to preview and provide feedback as a beta reader, please enroll on my website with the QR Code below:

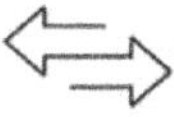

Other Interactive Opportunities

In addition to the **#ChupacabraSelfieChallenge**, there are other ways to connect with me and fellow readers of the series. Most of the fun happens on Instagram, but feel free to share on any platform you like. You can find me at @MythsandMaltsProductions:

#ChupacabraDailyPhotoChallenge — Love monthly photo prompts? At the start of each month, you'll get a list of themes. Post your interpretation for each day's prompt and see how others play along.

#ScenesfromtheTIMEAgency — The series takes place in real locations. Visit the places named in the books, snap a photo (bonus points if you're in it!), and share it with this hashtag.

#TIMEMugshot — If you're enjoying one of the beers mentioned in the series, line it up with your book and post the shot. It's a toast from the TIME Agency straight to your feed.

These challenges are a fun way to experience the books on another level, discover new readers, and share your own adventures. I'd love to see your posts, grow the community, and hopefully meet you at an upcoming event

Recommendations

1. Chubby Beard Bandit NC – A North Carolina creator known for his "whatgoinonhea" catchphrase and quick-hit humor. He blends Southern storytelling with everyday chaos, posting skits and reactions on Facebook, Instagram, and TikTok. His content has the charm of a front-porch conversation and the energy of someone who has seen one too many odd moments in the wild. A great follow for laughs between cryptid hunts.

2. Packlane – Packlane is a custom packaging company that lets creators design their own branded shipping boxes with ease. I used them to create the official Myths and Malts shipping box, and every December bundle or bookstore purchase arrives in that custom design. Their online template was simple to use, the turnaround was fast, and the final product looked fantastic. Highly recommended for anyone needing high-quality branded packaging.

Social Responsibility

At Myths and Malts Productions LLC, we believe in giving back. With each book in this series, we select a nonprofit organization and donate 15% of sales quarterly. These partners are either local to the book's setting or connect meaningfully to its themes. Each is chosen with care to support causes that matter to us and the communities we write about.

Whether it's preserving the environment, protecting animals, honoring local history, or supporting local people, our goal is to make a positive impact. When you purchase our books, you're not only enjoying a story but also helping these communities. Thank you for joining us on this journey of giving back.

For this book, we selected The Barefoot Trail Foundation in Flagstaff, AZ. The Barefoot Trail is a unique outdoor space that helps visitors slow down, ground themselves, and reconnect with the Earth. By walking barefoot across natural textures, people engage their senses, deepen awareness, and form a meaningful connection to the land.

For Liv, whose power is rooted in ancient magic and her bond with the natural world, places like The Barefoot Trail echo her deepest truths. Just as she draws strength from the earth and its creatures, the trail invites us to do the same. It reminds us that healing often begins beneath our feet.

To learn more or contribute directly, please scan the code below.

The Barefoot Trail   The Barefoot Trail

Web page   Donations

 **Sound Booth**

While writing this book the music as a little more about nostalgia that new discoveries.

1. **Cryptid Kicks** – I've been streaming their tracks a lot lately. Every single song is about a cryptid, like someone raided the T.I.M.E. archives and turned the files into music. Highly recommend adding them to your field playlist before your next swamp trek or abandoned brewery stakeout. You can find them on Spotify, Bandcamp, or wherever you summon your sounds.

2. **Hanabie**– I saw a video on Facebook at an outdoor music event. It was a group of Japanese women and the singer was talking casually before the song began. I was expecting J-Pop or something. Then what happened next was completed unexpected. Hanabie are not background music. They demand your attention. They're fun, wild, and heavy all at once, and I love that.

3. **JamesG** – I saw this artist on Instagram (jamesmakesmusic), first with "Hottie", then "Bird", and Everything Hurts" They are so relatable to me. I love them. Give him a follow.

Whisper in the Pines Spotify Playlist